Her Heart's Surrender . . .

Rogan chuckled, easily straddling her. "You had your chance. Now we will do things my way."

He grabbed her wrists and jerked them over her head. The more she struggled, the more he laughed at her, and the more furious she became.

"Let me go, Rogan, or I'll scream!"

Rogan grinned, lowering his head until it was but inches from hers. She stilled.

"Scream all you wish, my lady, there are none here to heed you. The servants have been dismissed for the evening and Fredric and Emma left over an hour ago. It is just you and I—alone."

Rogan leaned on his elbow, scanning the length of her. She was clad in a lacy chemise and stays, her breasts heaving beneath the taut fabric. He reached out and traced a finger along the line of her collarbone to the hollow of her throat. He could see her pulse drumming wildly, the heat of her skin warm against him as she flushed a deep crimson beneath his touch. . . .

JACLYN REDING

DIAMOND BOOKS, NEW YORK

This book is a Diamond original edition,
and has never been previously published.

DECEPTION'S BRIDE

A Diamond Book / published by arrangement with
the author

PRINTING HISTORY
Diamond edition / December 1993

ISBN: 1-55773-966-8

Diamond Books are published by The Berkley Publishing Group,
200 Madison Avenue, New York, NY 10016.
DIAMOND and the "D" design
are trademarks belonging to Charter Communications, Inc.

PRINTED IN THE UNITED STATES OF AMERICA

10 9 8 7 6 5 4 3 2 1

Everybody needs their own
guardian angel.
I dedicate this book to mine,
Catherine Coulter,
a true and wonderful friend,
who taught me that my heroine
should always laugh,
and never whimper
in the face of danger.

Thanks, Catherine
With much love,
Jacci

Oh! how many torments lie
in the small circle of a wedding-ring!
—COLLEY CIBBER

Deception's Bride

Prologue

Castle Drummore
Lothian Region, Scotland
1752

A flash of lightning cut the night sky and for the barest of seconds the tiny chamber was filled with brilliant light before the onyx shroud of darkness came to reclaim it. Alone in her bedchamber, Chelsea Estwyck lay still beneath the thick folds of the goose-down coverlet, counting the seconds until the thunder that followed would come.

Fifteen seconds later the thunder came rumbling across the inner bailey, rattling the bottles of toilet water and attar that lined the top of her rosewood dressing table. She thought back to the night when her father had taught her to count out the storm. She'd been six years old then, frightened of the shadows the lightning had cast on her chamber walls, spirits of the soldiers who'd fought and died at the castle, she'd told him while huddling further into his arms as each bellow of thunder came. Nineteen now, and without her father to run to when the night's demons came to disturb her dreams, Chelsea was no longer afraid of storms or the prospect of spirits. Still, each time she counted.

She looked to the timepiece on her bedside table. She could not see the hour for the darkness, but guessed it to be early morn. Soon the dawn would be upon them. Her chamber would be filled with the sound of her mother ordering the maids about, instructing them to press her marriage gown and scatter the great hall with the hothouse blooms grown by Drummore gardeners. Soon she would become a wife.

The rain fell harder now, tapping a cadence against the mullioned windows, the droplets running in thick, crooked streams like tears of a brokenhearted maiden. She remembered Haggat, the crone who lived in a thatched cottage at the edge of Drummore land once telling her the prophecy of the rain on one's wedding day. " 'Tis a bonny thing," she'd said in her jagged voice, her dark eyes glimmering in the low candlelight. " 'Tis tears of the angels, they are, blessing the union of lovers who marry beneath the drizzle."

Chelsea wondered if the downpour now raging outside would portend an even greater blessing for her when she met her betrothed at the marriage altar. Even now she could hear her mother bemoaning her ill fortune, as if planning her daughter's nuptials in December would keep the Scottish winter from blowing. She would, no doubt, fly into a fit of hysterics at the first unfortunate who left a muddy footprint on her fine Turkish carpet. But Chelsea cared not. If rain on her wedding day was a presage of good fortune, then let it flow from the battlements, where centuries ago flags of red and yellow and black had flown over the mighty fortress then known as *Dree Murk,* castle of enduring darkness. It was her wedding day, her long-awaited wedding day, and not even a raging squall could dampen her lofty spirits.

Turning on her side, Chelsea nestled deeper into the mound of soft pillows beneath her head, the sweet perfume of wild heather filtering to her from the sheets, calling her back to the day he'd first kissed her.

How gently Gregor's arms had held her that day as they sat taking picnic in the tree-shrouded glen beyond the creek's edge. He'd laid her back on a carpet of the small purple-blue flowers, soft as thistledown, and when his lips had touched hers for the very first time, she'd giggled from the tickle of his beard-roughened chin. How cross he'd grown at her reaction; she'd like to have swooned from the mastery of his kiss. But swooning was for schoolgirls, she'd told him, and still, she liked the kiss all the same.

And now they were to wed.

The thought of Gregor as her life's mate still sounded curiously strange to her. She knew not why; she'd had long enough to accustom herself to the thought, but once they were wed, she was certain it would seem as if it had always been meant to be.

Her musings were interrupted when she heard the sound of a door opening outside her chamber. It creaked loudly, echoing in the night, then hesitating as if to avoid notice. She tightened her fingers around the edge of the coverlet. It was Gregor, she somehow knew. He was coming. Coming to her. Several moments passed. Silence. Still her door did not open. She heard his muffled footsteps moving down the corridor, away from her chamber. She looked to the door. A candle glowed in the narrow space beneath its wooden frame, its flame flickering with each step he took. In seconds the light had faded to darkness.

Flipping back the coverlet, she slid from the feathered mattress and skimmed the carpet barefoot to the door. She pressed an ear against the thick, carved wood, sweeping a lock of hair from her eyes as she strained to hear to the other side.

Silence.

Slowly she lifted the heavy latch, wincing as it grated in protest. She pulled the door open just an inch to peek through. The corridor outside was dark and empty, long shadows splaying across the faded tapestries that covered the stone walls to keep out the winter's draft. She stepped from the chamber, searching for him in the darkness but he was not there. An icy current wafted along her bare legs through the thin linen shift she wore. She turned. The door to the chamber across from hers stood slightly ajar. Perhaps it had not been Gregor she'd heard. Perhaps it had been someone else. Perhaps he was still inside.

She stepped forward.

"Gregor?"

There was no response.

She pushed the door inward. A blast of cold air struck her like a face slap, chilling her to her toes along the bare stone floor. Across the chamber, the fierce December wind blew in through an open window, whipping the damask curtains about in a tangle. The rain from outside swirled within. Stepping inside, she near tripped over a pair of black leather boots lying near the door. She wondered why Gregor would leave the windows open on such a rainy night. She wondered where he'd gone without his boots. She wondered where he could be.

"Gregor?" she repeated, more loudly this time, knowing there would be no answer, yet still hoping there might be. Her breath fogged from the cold. She peered toward the bed. It was empty as she expected, the coverlet rumpled as if it had been occupied earlier.

As she pulled the windows closed against the storm, she spied a bottle, half-filled, on the carved writing desk beside her. She lifted the clear crystal vessel, sniffing its open top. The strong smell of Scottish whiskey caused her to draw back. She set the bottle down. A goblet teetered at the edge of the desk, immersed in a puddle of the dark-colored liquid that had spilled from inside. She recognized the goblet. It was one of a pair she and Gregor had received as a gift from some well-meaning relative. She set the goblet aright, frowning at the thin crack that veined off across the delicate crystal and turned to leave.

Where could Gregor have gone at such an hour? Had he decided not to wed her after all and sped away in the midst of the night so as not to alert anyone to his leave-taking? Chelsea shook the thought away, thinking it was more likely he had gotten a taste for a helping of the cook's sweet lemon tart and had sped away to the kitchen for a slice of it instead.

As she reached the end of the corridor, she peered down over the wooded railing at the rush-strewn floor of the dining hall below, where, hours earlier, hundreds had gathered to toast the bride's beauty before the warmth of a blazing fire. Now a lone maidservant with a crude twig broom was all that remained, sweeping the floor where soon she would become Gregor's wife. A young man cleared the tables beside her, swilling down the sweet Madeira wine left by the other guests.

Still, her bridegroom was nowhere to be seen.

Gregor Moultrie, master of Ballingall Castle, had hair as black as midnight and eyes so fierce they could render a man senseless with the slightest glance. He dwarfed her, as he did most men, but Gregor never frightened her. He'd never lifted a hand to her as she'd seen many of the men around Drummore do with their women, even when she'd angered him by proving him wrong on a sum he'd been totaling in the castle ledgers.

"The lamb that had tamed the lion," she was called, a title of which she was most proud. Her mother, Annora, first told her on the eve of her sixteenth birthday of her parents' wish that she marry Gregor. His family's lands at Ballingall bordered on Drummore to the west, and as it would fall to her one day, being allied with a Scotsman, a Scotsman such as Gregor, would ensure that Drummore would never be taken by the English king who had taken her father, or so her mother often said. A perfect union, her mother had proclaimed it, and perfect it would be, if only her father could be there to walk her down the chapel aisle instead of in exile somewhere across the Channel.

Damson Estwyck, once a peer and a member of the House of Lords, had narrowly escaped the hangman's noose after being accused of treason for his part in the 1745 Jacobite uprising. Chelsea had written to him only twice since he'd gone, though she doubted her letters had ever reached him, more likely having gotten lost somewhere among the multitude of hands they would have passed through before ever finding him.

She turned from the railing to continue her search for Gregor and heard the sound of laughter, lilting and female, in the distance. Chelsea tilted her head to listen. A throaty chuckle, deep and male, followed after it. The muscles in her stomach tightened. She knew that laugh. She'd heard it so many times. *Gregor.* She looked down the hall leading to the eastern wing. She started toward it with alacrity.

As Chelsea moved along the darkened corridor, she thought back to the first time she'd learned of Gregor's wandering eye, when she found him lifting Mary MacDonnag's skirts in a dark garden corner at a ball they had attended. Heartsick at his betrayal, she threatened to break their betrothal, refusing to wed such a faithless cur as he. After the ball, Gregor begged her for forgiveness, vowing he would never again take another woman, pledging he would wait for her. And she believed him. She believed him with the blind trust of a foolish girl, believing his promises to be a faithful husband. But he was not yet her husband, was he?

Perhaps she was mistaken, Chelsea told herself even as her step quickened. Perhaps it had not been Gregor she had heard. Perhaps it had been someone else.

She slowed when she spied the hazy glow of firelight that spilled from an open doorway ahead. She recognized the doorway. She refused to believe it true, but still she heard them. Sounds. Muffled and low. Man and woman. She started forward and did not slow until she had reached the threshold. She hesitated just outside the doorway. She did not want to enter. She did not want to see what she feared lay beyond. But she had to if she was to know. And she had to know.

Slowly, Chelsea stepped inside. A fire burned in the hearth across the room, its shadows twisting on the walls around her. Pieces of clothing were strewn haphazardly about; a lace cravat thrown to the floor, a single silk stocking flung over the door handle. Discarded with the other garments lay Gregor's *marriage-sark,* the white betrothal shirt he was to wear at their wedding, the shirt on which she had spent months carefully stitching his initials. A near-empty bottle of Madeira rested beside it, its last liquid remnants spreading across the fine silk in a dark crimson stain.

Chelsea looked hesitantly to the bed. Draped in scarlet and gold; the striking colors seemed to add a degree of warmth to the already stifling chamber. And then she saw him, the taut muscles in his back outlined in the firelight. He rose up on his arms, his hips moving smoothly, drawing back between two pale knees before driving forward again.

The gold brocade coverlet had slipped to his knees and he was groaning now, thrusting his hips forward while Chelsea watched as if in a trance. She heard the woman moan his name, watched as she wrapped her legs around his taut buttocks. They were unaware of her intrusion as their moans rose to a crescendo. Chelsea felt her throat tighten and found it difficult to so much as swallow. She wanted to leave, but her legs had suddenly turned to stone. Helpless, she watched as the man who had vowed eternal faith to her drove forward with one final thrust, dropping his head to his lover's breast.

She wanted to scream. She wanted to shriek like a bedlamite and expose their perfidy. But she did not. Somehow she found the strength to move and backed from the room, her heart pounding against the tightness that had wound around her chest. She did not stop until she reached the wall behind her. She hugged her arms around herself and sagged against the hard stone wall.

It could not be. It just was not possible. It had to have been a dream, a horrid, wretched nightmare. Slowly, hesitantly, she opened her eyes. She was still standing just outside that door. It had not been a dream. No dream could be so horribly cruel.

The thunder outside exploded like a cannon shot. She shoved herself away from the wall. Tears stinging her eyes, she fled down the corridor, away from the nightmare, away from the chamber where she had found her betrothed.

Her own mother's bedchamber.

Chapter 1

"Damn it, boy, I will not have it!"

Rogan Doraunt, Viscount Ravenel, and future Earl of Ashbourne, felt his jaw tighten as his father pounded his bony fist upon the desk. Meant to frighten him, the gesture only resulted in making the animosity inside him swell, while toppling an ornate silver inkwell from its gilded stand to bleed a pool of ink across the smoothly polished mahogany desktop. Its river of black spilled over the side, falling to an ever-widening blot on the centuries-old Turkish carpet.

Oblivious to the damaging ink, Townsend Doraunt waved the letter he had been reading in the air.

"I have warned you, Rogan, time and again, but you stubbornly refuse to heed my word. While it may be considered fashionable to bed another man's wife, you cannot continue defiling the wives of my colleagues. Most men strive to keep their identities confidential in such matters. You seem determined to have the entire *ton* privy to who your latest bed partner is, including the woman's husband. First, I read of you in the gossip pages of *The Spectator*, then my close acquaintances hint at your number of mistresses, and now"—he paused, taking a great breath—"now I learn from complete strangers of my son's philandering ways."

Rogan stared at his father, but did not listen. In his twenty-nine years he'd perfected the art of appearing to heed his sire's tirades when, in fact, he did not hear a word. He could have been citing Shakespearean sonnets, but Rogan simply watched his face grow mottled with rage and wondered when he had aged so. Had it really been ten months since he'd last seen him?

Townsend narrowed his black eyes on his only son. "Bedding the wives of my colleagues will only land you in the dueling field and one day your aim will not be so precise. I've no desire to have my son known as, 'the Doraunt who died in the Field of Forty Footsteps.' For centuries, your forebears have served the kings and queens of England, earning their favor and respect, yet you try at every turn to destroy their efforts. You are a disgrace, Rogan, both to me and the Doraunt family name. I always knew you'd not be worthy of holding the title of the Earl of Ashbourne. Now it seems you must needs prove me right."

"It is something I live for," Rogan replied, already growing impatient to leave. He looked to the gilded clock behind his father's balding head. He had only arrived a quarter hour earlier. The horses had not even been rested yet.

"Is that all you have to say for yourself against these

accusations?" Townsend knotted the sash to his loose dressing robe over his shirt and breeches. "Are you not even to try denying them this time?"

Rogan said nothing, affecting disinterest. He wondered for a moment who had written the letter to his father, who'd sought to make his private life public, but discarded the thought just as quickly. Most of the allegations and, he was certain, the ones Townsend had yet to disclose, had been true at one time or another. Yes, he'd taken other men's wives as mistresses and yes, most probably wives of his father's acquaintances. But not now, not in the time since he'd made Diana his sole mistress, ceasing with the seductions of his reckless youth. The accusations contained in that letter written by a mysterious hand were only lingering rumors, torrid tales made up by fashionable ladies tittering over Eccles cake and a china cup of Earl Grey, trying to alleviate their boredom with unfortunate stories of every available sod left in London.

He cared not who had written the letter or what words it contained. Nor would he cower before his father in shame because he'd learned of some assignation, true or not. He'd no duty to explain himself. He was twenty-nine now, in his prime, one could say, not some dotard left to staring at a woman's breasts and dreaming of what had been. Hell, had his father his wish, he'd have Rogan living like a vicar in chaste confinement, not so much as glancing at the fairer sex until his wedding night and then only to produce the next Ashbourne heir.

Watching him now, Rogan wondered if he truly did share the Doraunt blood, so vast were the differences between them. They did not even share a resemblance, Rogan's mahogany hair and silver-blue eyes quite unlike his father's dark ones. Perhaps he'd been left at the doorstep. Perhaps some unfortunate village girl had abandoned him there, hoping to give the result of a midnight hayloft toss a better life. At least it would offer some explanation for his father's lifelong hatred toward him.

As Townsend began reciting whole passages from that damnable letter, Rogan thought back to a time when he had sat in that very chair as a child, trembling so much in fear of his father's thunder that he'd wet his own breeches. Then he had been lectured on the importance of tackling his studies or how no accomplished gentlemen practiced his fencing less than three hours each day. As an adult he fared no better in his father's eyes, this son who'd not followed his father to marriage and children and a life of running an estate in the country. Rogan wondered if he should remind his father that he himself had not wed till the ripe old age of forty after taking his tour in Europe, leaving a passel of mistresses and, no doubt, bastards in every port of call. In the end he decided against it, knowing it would serve no purpose.

Still, why he traveled to the country twice a year was a question he could never quite answer. Each time he came, it was to the same reception, and each time he vowed it the last. Yet he did come out of some sense of bounden duty as a son, only to be reminded of what a failure he had become. When he took his leave, which, judging from this afternoon's confrontation would be soon, he would return to his town house in London to down a full bottle of brandy and curse at the housemaids the following morning for the devil of a headache he'd surely wake to. It was always the same.

Townsend droned on, moving now to the responsibilities

of the eldest child, of Rogan's duty to supply Ashbourne with an heir to carry on the Doraunt name. Needing to separate himself from the image of the boy cowering before his father, Rogan stood and strode to the wide bay window across the room. At that moment he did not think he would ever want a son to curse with the moral obligations of being the next Ashbourne earl.

He stared out over the winter-dried lawns of Ashbourne, noting how very little the estate had changed since his childhood. The small stone gazebo where he'd sat with his mother while she read aloud to him and his sister, Emma, from her book of sonnets, had weathered only slightly to a sun-faded pink. The stables that housed the renowned Doraunt steeds still stood nestled in the shadow of the age-old orchard. Its trees, now winter bare, would be filled come summer with bright red apples, the horses grazing on its castaways through the crooked fence line.

Ashbourne was his ancestral home. He'd come of age among the carefully tended gardens and lawns, climbing every tree that stood in the forest where, he'd concluded at the all-knowing age of nine, the fabled Robin Hood had dwelt. He'd spent his days exploring every crumbling stone of the castellated ruins of the Norman keep that once stood on this same land, knowing it would be his someday. It would be passed down to him as it had been to his father, and his father before, something he had always known, something he held in the highest regard.

The portrait gallery in the eastern wing was lined with images of the Doraunt men who had ruled before him, back to the days of Queen Bess and the first earl, Radcliff Doraunt, on whom the good queen had bestowed the title of Ashbourne. How Rogan had wanted to be counted among them. To have his portrait hanging on that walnut-paneled wall beside his father's image as a lasting testament to his heritage. To be counted among the prominent men who had held the grand estate. How he had wanted that exalted position above all else, striving toward it with every ounce of will he possessed, until the day on which he'd reached his twelfth year; the age at which he learned his father would never love him.

On that morning Rogan woke determined to prove himself to his father. In all else he'd failed, but that day he'd had a plan, a plan that had been months in the making, a plan that would finally succeed. It had been on the north lawn, the very lawn he now looked down upon, on a frosty autumn morn in November of that year. The leaves on the stately Ashbourne oaks had been a mixture of bright orange, yellow, and red, cloaking the ground below in a colorful carpet of fire.

Staring out over that lawn now, Rogan could see his mother, so young, so beautiful, standing at the edge of the clear-watered swan pond, holding the hand of then three-year-old Emma as she tossed biscuit crumbs to the long-necked birds floating there.

Rogan saddled his father's favorite stallion before dawn; Valiant, a magnificent red chestnut standing well over eighteen hands. He wasn't permitted to ride the stallion, was never allowed within more than two yards of him, but he wanted to prove how well he could ride, to finally make his father proud.

With the sun just breaking over the treetops, Rogan began taking the horse through its paces while Emma clapped her hands and his mother just smiled. Townsend roared at him to dismount. When he begged his father to allow him to continue, Townsend just stared at his son with his cold eyes, watching and waiting for him to finish his equine display.

Fearing Townsend's anger, Rogan strove harder to succeed, urging Valiant on at a reckless pace. But after nearly a half-of-an-hour of displaying every riding skill he possessed to no result, Rogan turned Valiant back to the stables, his head hung low, knowing the beating that was certain to come.

Then Rogan caught sight of the fallen tree across the yard. Hope sprang anew. How impressed his father would be to see him jump clear of it. Despite his mother's protest and amid Emma's delighted squeals, Rogan spurred the horse around. Steam blowing from Valiant's nostrils, the wind whipping his coattails out behind him, he raced across the lawn toward the massive oak. Joy surged through him with each beat of Valiant's flashing hooves. He wanted to shout out loud, knowing he would clear the tree, knowing his father would finally be proud.

He had not seen the deep trench hidden behind the tree until it was too late. He yanked on the reins as Valiant twisted beneath him, trying in vain to pull back to safety. He could never be sure if it was the horse or his mother whose screams he'd heard as the stallion's legs snapped brokenly beneath him.

For years afterward Rogan would wish he'd been crushed beneath the horse's thrashing legs instead of landing safely at the berm. He could still see the rage that twisted Townsend's face as he tore across the lawn to him. He'd tried to run, but Townsend's longer legs easily caught him and he dragged him by the collar to the edge of the ditch.

Rogan would never forget the sight of that mighty animal

lying crippled and twisted in that ditch, its eyes rolled back into its head in agony, its desperate breath fogging from the cold. Nor would he forget his father forcing him to pull the trigger that had ended its short life.

Rogan turned from the window, forcing back the memories as he crossed his father's study to the sideboard.

"She has been chosen, Rogan."

He poured himself a liberal amount of his father's brandy and took a long swallow before responding.

"She, sir?"

"Yes, she. Your wife. Since you have shown no interest in finding one on your own, I have taken the liberty of choosing her for you. She is a fine girl of good sound stock, well worthy of the son of an earl."

"And has she a good bite and take well to the saddle?"

"Keep a civil tongue, boy. She has been chosen and you could not have made a better match for yourself. You will wed Gwyneth Pierpont within the year."

Rogan's fingers tightened around the glass. He knew the name well. Who in London would not know the daughter of one of the most powerful men in England, a man who would be certain to keep his wayward son-in-law in check?

"And have you proposed marriage for me as well?"

"No. That I leave to you. See to it as you wish, but have it done with quickly. I wish to see you wed before summer."

"And if she refuses?"

Townsend lifted a brow. "She will not. I have already learned, on good authority, that she is quite agreeable to the match. She would be a fool not to. You are the future Earl of Ashbourne."

"And if I refuse?"

"Why would you? She's well dowered, certainly pleasant enough to look at."

"She has small breasts."

Townsend was not amused. He neglected to rise to Rogan's taunt. "If you refuse, which I do not believe you have the idiocy of doing, you will be given a choice."

"Which is?"

Townsend opened the top drawer to his desk and removed a rolled and bound parchment from inside. Rogan could have sworn he saw a flicker of a smile touch his father's lips as he tossed it heedlessly upon the desktop.

Rogan took the roll and pulled the string that held it, reading the first line. *I, the Right Honorable Townsend Doraunt, Earl of Ashbourne, do hereby bequeath . . .*

He looked to his father.

"You need not read further. I will tell you that which concerns you." Townsend paused as if what he was going to say held great meaning. "In the event that you do not marry by the time of my death, that which was to have been left to you by me, every shilling I have, will be given to your cousin Beecher Prestwood."

Rogan sprang forward. "What? You cannot take Ashbourne. It is mine, by right of primogeniture. Even you cannot breach that."

Townsend smiled at his son's reaction, a smile that brought a chill to Rogan's blood. "Ah, yes, primogeniture." He crossed his hands before him, inspecting a gnarled knuckle before continuing. "You are correct in that assumption, Rogan. Legally I cannot take Ashbourne from you. It is yours by right, by law, and by consequence. But"—he paused—"I do have the ability to take all funds from Ashbourne and give them to whomever I choose. I have chosen Beecher. And do not think to protest. I have had the foresight to check with my solicitor. It is all within the law, so you see, I do not have to take Ashbourne from you. Even your income from your holdings in the north and that fool shipbuilding venture of yours could never amount to enough to run this estate."

Rogan felt his jaw tighten. Suddenly he never hated his father more. "You would leave this estate broken." He was beginning to feel powerless, a feeling to which he was unaccustomed, a feeling he did not like. "I know you care nothing for me, but have you not an ounce of care in you for Ashbourne? For your ancestry?"

Townsend smiled, the lines on his aged face turning to deep crevices. "It is as I thought, Rogan." He rose and crossed the room to the window, his hands folded behind his back. "It is in your blood, boy, as it was and still is in mine. Despise it as you may, you and I share a common bond. This great estate. You live and breathe it, what it stands for, and for all your words that you do not want it, for all your wasteful and salacious attempts at defying me, you could never allow Ashbourne to perish."

Rogan stared at his father's back, hating him for being so right. "Yet you would."

"My decision has been made. Since I cannot gain your agreement through normal means, you have forced me to this unfortunate action."

"Gain my agreement? Do you not mean my obedience, sir?"

"Call it what you wish, Rogan. My decision still stands. I did not ask for your opinion, nor does it matter to me. I will do what I must to see Ashbourne flourish—or I will see it felled by your hand. The decision is yours. You can marry the Pierpont chit and curb your licentious ways, else find yourself without fortune, without name, and thus, in the future, without Ashbourne."

"Have care, mistress! Make way!"

Chelsea pitched forward, dropping the package she held as two rough hands shoved her from behind. She landed on her bottom in a sludgy puddle, her fingers sinking beneath the surface as she attempted, and failed, to break her fall.

She cursed under her breath and looked up to see the carriage, shining black and emblazoned with gold, speeding recklessly past, red-liveried footmen running along it on all sides, pushing other unsuspecting pedestrians out of its way. She glanced toward the crowded footpath. With the exception of a few smirking gawkers, none of the throng walking by chose to take notice of her fall. She started to rise on her own, noticing the package she'd been carrying, the fine parchment stationery she'd just purchased with the near last of her funds lying ruined in the mud beside her, her new feather quill snapping beneath the polished red heels of a passing dandified gent.

"May I, milady?"

Just when she had begun to question the existence of any solicitous-minded soul within the whole of London, a deep, cultured voice from behind offered hope. Chelsea turned as best she could to find a black kid-gloved hand extended toward her, the rest of the bearer's body hidden from view.

"Thank you, kind sir," she murmured as he pulled her gently to her feet. She moved to wipe the muck from her hands on her skirts, but the stranger took her arm.

"Here, milady, do not soil your gown further." He offered her a fine-looking silk handkerchief.

"Oh, no, I couldn't . . ." Chelsea fell silent as she lifted her eyes to the man. His eyes, a deep, dark green, drew at her memory. She quickly took in the rest of him. He was an older gentleman, evidenced by the crinkling at the corners of his eyes, and was dressed in an elegant suit of silver-gray velvet. He was wealthy, his clothes bespoke it. And he'd be about the right age. She realized with a glimmer of hope that he could be the man she had been seeking since her arrival in London three weeks earlier.

"Excuse me, sir, but have we met before?"

He bowed to her, and she was afforded a view of his powdered ramillie wig, which was curled and tied back with a neat black bow. Her confidence soared. Everything about this man met the image she'd formed in her mind. It had to be him. She just knew it.

He smiled. "I am most flattered, dear child, though I fear you are mistaken. Although at my advanced age my memory is not as clear as it once was, I feel I most assuredly would recall meeting someone quite as beautiful as you."

Chelsea smiled at the compliment, yet remained unconvinced. It was his eyes. Such an odd shade of green, like the moss that grew along the rocky creek bed below the falls at Drummore. Where had she seen them before? "You look very familiar to me. You are certain we have never met?"

"Quite." His gaze swept over her person. "Now, if I may be assured you are uninjured, I would be most honored to see you safely to your door."

"Oh, there is no need. I am quite fine, not a scratch upon me. Besides," she said, turning, "I am staying right here at this boardinghouse. Thank you again for your kind assistance."

Still smiling, he tipped his tricorne and turned about, muttering a low "good day" as he started off.

"But, wait." Chelsea halted, watching as he disappeared from view around a near corner. He had left before she could return his handkerchief to him.

She glanced at the soft cloth. Embroidered across its center in fine elegant stitches was a tiny odd-shaped flower underlined with a distinctive scroll of some sort. The stitches were made with threads of gold and it was edged with the finest Mechlin lace. Why would he leave the fine piece with a stranger?

She tucked the cloth into her reticule and started back toward the boardinghouse, the encounter soon forgotten as her thoughts returned to the troubles at hand.

Would she ever find employment? All morning she had been going from shop to shop along St. Martin's Lane, asking, nay, pleading for any menial chore that might supply her with an income. Nothing. She had just returned from yet another false hope, quashed when the shopkeeper informed her that she was "too bloomin' delicate for the job."

What was she to do? The weekly rents were due tomorrow and her funds were nearly emptied. She had to remain at the boardinghouse at least until her great-uncle Leland could answer her message to come for her. *If* he would come for her. The young clerk at the House of Lords had promised he would deliver her message to him, yet over a week had passed and still no reply. What could be taking him so long?

Chelsea felt a small tug on her cloak.

"Pence, please, miss."

A child of no more than five years stood before her, holding out a dirty hand. His tattered shirt was devoid of one sleeve, his breeches ragged across the knees. No shoes covered his tiny feet.

"Please, miss?" he repeated, his large brown eyes peeking out from behind a smudged face.

Chelsea's heart softened. She searched in her reticule for something to give the boy. A single pence was all she could find.

The boy grasped the coin before she could offer it and scurried down the street, weaving his way through the stream of pedestrians before disappearing into the thick crowd. Chelsea spotted him next at the far corner, handing the pence to a frail-looking woman. She was undoubtedly his mother. In her arms she cradled an infant, whose squalling could be heard through the din of the street hawkers. The boy pointed to Chelsea and the woman smiled, pulling her ragged shawl more closely about her shoulders before she turned and disappeared around the street corner.

A shiver ran through Chelsea as she started up the narrow stairwell to her tiny rented chamber, having seen so many like souls banished to the streets since her arrival. It seemed every alleyway was teeming with them, the poor and the hungry, whole families living off the fetid refuse piles dumped outside the market stalls each day. And the children, so many children, their tiny faces forever masked by layers of soot and grime. How long would it be before she, too, would be left to begging for a pence from strangers passing by?

"Miss MacKenna! Miss MacKenna!"

Chelsea halted on the step at the familiar screech from behind, wondering what the Widow Andrews would have to complain about this day.

"Miss . . ." The rotund Widow Andrews hobbled as quickly as she could on her good leg into the entryway, her white lawn mobcap hanging slightly askew. "Well, aren't we the pawpular lawdy this day."

"Yes, Widow Andrews?"

She stopped at the foot of the stairs and leaned her full bosom against the weathered banister. " 'Ad two gentlemen callers t'day." She tossed her head in the direction of the door. "Jess missed one leavin'."

"Two callers?"

"Aye. The lawst one looked mighty rich. Just you remember, I'm not allowin' any whorin' in my house!"

"Did they say what they wanted?"

"Aye, lookin' for ye, they was. First one was a bloomin' giant, must've stood ten foot, demandin' to know where's ye were an' all. 'E called ye by a different name. Estwyck, I think. I told him I 'ad a Chelsea MacKenna and that ye was out, but he din't believe me. Said he was goin' to wait."

Chelsea glanced around the front hallway. It was empty. "Where is he?"

The widow scratched her hindquarters before responding. "He slipped out when the other gentleman came callin' for ye. This one asked for ye by MacKenna. Was yer maiden name Estwyck? Ye said your husband 'ad died in the Forty-five Rebellion, though I still don't believe ye're old enough to 'ave been married that long."

"I was married at fifteen when my parents died," Chelsea lied, hoping she could pass for at least three and twenty. "What did the second gentleman want?"

"He left this note for ye." The widow pulled a folded piece of parchment from the pocket of her stained apron. She held it back. "Said I was to give it to ye only, but I can assure ye, I din't read it."

Chelsea rather doubted that the woman could have read it had she tried, but continued to listen as the widow prattled on. " 'E was a mighty fine gentleman, rich as they come, and 'ad the greenest eyes I ever seen."

Green eyes? Chelsea quickly snatched the note from the widow's fleshy hand. The man who had just helped her up from the street—he had green eyes. "Thank you, Widow Andrews," she said, shoving the note into her reticule and away from the widow's curious stare. Perhaps the second visitor had been her great-uncle Leland. Perhaps he had not recognized her after all the time since he'd last seen her. She had not seen him since she was but a child, and the man in the street had looked familiar. . . .

"Did either man leave a name?"

"No, an' I asked them, too, 'cus ye told me ye were waiting for yer uncle to come, but they both said they weren't him."

Chelsea's hopes plummeted. But what of the other caller? "The first man who came, did he perhaps speak with an accent?"

The widow rubbed her chin. "Yea. I believe 'e did, ye know, sounded Irish."

Or Scottish. "Thank you again, Widow Andrews. If either of these men return, please do not tell them where I am. Neither appears to be my uncle and he is the only person I wish to see in London."

She moved to the door, hoping to exit before the widow could question her further.

"How am I supposed to tell anyone where ye are if I don't know meself? I got to look out for ye, ye know. Ye ain't got no other family 'ere to do that!"

Chelsea hurried out the door, stepping quickly into the pedestrian traffic along the busy avenue. She threaded her way through the milling mass, shielding her head beneath the hood of her cloak as she cast a watchful eye about at every turn.

How had Gregor found her so quickly? She had been so careful since leaving Edinburgh, making certain no one along the way knew who she truly was. Everywhere she had gone, she had used the fictitious name of MacKenna, hoping to deter those certain to be on her trail. And now he was here in London. There was no doubting it was he. No other man fitting that description could have come calling for her.

Yet what of the other caller? If he truly was the man who helped her in the street, why had he not admitted to knowing who she was? And how had he known to use the name MacKenna?

The note.

Slipping into a narrow alleyway, Chelsea pulled her reticule from inside her cloak and searched its folds for the parchment. It was sealed with a blob of red wax and imprinted with the same peculiar flower-and-scroll design that decorated the lacy handkerchief. The man who had helped her in the street had been her second visitor. Why, then, had he denied knowing who she was?

She broke the seal and began to read the elegant script written within. *Miss Estwyck . . .*

Chelsea stopped reading as a large darkened shadow spread across the heavy parchment. She did not need to look up to know who stood before her.

"Chelsea, lass, I found you. Now stop this fool running away and come here to me!"

She quickly shoved the note back in her reticule. "Gregor, what are you doing here? Why have you followed me to London?"

He took a step forward. "Now, Chelsea, 'tis all right that you got scared before the *braithel*. I, too, got a case of the nervous shivers and—"

"—and thought to warm them in my mother's bed?"

Gregor froze.

"Oh, you didn't think I knew about your late-night visits to my mother's chamber? Well, now you may spend every night there if you so choose. Rut her till your eyes turn blue, for all I care. I will no longer be there for you to hide from."

"Such filth will not come from your innocent tongue, Chelsea. Now come along, we've a long journey back to Drummore."

He reached out to take her hand, but she stepped away. He looked at her, his eyes narrowing.

"I'm not going back to Drummore with you, Gregor."

"Enough of this nonsense now, lass. You're coming home and we are going to be wed."

"Why, Gregor? Why did you come after me? You cannot think that I would believe it is your love for me that brought you all the way here from Scotland. No, 'tis something else." She paused for a moment to think, then said softly, "The land."

Gregor remained silent, affirming her assumption.

"Yes, 'tis Drummore that brought you chasing after me, isn't it? Of course. What an idiot I've been not to have seen it sooner. As laird of Ballingall *and* Drummore land, you'd have control of the eastern Lothian region. Without Drummore, you have naught but a small holding of land that is neither arable nor fit to feed a sheep on."

Gregor's eyes darkened. "What do you know of land?"

"Your family lost many of their holdings in the Forty-five. The only reason we still have our land is because my mother has affiliations with court and somehow managed to keep it. Probably bedded every member of the House of Lords to do it. But then there was me. My father had stipulated that Drummore be my dowry. What better way for my mother to keep it from falling into the hands of some English *sassenach* I might choose than to wed me off to her Scottish lover?"

Gregor advanced. "Always told your *midder* allowing you to read those books would make you into nothing but a *dandillie*. But that matters naught. You're still coming with me back to Drummore to be my wife." He grabbed her arm then, squeezing it painfully, and pulled her close until his breath was touching her nose. "And when we get back, you're going to learn in every way what it means to honor and obey your husband."

With a growl, his mouth descended on hers, crushing her lips beneath his. His fingers squeezed her jaw, forcing her lips apart. Unable to fight against his strength, Chelsea had only one alternative. She opened her mouth, and as he pushed his tongue inside she bit down hard, sinking her teeth into its meaty flesh.

Chapter 2

"Give us another round in here, tapster, my boy needs his wits completely sotted afore he goes!"

Settled at a crowded gaming table in a smoke-filled chamber off the main taproom of the Fleece Tavern, Rogan looked to the narrow open doorway as his friend and brother-in-law, Fredric Ellingsford, shuffled into the room, swinging his ale tankard before him.

"Aye, he need be squiffed in order to complete the task before him now."

"What's this?" Rogan said, chuckling at Fredric's inebriety. "One would think you were unhappy with marriage to my lovely sister. You, the one who has been belauding the marital state to me for weeks."

" 'Twas your sister's idea. Said your marriage was inevitable. Said, I believe, your trying to avoid it was like casting stones against the wind and I thought it wouldn't hurt to . . ." Lean as a shotten herring, Fredric near tumbled onto the table before them. The contents of his tankard sloshed over its sides. The cards being played fluttered to the floor. When the others sitting at the table protested the disturbance, Fredric stood, wavering only slightly, but attempting a stance of some dignity.

"Now, gentlemen, no need to get shirty. 'Twas an accident. It's only a game and . . ."

He looked ridiculous. His shirttails hung out the back of his breeches, his cravat was stained with ale dribblings and drooped limply around his collar and somehow, somewhere, his powdered club wig had gotten turned askance over one brow. As if suddenly noticing its lopsided condition, he swiped the frazzled peruke from his head and looked at it as if it were unrecognizable. "Hey now. This isn't my wig. It looks like a bloody drowned rat. Who's the bloody bounder that took my . . . ?"

Fredric's last words dropped off and he became entranced with the serving wench's breasts as she leaned over the table to remove their empty tankards. His head lolled back and forth, following the fleshy mounds as they moved about the table, his eyes wide with wonderment.

Rogan drew a knave from his hand, discarding it to the table.

"Shunna done that, Rogue," Fredric said, his eyes never leaving their spot, "he needed that one . . ."

Rogan surrendered his cards to the table. "Thanks to you, Fredric, I've now lost four straight hands to him. Care to make it five?"

"Don't be blaming me for your lack of luck today, my boy. Isn't my fault your mind's elsewhere."

"As is yours, my friend. And if you haven't sobered up

before you get home, you'll be catching the devil's tongue from my dear sister, Emma."

"Bah!" Fredric finally pulled his eyes away and waved a hand through the air in drunken indignation, nearly toppling himself over with the effort. "I'll let no woman tell me what to do. I'm the man of my house and no woman, not even your sister mind you, is to tell me when I've had my fill."

He puffed out his under-fleshed chest and raised his tankard high in salute to his words.

Rogan shook his head, knowing that on the morrow, when Fredric's head was clear and he had his usual wits about him, he'd deny ever saying such things. He worshipped Emma like a stray puppy, more so now that she was with child. Rogan wondered what it was about some women that caused men's minds to turn to mush, and thanked the heavens he hadn't yet been admitted to their ranks. Mayhaps, he prayed, he never would be. It was far better to keep emotions out of it and sample a variety of sweets than to lose one's wits over a termagant and spend the rest of one's life under the cat's foot.

He flipped a coin on the table as the serving wench set down a round of newly-filled tankards. He reached behind her to pull her soft bottom onto his lap. "Come here, love," he said, nuzzling her neck with his mouth. "How would you like to keep this man from a fate worse than death?"

The saucy redhead, known to him only as Moll, smiled in ready acceptance. She pressed her full breasts, already near to bursting from the tight confines of her bodice, against his black frock coat and peered up at him with provocative blue eyes. "Be me pleasure, milord. Shall I tell me boss we'll be taking a room upstairs then?"

Rogan toyed with the flame-colored lock of hair that settled just above her breast. "That I'd not this wretched performance to give today, Moll, I'd be most willing to while the afternoon away with you upstairs between the bedsheets. Your offer sorely tempts me."

"I'd wager I know of a way to convince you." Moll ran her hand down the front of his greatcoat to the more than evident bulge in his breeches.

"Come on, man," Fredric said, interrupting with the timing of a diligent matron, "up with you now. 'Tis time for you to buckle to. You are only prolonging the inevitable, you know. You've held off longer than the rest of us. 'Tis time for you to go now before you lose all your funds and haven't a brass farthing left to hire you a hack!"

A round of male laughter rumbled around the table at that last remark.

"Moll! Stop ye're bawdy rollickin'! Ye've got other patrons to serve!"

Moll scurried from the room at the tavern owner's shout, dodging the groping hands of a down-on-his-luck baron thoroughly in his cups. Rogan called after her for a brandy before turning back to the game. "One more brusher to keep me on the journey, lads, then I'll be off."

Inwardly he was in no hurry to be on his way. He was in no hurry to do anything but avoid what this day was leading to, even as he knew he could avoid it no longer. His future, as laid out by his father, was certain. The only thing Rogan was more certain of in his life was death and that, at the moment, seemed preferable. He drew up his hand and nearly groaned aloud. Even the cards were against him. Not five minutes later he was tossing his cards to the table in defeat.

"Seems you're the holder of my card, Dan. You win again."

Rogan's opponent sat back in his chair and smiled a victorious grin. Though only two years his junior at seven and twenty, the lanky Daniel Haythorne could have passed for a lad of eighteen without question. The youngest of seven sons to a wealthy old earl from Dorset, he had large brown eyes that made the ladies swoon, topped by a mop of ruddy hair which curled wildly at his forehead regardless of the amount of pomatum he pasted in it.

Daniel tipped his tankard to Rogan. "Seems your mind is elsewhere, my friend. Weddings and such fripperies. You know, I can recall a day when you and I were at Oxford, not too many years ago . . ."

" . . . vowing never to fall victim to the London marriage market," Rogan finished. "We were to spend our days in cakes and ale, gaming and chasing unchaste women as we watched everyone else march off to the prison of wedlock." He paused, his voice turning sour. "Aye, what a fitting word it is, *wedlock*—to be locked in wed."

Rogan had told no one, not his closest of friends, not even his sister, Emma, about his father's damnable plot to force his hand in marriage. He hated his complete inability to alter the situation. He took a deep draw of the brasher of brandy just served, swallowing it down with a frown as it burned a direct path to his stomach.

"Didn't Beecher say he would be joining us here today? He is family, Rogue. He should be here on your last day of unbetrothed freedom."

Rogan's mood was quickly plummeting and Daniel's mention of his cousin only made it more so. Beecher and Rogan were distant in relation, Townsend's half-sister being Beecher's mother. When Beecher's mother had been left a widow with an infant son and not much of a portion to keep her, Rogan's father had installed her at Ashbourne, taking the responsibility of Beecher's upbringing to heart. They had come of age together, taking instruction from the same fencing master, yet for as long as Rogan could remember, they had been in competition against each other in every way, though most often for Townsend's miserly doled affections.

Beecher seemed to make the most of Townsend's endless disdain for his son, always finding some way to best display Rogan's shortcomings in his father's eyes. Rogan could still remember the day Beecher had challenged him to a race in front of the girl they had both taken a fancy to. They'd been young, but needing to prove their manhood. Rogan accepted the challenge and proved the better of the race and for the girl's affections. Beecher was furious, throwing the first fist. When Townsend came to break up the scuffle, it was Beecher he consoled while Rogan's mother stitched the gash left in her son's arm from Beecher's hidden pocketknife.

Rogan now ran his finger along the thin white scar on his forearm, frowning at the memory.

"A toast . . ." Fredric suddenly announced. He raised his tankard high. "To our good friend and colleague, Rogan Doraunt, Viscount Ravenel, and future Earl of Ashbourne. We sadly bid you adieu as you go off to your future bride, the lovely Lady Gwyneth. May you find happiness and joy as much in life with her . . ."

" . . . as you will between those lily-white thighs!" Daniel countered, downing the remainder of his ale with one quick swallow. "What a fine ending it is to one of London's most celebrated bachelors. Perhaps Beecher and I can save the grieving beauties from throwing themselves into the murky Thames when they hear of your engagement to Old Man Pierpont's most prized possession."

"Yes, well, seems delaying this thing any longer will do me no good." Rogan stood and moved across the tap-room to the dirt-streaked window of the tavern. Outside, the crowded market in Covent Garden brimmed with every sort of humanity imaginable, prostitutes lingering at every available corner, while hawkers and costermongers walking along shouted their wares for sale.

"Fine Kentish cherries! Pence a pound!"

"Hot ginger loaves!"

"Chestnuts! Three-pence a hundred!"

" 'Ere ye are, milord," Moll said, breaking him from his thoughts. She handed him his cloak and black tricorne, straightening its gold cockade. "I 'ad the boy run out t' find ye a hack."

"My thanks, Moll, but there's no need. I think a walk would do me well to clear my head of this afternoon's drinking. Wouldn't want Lord Pierpont turning me away at the door for being sotted."

The smile that passed over Moll's full lips could only be called consoling.

Rogan leaned toward her. "Think I might steal a kiss for luck, Molly dear?"

"Luck that she'll say yea or that she'll say nay?"

"I'd rather the latter, but suspect the former." With that, Rogan tipped her chin with his finger, kissing her quickly before starting for the door.

"Ye don't have to stay away long, ye know, milord," Moll said breathlessly as he moved away. "I'll not be leaving here anytime soon."

Rogan donned his cloak, tipping his hat before moving toward the door. "Tapster," he said, calling for the barkeep, "many thanks for your unending efforts."

The man uttered an inaudible response, never looking up from his newspaper as Rogan flipped him a coin, before turning to leave. The barkeep caught it without losing his place on the page.

Outside, away from the warmth of the taproom hearth, the skies were hung with fat, dismal clouds, the air heavy with the smell of impending rain and stale fish. Though the season had not been harsh enough to freeze the Thames for a winter frostfair, the air had a brisk bite that had lingered through the early weeks of February.

A dismal day for this dismal task, Rogan thought to himself as he made his way steadily through the crowd. He side-stepped a running child, striding quickly over the waste gutter that ran down the middle of the crowded street. A prostitute loitering at a nearby doorway called out to him, offering him an afternoon the likes of which he'd never spent. He chuckled, doubting she could provide such a time, and waved her off.

As he turned down an alleyway, a seedy looking specimen stepped from the shadows and stood waiting for him several yards ahead. Tufts of matted and no doubt lice-ridden hair covered the better part of his bulbous head and upon closer inspection, Rogan found the man lacked one eye, leaving an uncovered blackened hole in its place. The man now assessed Rogan with that eye, looking him up and down while his mouth curled upward, displaying a vacancy of several teeth.

"If I were you, I would turn around and go back to your hole."

"Well, yer not and I thinks you needs to give me your fine coat there, toff."

Rogan reached inside his waistcoat and pushed the fabric aside to afford the thief a good view of his pistol butt. "This coat?"

The thief's leer faded. Rogan didn't think the man fool enough to challenge his shot for he brandished no weapon with the exception of his ugliness. No doubt most dropped to their knees and emptied their purses at the mere sight of him. Rogan, however, was not like most, and the thief seemed to take this into consideration for, after a long moment, he merely grunted and turned away, disappearing into the alley from whence he'd emerged.

She has been chosen, Rogan. Your future wife.

Townsend's words echoed through Rogan's mind. Fair hair and bright blue eyes, Gwyneth Pierpont was the catch of the season, everyone said. She'd attended every social function, seeking him out and flirting with practiced expertise. She was an artful actress, portraying innocence quite cunningly, but Rogan knew her innocence to be false, falser than the red Spanish rouge that colored her pale cheeks.

It was common knowledge, actually old news now, the story of Gwyneth's deflowering. But it was not forgotten. Not long ago, in the prime of her virginal youth, Gwyneth had fallen in love with the son of a duke whose estates neighbored her family's. She had given her virginity to him, thinking to lure him into a proposal of marriage, but her choice proved fatal when her ploy backfired and the young man married her sister, Jeanette, instead.

Yet Rogan did not care. The marriage meant nothing to him. That she be a virgin mattered even less. At least she wouldn't be some mewling frightened bride shocked at the sight of a man's body when he took her on their wedding night. She was a woman of noble birth and passable enough in appearance to please the eye. And she had been chosen by his father, a fact he would never forget.

"Nae! Let abee!"

At the sound of the hurried footsteps approaching from behind, Rogan forgot all thought of Gwyneth. He started to turn about, thinking the wretch he'd faced moments earlier had found himself another victim and . . .

Ooooff!

He staggered back, his head striking the wall behind him, dazing him and blurring his vision. He shook his head to clear it and closed his arms around his assailant, fighting to stand beneath the squirming weight.

"Hold, man, stop your struggling."

A fist connected soundly with his jaw, clipping his chin upward. A firm toe struck his shin. He raised his hand, ready to knock the beggar on the head, pulling his punch just as he looked down and noticed not a man, but a woman, struggling to break his hold.

"What the . . . ?"

"Let me go!"

Rogan caught her forearm just as her hand swung back toward his jaw. She swung her other arm. He caught that too, and twisted it behind her.

"Stop it, you're hurting me!"

Rogan released her and she hit him again, pummeling his chest with her fists.

"I thought you said I was hurting you . . ."

He grabbed her wrists. He twisted her arms around her back, crossing them behind her and pulled her against his chest, this hellion with a punch nearly as strong as a man's for so slight a form. He growled at her. "Be still now, will you?"

Though meant to frighten her, his comments succeeded only in making her squirm all the more. She kicked and thrashed. She punched and struggled. She seemed to have sprung several arms for she pulled his hair and scratched his face, still screaming for him to release her. Somehow Rogan managed to pin her arms to her sides, throwing his leg out to deflect yet another blow.

"Enough already!"

To his surprise, she did as he asked, or rather told, or rather bellowed, and when he looked down at her, noticing her face for the first time, he did not believe he had ever seen a more lovely creature in all his days.

She was beautiful, delicate, and fragile, but with a strength shining from her eyes that belied her outward appearance. With her arms held behind her, her breasts were pushed forward, crushed against his chest. Rogan found he liked that. Her face was oval-shaped and arched with dark brows over deep blue-black eyes that flashed at him in anger. Thick waves of midnight-black hair curled wildly about her pale ivory face, her lips full and curved. He felt a sudden itch to kiss those lips and so entranced was he by the vision before him, he did not notice when she pulled her hand free and balled it into a fist, slugging his arm and instantly halting his perusal.

"Let me go, blast you!" she said, her punch quelling any thought of injury on her person. "And stop sizing me up like some harlot at Covent Garden."

"What kind of language is that for a lady to use, especially when she is being rescued by a gentleman?" He tightened his hold on her other arm. "Now, I will let you go if you promise not to hit me again."

She said nothing.

"Will you promise?"

She nodded. A woman with looks like that could be dangerous. He wondered if he should trust her, even as he gently released her. He started to step away from her, thinking she'd surely run now that she was free, but she pulled him back and clutched at his jacket.

"I thought you wanted me to let you go . . ."

His words dropped off when she looked up at him, her eyes reminding him of the stormy night sky, dark and turbulent.

"Help me, please."

Her voice was deep for a woman, breathy, a soft near whisper that somehow intrigued him even more.

"Help you, my lady? But I do not even know your name."

She glanced around the alleyway, seeming to be searching for something behind them. She looked back to him and repeated, "Please . . ."

Rogan started to speak, to ask her why she was running or from whom, but before he could utter a word, she was pulling his head down toward her and pressing her lips urgently to his. The innocence of her kiss told of her inexperience, but the shock it gave him sent a jolt running through his body more fierce than he'd ever before felt. He did not hesitate in his response, but pulled her into his arms and returned the kiss with pleasure.

Rogan didn't know what made him open his eyes while he stood there kissing her; he'd heard no sound to alert him they were no longer alone, but when he did, he saw the form of a mammoth man advancing upon them. His arm was raised to shoulder's height. In his hand Rogan could make out the distinct shape of a dagger, its pointed blade glinting at him in the single ray of sunlight that somehow filtered its way down to them. He had only moments to spare.

Rogan pulled the girl hard against his chest. She gasped at the sudden movement and tried to break away, but he held her tightly, deepening the kiss. Holding her to him, he reached for his pistol.

Chelsea was stunned. She opened her mouth to scream and nearly dropped to her knees when she felt the stranger's tongue slide easily into her mouth. He tasted of brandy, and the contact sent her senses soaring, but she was too shocked to protest, too weak to fight him. What was she doing? She could feel his thigh pressing between her legs, yet not until she felt his hand moving between them, brushing against her breasts as he fumbled at her bodice, did she realize what was happening.

"No!"

She tried in vain to pull away. His hold only seemed to tighten. She felt his warm breath touch her ear.

"Hold still, my lady, else you'll feel the sharp prick of the blade."

Sharp prick of the . . . ? Oh, God, what had she done? Visions of rape and violence filled her mind. Panic began to set in. He would kill her and none would know better. She had run down a deserted alley to escape one fiend and had thrown herself into the arms of another. This man was a stranger. He could pull her into a darkened cove and none would know the better. Even now his fingers were fondling her where no man had ever touched her before, his leg pressing against her in the most intimate of places.

She felt his hand move up toward the lacings of her bodice. She fought against him, but he held her firmly, his arm encircling her waist. She heard the fabric of her gown tear and tried to scream aloud, but his mouth took hers again, silencing her cry. His tongue plunged into her mouth, sending a shock wave of sensation spiraling through her. She felt something cold and hard touch against her breasts. She tried to scream, remembering his threat of the blade, but could make no sound. He was going to kill her. He was going to cut her throat right there. And there was nothing she could do about it.

And then the world was spinning before her as he swung her like a rag doll behind him. His hand closed around her wrist, holding her tightly. Chelsea fought to pry his fingers loose, but they seemed locked around her, pinning her to his side.

"Release me, or I'll scream!"

"Halt where you stand or feel my shot!"

Chelsea looked up when she heard the cock of a pistol. Her mouth fell open as the man who held her so tightly, the man who had moments before been assaulting her body, carefully lowered his gun toward the opening of the alleyway. Gregor stood but a distance forward, a nasty-looking dagger in his hand, poised and ready to strike.

Chelsea nearly dropped. The blade. He had meant that Gregor was coming at them. Five more yards and one of them would have been dead.

"What do you think you're doing with my *bund-sack*?"

Bund-sack? Rogan tightened his finger on the trigger.

"Nothing you need to be concerned with, friend."

His opponent narrowed his eyes and Rogan could have sworn he heard him emit a growl. He looked like a great bear ready to attack. A great black bear with fangs bared. The better part of his face was covered by a short dark beard, set off by a jagged, red scar that ran crooked above his right cheek. Straight black hair reached to his wide shoulders. That he wasn't at all pleased to have found him kissing this girl was apparent. What Rogan wondered was why. He pulled her closer. It was no wonder she was running. The man was menacing.

"Come here to me, lass!"

The girl tried to run, but Rogan yanked her back. "Not so fast, my lady. You were not going to leave me here to face him alone, were you? Besides, we are not yet finished, you and I."

Rogan turned then to face the great bear of a man. "What business do you have with this woman?"

"It is none of your affair, Sassenach." The man reached for Chelsea. "I said to come with me!"

Rogan pulled her back. "It would seem the lady does not desire your company."

From behind, Rogan could hear the sounds of horses and carriages and the city, and knew a main thoroughfare must be close by. Hoping he could reach it and lose his opponent in the crowd, he stepped back, still holding the girl at his side.

"Follow me."

He did not look to see if she agreed.

The other man stepped forward. "Come here to me, lass, or I'll kill your *coulie pockpudding* lover where he stands!"

Coulie? Pockpudding?

Rogan knew he had to remain calm. He kept his pistol aimed as he continued stepping back. With each step, the other man followed but somehow he seemed to be getting closer. Rogan kept moving. The sounds were louder now, but they were still a world away from freedom. The giant would reach them far before they reached safety. He needed a diversion. Where was a one-eyed cutpurse when he needed one?

Rogan took another step back. The other took two, lessening the gap between them. With each step he took, the giant followed with more until but a spit and a stride stood between them. At this close proximity, Rogan could see the promise in his opponent's dark eyes. No man liked having a woman taken from him and no man would stand idly by and watch it happen. Before it was done one of them would be dead. Rogan didn't wish to weigh the chances on whom.

Something overhead suddenly caught his eye. He looked up for just a moment as a window three stories above drifted open. A maidservant poked out her head, lifting a chamberpot onto the sill. Rogan looked to his opponent. He was oblivious of the pot positioned directly above his head. Rogan knew he had to keep him that way.

"What do you say we make a bargain?" he said, one eye on the chamberpot above.

"I don't bargain with English whoresons."

The maid pushed the pot to the edge of the sill.

"It will be worth your while . . ."

"What sort of bargain?"

She lifted it up.

"You allow me and the lady here to go our way and—"

She leaned out the window.

"And what?"

"I'll warn you about the chamber pot which is about to be emptied on your head!"

The giant looked up and the maid turned the pot over, dumping its foul contents directly on top of him. Rogan did not waste a second.

"Hurry, my lady, run, toward the street!"

Chelsea felt as if her arm were being wrenched from its socket. Her heart was pounding against her chest and she could hear Gregor howling behind them. She managed to pull her arm free from Rogan's grasp and lifted her heavy skirts to her knees, praying she would not trip on a cobble. Her sides began to stitch beneath the tight lacings of her stays, her chest so tight she could barely breathe, but still she ran. She ran as if the devil were at her heels, indeed he was, and more furious than she had ever before seen him.

People were looking out windows and doors, roused by Gregor's thundering, but she paid them no heed. She did not want to think of what would happen if Gregor caught them. She had heard of him killing others for less reason. In seconds, they reached the opening of the alleyway and emerged onto a busy thoroughfare, turning just in time to dodge a racing carriage. Rogan grabbed her arm again and before Chelsea knew what was happening, she was being shoved into the open door of a nearby waiting hackney coach.

"Whoa, guv'ner," the coach driver said, spilling his mug of ale on his shirt. "Where ye off to?"

"Grosvenor Square, and hurry!" Rogan said, pulling the door closed behind him.

Chelsea scrambled into the corner of the seat, her chest heaving as she took in heavy gulps of air. Gregor was still bellowing like a madman behind them. She managed to turn and peer out the back window just as he came roaring from the alley, his upper body soaked with waste. She saw him raise his hand and heard the sound of the dagger slicing through the air. Its blade whizzed by to lodge in the door frame beside them. Chelsea screamed and pressed herself farther into the corner, eyes wide, staring at the bone-handled dirk.

The coach lurched forward and she fell back in the cracked leather seat, banging her head against the back window. Through the weaving and bouncing of the speeding vehicle, she managed to grasp the window frame to pull herself aright.

"Are you injured, my lady?"

Two silver-blue eyes looked over her with concern. Chelsea didn't know what to do, what to say, and just stared at him as he ran his hands over her arms to check them for injuries. He fingered the tender spot on her forehead where she'd fallen back. He was probably the most handsome man she'd ever seen, and she couldn't believe she'd thrown herself at him like she had. She was like to die from the embarrassment.

Satisfied that she was in no immediate danger, Rogan removed the dagger from the door frame, glancing at the shiny blade before pocketing it inside his coat. "He'll not be harming you again any time soon."

Suddenly the carriage lurched, throwing Chelsea against his chest. His arms went around her, his face within inches of her own. Those eyes stared down at her intently.

"Well, my lady, now that we've gotten better acquainted, perhaps you could tell me just what a *coulie pockpudding* is."

Chapter 3

"Wherever did you find her, Rogan?" The woman's eyes shone warm and concerned as she took Chelsea's cloak and handed it to a waiting footman. "Poor dear. You look as if you've been through the deluge. Is that a bruise on your arm? Come and warm yourself by the fire here while Rogan tells me what has brought you to our parlor."

Without benefit of an introduction, Chelsea could only guess the woman to be a relation of Rogan's. When she'd opened the door at their arrival, clutching her delicate knit shawl about her shoulders, Chelsea had at first thought her his wife, which caused her to hang back behind Rogan, remembering the way she'd kissed him in the alleyway. But watching her now, it became obvious they were related by blood for they shared the same facial features and mahogany-colored hair, hers upswept in a fashionable twist beneath the trailing tippets of a frilly lace pinner cap.

She turned to Chelsea. "I'd wager you could use a cup of our cook's celebrated tea. It's her own blend, guaranteed to soothe any frazzled nerve. By the by, since my brother lacks the social graces to introduce us properly, my name is Emmalyne Ellingsford, his sister, but you may call me Emma. Now, Rogan, what is this all about?"

Chelsea followed them to a bright and airy chamber off the main hall, its walls papered with silk in a yellow floral pattern strewn with small colorful birds. Across the room, tall mullioned windows that reached to the ceiling lined one wall, and on a summer's day Chelsea could imagine the bright sunlight streaming inside. Now all they revealed was a canvas of gray and dismal clouds hanging low on the horizon.

As Rogan began to relate the details of the past hour to his sister, Chelsea took a seat upon a comfortable looking armchair beside the wall of windows. She had begun to wonder if her heart would ever cease its pounding. Her throat burned from running in the icy winter air and she felt certain it hadn't been until after they were a safe distance away from Gregor that she'd actually drawn a breath. What would she have done if Rogan had not been in the alleyway at that precise moment? What if Gregor had caught her, as he surely would have had Rogan not been there? She'd be on her way back to Scotland this very moment, not standing in this cheery parlor by a warm fire. She'd be on her way to marry Gregor, with his lover, her mother, standing proudly on.

Except for the man who had saved her.

As she listened to Rogan recount the confrontation with Gregor, she found herself studying his profile from across the room. He had a voice that was deep and strong, filling the room each time he spoke. His jaw had a stubborn set to it that made one think he was used to getting his way. His face was clean shaven and handsome as she had ever seen, set off by a sort of cocksure grin that lifted one corner of his mouth, a mouth that had kissed her so very boldly . . .

So intent was she on her perusal of him, she did not notice when Rogan looked over to her, until he smiled as if clearly reading the direction of her thoughts. Chelsea glanced away and peered out the window, feigning oblivion of him and Emmalyne and their conversation, while trying to hide the flush that spread across her cheeks.

She closed her eyes and rested her head against the windowpane, allowing the cold glass to ease her aching temple. How had this happened? How she wished she could somehow erase the last two months from her life. Staying at Drummore, after finding what she had that night, had been an impossibility, she knew. She would not have been able to face her mother and Gregor without revealing what she knew, would never be able to return to Drummore again without recalling that horrible night. And she would never have been able to wed Gregor after learning he'd been her mother's lover.

She'd left that very night, taking only what she could carry, a valise stuffed with two gowns and whatever valuables she could procure, just as the first rays of morning were dawning over the heather-carpeted hills around the castle walls. Old Stilch, the castle smithy, had aided her in her escape. The white-whiskered man, more ancient it seemed than the centuries-old keep where he'd worked his entire life, had always held a soft spot for the master's daughter, she knew, as if she had been his very own. He hadn't asked for the smallest of explanations when she tapped on his door to enlist his aide in fleeing the bailey. He'd just nodded, as if somehow already knowing, his wise old eyes glimmering in the candlelight.

Her wedding dowry had been easily found, secured in a coffer and waiting to be given to Gregor that morning. Stilch had broken the lock that secured it and instead of being a reward to Gregor for wedding her, it had paid her coach fare out of the country and away from the life she had known.

Rogan had quizzed her about her affiliation with Gregor and she'd staunchly denied knowing who he was. She claimed he was a stranger, a drunken stranger who'd obviously mistaken her for another. She knew Rogan did not believe her, it was silly to think he would, but somehow she could not bring herself to tell him the truth of it all. If anyone discovered that she had been betrothed to Gregor and had disappeared without explanation, she could easily be brought back to Scotland, back to face her mother—back to face Gregor. One could not leave a promise of marriage without, at the very least, an explanation and she could not do that. Not now. Perhaps not ever.

Her only hope was to locate her father. Damson Estwyck would save his little *dautie,* of that she was certain. But he was so far away, somewhere across the Channel. The only way she knew she would ever find him would be first to find the one other person who knew his direction. Her father's uncle, Leland Estwyck, Viscount Hollinsford.

Chelsea had not seen her great-uncle since she'd been but a child in the schoolroom, but she remembered him as being kind and sincere, drawing her upon his knee and tickling her till she squealed with delight. He would know where her father had gone. He would know how to reach him. But her messages to Leland had gone unanswered and now she was alone in a foreign place with no other family to call upon, out of funds and soon to be out of her room at the boardinghouse and relying upon the kindness of an absolute stranger.

A footman knocked on the door, then entered the room. As he conversed quietly with Rogan, Chelsea glanced over to him. She had never before seen a man stand up to Gregor so, or live after attempting it. He'd not hesitated when she'd begged him for his help, but gallantly defended her without question. She remembered how it had felt when he'd kissed her, how oddly her body had responded to him, like she—

"Miss MacKenna." Rogan's voice suddenly broke into her thoughts. "It seems your suitor has learned where we are."

Chelsea looked out the window to where he'd indicated. She nearly dropped when she recognized the form that waited at the other side of the iron gate at the front of the house. It was Gregor. He had followed them there. Somehow he'd learned where they had gone and had followed. And now he stood waiting for her like the very Devil himself.

Should she have expected him not to? They had exchanged betrothal promises, a bond nearly as unbreakable as the marriage vows themselves. And Chelsea knew Gregor well enough to know he would never relent. He would never leave London without his prize in tow, and he could never return to Scotland without her. Besides his greed for Drummore, he couldn't allow himself the humiliation of facing his people alone. A man could walk out on a woman whenever he pleased, but a woman walking out on a man spelled certain disgrace for him with his own kind. He'd be ridiculed, his authority questioned, for any man who could not manage a woman certainly could not manage an entire estate.

"I will see what I can do to convince him to leave. In the meantime, I will post my stablemaster, Krune, at the door for protection. You've no need to worry. Krune is twice his size and wields a nasty shoeing iron. I've a personal matter to attend to myself. I will be back directly. If you would but stay here with my sister until my return, then we will see what we can do to help you."

Chelsea must have looked beyond frightened for he added, "Don't worry. He cannot harm you here."

She nodded and watched as he bowed and turned to leave. She wanted to go with him and chided herself for her foolishness. Still the room seemed suddenly empty without him.

"Miss MacKenna, is it?"

Chelsea looked over at Emma. "Please call me Chelsea," she said, knowing she would most probably forget to answer to the false name of MacKenna.

"Wonderful." Emma patted the cushion of the settee beside her. "Do come and sit with me. Rogan has just told me what you suffered at the hands of that awful ruffian. You poor, poor dear."

Emma leaned forward to fill a china cup from the teapot. She offered the vessel to Chelsea. "You needn't worry about him any longer. Rogan and I agree you shall stay here with us until we can see you safely to your family."

Chelsea took a small sip from her cup, a delicate china

decorated with tiny roses. The tea was fragrant and lemony, warming her instantly.

She thought to tell Emma that Gregor would never leave without her, but said simply, "I have no family here."

"Oh?" Emma raised a brow. "Where have you family?"

Chelsea hesitated. Her fears of being sent back to Scotland issued forth. "I have no family—anymore," she lied. "My father and brother were killed fighting in the Forty-five and my mother died after birthing me."

Chelsea set her teacup in its saucer and it clattered in her trembling hand. She clenched her fingers into a fist at her side to hide her nervousness. "I remained at home as long as funds would permit, but they were soon gone. I have come to London in search of employ."

More lies. She had lived so many in the past weeks that she now began to question her own true identity. When would it end? Or would it ever?

Chelsea watched Emma carefully to see if she would believe her. It wasn't entirely a falsehood. Her brother, Jamie, had died in the Jacobite uprising and her father was now in hiding somewhere on the continent for his part in the revolution. As for her mother—she had died to Chelsea that night three weeks earlier when she'd found her sprawled on her back beneath Gregor.

Chelsea took another sip of tea, swallowing hard to rid her mouth of its sudden sour taste.

"I see," Emma said thoughtfully, running a manicured finger over her chin. "If you do not mind my asking, where have you been staying since your arrival in London?"

"At a rooming house near Charing Cross. I have been trying to find employment since my arrival, but I am afraid I have not been very successful."

She had tried everything she could think of, every vocation she might be able to perform and no one had wanted her, but they all had the same advice to give for swift employment—a thought she could never even consider.

Chelsea had seen the painted-faced ladies of Covent Garden not long after her arrival in London and knew what they did when they took their patrons inside. They waited outside the ornate bagnios and crowded alehouses, eagerly attaching themselves to the coat sleeve of any passing gentleman who might provide them ample coin for the evening.

A chill swept through her at the thought that her life might turn to such desperation and she vowed never to fall to such depths. Yet what funds she had remaining were quickly slipping from her fingers. Her dowry had proved minimal, since most of the marriage settlement had included the ownership to Drummore and its surrounding lands. What would she do when she had nothing left?

Emma took her hand as if reading her thoughts clearly. "I just had a thought. I shall offer you employment. You will stay with us, as my companion. I can use any assistance possible now with my time coming nearer."

She patted her stomach proudly and Chelsea suddenly realized what she was saying. "When is the child due?"

"Oh, not for four more months. My belly hardly swells, but when I do grow larger, I shall need to engage the help of a lady's companion. Fredric and I will be leaving this house in a couple of weeks when the renovations on ours are complete. I shall hire you now and you needn't worry about employment any longer, that is, if you would agree to it?"

"Do you really mean it?"

"Of course I do. You would be doing me more favor than I would you."

Chelsea's head was spinning. She felt as if the weight of the world had been lifted from her shoulders. Now she could concentrate all her efforts on finding her father. As soon as she could slip away, she would send off another dispatch to her great-uncle, Leland, pleading for him to come to her.

Chelsea nodded.

"Wonderful. I'll have Rogan send someone for your belongings. At what rooming house were you lodging?"

"At the Widow Andrews's, Number Four St. Martin's Lane."

"Good." Emma stood. "Now, I'm due for my afternoon's rest. I'll have one of the maids show you to your room. Once you are settled, then perhaps we can discuss what to do about our unwanted visitor outside."

Rogan was just leaving when Fredric arrived home, looking much the worse for wear after another three hours at the Fleece.

"If I were you, I'd get my arse up to your chambers before Emma sees you in the state you're in."

Fredric raised a haughty brow, his voice crowing loudly. "I've every right to partake on the day my brother-in-law get his wings clipped."

Rogan chuckled, noting that despite his bravado, Fredric's words broke off softly as he looked around the hall like a child about to be punished for a misdeed.

"What are you doing here anyway? I thought you'd still be at the Pierpont home, sharing a premarital glass of brandy with the proud Lord Pierpont. Did the negotiations go that easily?"

"I haven't yet gone." Rogan glanced back toward the parlor, his thoughts drifting to the beautiful girl sitting there. "I was unavoidably detained."

Emma came forward to join them. "Rogan, Miss MacKenna's things are at the Andrews boardinghouse on Charing Cross."

Noting the outward appearance of her husband and the odor of ale that emanated from him, she shot Fredric an angry stare, her last words a mere afterthought. "Please see about retrieving them for her."

"Perhaps Fredric could see to it," Rogan said, coming to his brother-in-law's rescue. "I'm overdue for an appointment."

The mention of his impending engagement momentarily distracted Emma's attention. "Am I to believe this appointment is with a certain Gwyneth Pierpont?"

"I've not much of a choice, have I?"

Emma neglected to answer. She knew well of the condition Townsend had attached to his will for their father had told her of it in a recent letter. Though she did not agree with her father's tactics, she believed he had Rogan's interests at heart and knew, too, what her brother did not—that Townsend's time with them was limited.

"Rogan, have you ever thought that Father might have a reason for adding that condition to his will?"

Rogan nodded. "He wishes to prove he can still control me."

Emma frowned. Sometimes she wanted to clobber him for his stubborn pride. "Rogan, is it not obvious to you? He is making his arrangements, settling all his loose ends before . . ." She broke off, her eyes glistening with unshed tears. Her voice cracked when she spoke again. "He didn't want you to know, but, he is dying, Rogan. His physicians have told him he will not last the year. He needs to be assured Ashbourne will carry on. He needs to ensure the continuity of the Doraunt line. His father had the same duty for him and you will with your sons. I cannot inherit. I know you tell yourself none of it matters to you, but it does. I know it does. Do you think I do not remember the way you used to stare at those portraits of Grandfather and the others? How you dreamed of becoming one of them? And well you should. It is your right and your duty. And now it is your time. You simply cannot ignore your responsibilities any longer."

Rogan felt a twinge of dutiful sadness at the news of his father's true condition, but pushed it away. "You, too, preaching to me about my duty? You make a good substitute for our father, Emmalyne. I would that you had been born the son instead."

Emma smiled, touching his arm softly. "Gwyneth will make you a good wife, Rogan. I am certain of it."

He just stared at her, revealing nothing. She hated when he became this way, stone-faced and hardheaded, refusing to show any emotion, give in to any plea. It was a habit that was years in the making, a trait he'd inherited from their father, whether he liked it or not.

"Do not try to placate me with the long-dead dreams of a foolish boy. I am not doing this thing because he is forcing me to it, Emma. I need his favor no more than I need a wife. I want what is rightfully mine and I will do whatever I must to have it. Yes, Ashbourne will continue. But this marriage is only a matter of convenience. Gwyneth does not matter to me. She is simply going to provide me with the requirement I need to get what's mine. I will not change. My life will not change, and this marriage sure as Hades will not make me into its liege."

He set his tricorne on his head and turned toward the door. "I'll try to have this business done with quickly and be back by nightfall."

Emma's eyes brimmed with tears as she watched him sweep his cloak over his shoulders, knowing the hurt her brother was fighting so hard to subdue. Townsend had always been so very hard on Rogan, trying to force him to be the sort of man he was. But he had never shown Rogan any affection or encouragement, believing a man who showed emotion was a weak man. And, in doing so, he had instilled that same trait in his son. Rogan did not care for Gwyneth. He would never know the happiness that could be found in marriage. He would never have the joy that she and Fredric shared in creating their child. And he would never know the true fulfillment of love.

Fredric followed Rogan, slipping on his cloak along the way.

"Good luck, man. Try not to think of it as badly as you do. There are throngs of swains dying for a chance with Gwyneth out there."

Rogan nodded, yet Fredric's words did nothing to appease him. It was just a task to be completed, nothing more. The sooner he took care of it, the sooner he could get on with his life.

"Oh, yes, I meant to say earlier," Fredric added, "that cousin of yours never did show his face at the Fleece. Are you certain you told Beecher to meet us today?"

"Yes, I am sure of it. It would seem he found himself some willing female to spend the day with instead."

Her lips curving into a full smile, Gwyneth Pierpont stretched her arms high above her tossled head, knowing well her actions raised her naked breasts over the top of the sheet that covered her. Much to her expectation, the man beside her lifted his head and brought one soft nipple to his mouth.

At the sensation that shot through her, she arched her back, gasping aloud as he tugged at her sensitive flesh, teasing it to erection. In a moment he was atop her, parting her thighs with his knee as he lowered himself slowly onto her. He entered her fully, pressing his hips forward. She easily took his length and arched her back even more, wrapping her legs around him as he began to move rhythmically within her.

"Yes . . ."

Though barely a whisper, that single word spurred her lover onward. He threaded his fingers through her thick blond hair as his mouth started a steady assault down her neck to her breasts. She cried out as he bit lightly at her nipple, gasping for breath.

"More," she panted as he pressed his hips forward, filling her completely.

Before he could reach his climax, she pushed him back onto the bed, rolling atop him. Her legs apart, Gwyneth threw her head back and ground her hips over his in the manner she'd perfected. Her movements were fluid as her body rose and fell, and she felt his hands tighten their hold on her hips. She smiled with the pleasure it gave her.

The power alone was a drug to which she was hopelessly addicted. She alone commanded his desire and she would give him satisfaction as only she knew how. She taunted him, drawing up from him until he begged her for release, then she tightened her inner muscles around his rod, driving him to a near frenzy.

His moan sounded almost pained when she finally allowed him to climax. She curled her fingers through the hair on his chest as she felt him tense and release his seed within her. Only then did she allow herself the same abandon. With her lover panting beneath her, Gwyneth reached to where he still lay sheathed within her and teased her aroused flesh with her own fingers until she was taken by her equally satisfying climax. She cried out loud, mindless to who might hear, throwing her head back before collapsing breathlessly atop her lover's equally heaving chest.

"You are insatiable," he said a moment later, his voice hoarse from exertion.

Gwyneth lay still, listening to the erratic beating of his heart. She smiled to herself. "And you equally so."

Together they lay there for several minutes, basking in the afterglow of their coupling, before she lifted herself from him and slid beneath the thick down-filled coverlet. She could feel the wetness of his seed trickling down her thighs, staining the sheets, but gave no thought to the fear that she could become pregnant with his child. After he left her, when she was alone in her room, she would remove the small sponge soaked in vinegar she had inserted within her earlier. This was a device taught to her by her maid and dear friend, Eula, who'd learned it from the women in the brothel she had worked for prior to coming into her present employ.

The timepiece on the mantel chimed the four o'clock hour. Gwyneth waited until it silenced before she pushed back the coverlet and stood slowly from the bed.

She crossed the room in full nudity, her movement fluid, her stride slow and seductive, stopping before the full-length cheval glass near her window. Carefully she inspected her appearance, smoothing back a limp tress which had come loose from its pin.

"Is it not time you went to meet him?" she said. "He could have left the Fleece by now. He could be on his way here this very moment."

Lying on the bed, watching the reflection of her gloriously naked body in the glass, Rogan's cousin, Beecher Prestwood, smiled in languid satisfaction.

Chapter 4

Beecher clasped his hands behind his head and leaned back against the down pillows, watching as Gwyneth lazily brushed her golden hair. "Is it not time I went to meet whom? Your future bridegroom?"

Her movement halted as Gwyneth's eyes gazed back at him in obvious irritation in the reflection of the glass. "Who else would I be speaking of? You were to meet him and that dreadful Fredric at the Fleece today, were you not? Rogan is sure to wonder where you have been all day."

Beecher rose, noticing the difference in her tone from the sweet, lilting chirp when he had been riding her moments before to the sharp aggravation now. "I wonder what my dear cousin would think if he could see us now? His cousin bedding his future bride." He came up behind her, kneading her shoulders as he pressed his hips against her buttocks. "I wonder what he would think if I told him about the lovely little birthmark you have on your delicious little bottom?"

Gwyneth's frown deepened and she pulled away from him. "What a ridiculous thing to say. It would ruin everything we have planned all these months. The courtship, the engagement, the wedding. Soon we will have everything we want, each other and use of Rogan's funds. Let us not ruin it by becoming careless when our goal is so near."

Beecher stared at their reflection in the glass. Gwyneth was a perfect complement to him. With their blond good looks, they would make a beautiful blond child. He pictured Gwyneth's flat stomach growing round with his child and suddenly he wanted nothing more. A longing so fierce it pained him shot through his body at the thought of losing her to his cousin.

He belonged with her, not Rogan.

"I am not at all pleased at having to share you with anyone, especially my grossly overprivileged cousin."

He spun Gwyneth around and pulled her against him, crushing her lips to his.

"Stop it," Gwyneth protested crossly, pulling away from him. "I am not your possession to share with anyone." She touched a polished fingertip to her lips. "How am I to explain to Rogan the presence of bruises on my lips? You know this is the way it must be. My father would never allow me to marry a man without a title above that of a baron and he especially would not allow me to marry a man without funds."

Beecher released her abruptly, her statement stinging deep. Rogan had everything—the title, the wealth, and the respect of his peers. Beecher had nothing but a pittance and funds equal that to come with it. His bloody father had lost it all—the country house, the money, all that was to become his—on some empty venture in the rum trade, leaving him with naught but derision and a shameful legacy to outlive. He deserved more. Much more. And he would have it.

The accident of his spying Townsend's will on his solicitor's desk that morning had been almost overwhelming. It was as if it had been planned that way, as if he had been meant to see it, to know that if Rogan did not marry Gwyneth, it would all fall to him at Townsend's death.

Beecher smiled to himself at this knowledge. All he had to do was wait, wait until the right moment. Townsend's health was descending daily. With it, so was Rogan's time. Once he proved to Rogan that Gwyneth was his lover, he had no doubt the marriage would be called off. Rogan would never marry a woman with whom Beecher had lain first. He could never live the rest of his life knowing Beecher had bedded her, wondering if he was the better lover of the two, fearing she would return to him. But he had to wait in revealing this bit of information to Rogan until after their engagement became public so his cousin would suffer the scandal of everyone in London knowing he had been cuckolded, as it were, before the fact.

Moving to the bed, Beecher watched as Gwyneth slipped into a silky pink wrap. She moved like the wind, soft at times and at others, fiercer than the sharpest gale. God, but she was beautiful. She had a body made for coupling, soft, yielding to the touch. No woman, whore or lady, had ever made him feel the way she did. She knew things to do with his body he'd never dreamed of doing, things that gave him more pleasure than he'd ever experienced before. He felt himself begin to harden anew at the sight of her dark nipples outlined clearly through the sheer fabric of her wrap. He wanted her again, even though he'd just had her. He knew he'd never get enough of her. He quickly turned away.

As he pulled on his breeches he thought of the day when he would not have to climb up a trellis furtively to her chambers. He would fling her over his shoulder and march to her chamber door, kicking it open for all to see. And he would throw her on the bed and make her scream with pleasure so everyone would know when he took her. And take her he would, every day and every night, so she would never forget it was he who she loved.

But until that day, until he could make her his bride as he planned, he could never tell her what he knew about the provision of Townsend's will. He knew, at that moment, she desired Rogan more, because she hadn't had him, because he had the title and the wealth. If he told her too soon, she might let it slip to Rogan. She might get greedy, thinking she could have them both, and try to thwart his plans. Without the fortune and Ashbourne, she would lose that attraction for Rogan quickly as she would a new ball gown after she'd worn it the first time.

Tucking in his shirttails, Beecher could not help the smile at the knowledge that he'd had her first, had tasted the honeyed sweetness of her passion, and with that had finally bested Rogan at one thing. And when he inherited the fortune, she'd beg him to marry her. And he would. Not to please her, but to please himself.

He peered toward the clock across the room. Time. Time was all it would take. Time would be the answer to his dreams. Time . . .

"I really think it is time you left."

Gwyneth's irritated tone roused Beecher from his thoughts.

"Bored with me already, my sweet?"

She stood framed in the double doorway leading to the balcony, his usual exit from her room. Her mouth was set with a frown at his chiding tone. "I've a marriage proposal to ready myself for. It's not every day a girl gets betrothed."

She turned then and walked to the balcony, dismissing him in an instant. "Do not forget your coat on your way out."

As she stood in the doorway, the sun filtering down to her, she appeared ethereal in the light. The filmy fabric of her wrap looked like the wings of an angel. With the heart of a witch. Someday she would look upon him with adoration, as she did for Rogan now. Someday she would beg him to stay instead of urging him to leave her. Someday—soon.

"When shall I see you again?"

"I will call for you in the usual way."

She moved to the railing. She was becoming impatient with him, he could tell.

"Do I get a parting kiss from my lady's sweet lips?"

When Gwyneth reached up to peck him quickly on the cheek, Beecher pulled her forward and crushed her mouth against his. His hands kneaded her buttocks beneath her wrap, pulling her against his hardened sex. Her head lolled back, and she looked at him breathlessly when he pulled away. Deny it as she might, the light burning in her eyes right then told him he did give her one thing she wanted—pleasure.

"Just so you do not forget me, my love."

With that he swung one leg over the railing, tipping his hat gallantly and laughing aloud as he disappeared below.

In the distance, beyond a break in the trees lining the street below, Rogan watched as Gwyneth's lover dove between the hedges.

He had been unable to see her lover's face from his vantage point. He did not care. The man's identity was of no importance to him anyway. All that mattered was that he now had a reason to refuse to wed Gwyneth. He could rightfully and reasonably deny his father's wish. Let him spend months trying to find another chosen bride.

He had but one thought as he turned to start back the way he had come only moments before: at least he had not yet proposed.

Chelsea opened the door to the chamber she had been directed to and paused at the threshold, her eyes slowly traveling along over each wall, each furnishing. The tall rosewood bed, its four posters intricately carved, was decorated in shades of pale blue, yellow, and pink. A fine Turkish carpet of the same colors covered the polished hardwood floor, and soft blue damask draperies framed the tall sunlit windows.

Chelsea moved to them and peered out over the back of the town house, noticing the garden below, a small carriage house and stable situated beside it. The D-shaped flower beds were bare from winter's cold, the roses cut back to bare twigs rising from the frozen ground, but she could close her eyes and imagine them teeming with bright flowers along the graveled walkways.

Peering in the small glass at the dressing table, Chelsea cringed at the sight she presented. Her hair had long since come loose from its pins and was tangled about her face. She hadn't noticed, but she had somehow gotten a thin tear in the sleeve of her gown that ran its length to her elbow.

She took the elegant gilt-backed comb lying there and started working through the tangles, picking out the pins that remained. When finished, her hair fell in smooth waves around her shoulders. She twisted it back serviceably at her nape and secured it with a pin.

She spotted her valise lying on the bed and, taking a seat beside it, slowly began removing her belongings. Everything was there, her two other gowns, the jewelry from her dowry coffer, and the small leather pouch that held her few remaining shillings. Nothing at all was out of place. She spied her small red velvet reticule lying on the bed and suddenly remembered the note Widow Andrews had given her earlier. She had shoved it back inside the tiny bag when Gregor had come upon her in the alleyway and had completely forgotten about it in all the commotion.

Pulling the corded drawstring open, she emptied the reticule's contents onto the soft coverlet atop the bed. The folded parchment dropped easily from inside. Quickly she unfolded the heavy paper, carefully reading the words contained within.

Miss Estwyck,

I have news of your father. Please meet me at five o'clock in St. George's Church Yard. You must believe I have your best interests at heart.

It was signed "James," after which was set the same strange flower-and-scroll design that graced the handkerchief he'd left with her.

She wondered who he was, how he knew about her. Suddenly, she didn't care. All that mattered was he had news of her father. He must know where Damson was. Hope sparked within Chelsea at the thought of seeing him again soon. It had been so long, so very long. She wondered if he'd look any different, if she would recognize him should she pass him on the street. She'd been nine years old when he'd left, still young and filled with thoughts of dolls and grand balls, yet that day was as clear to her now as if she'd lived it only yesterday.

She had been standing on the shore.

Leaning back against the soft pillows on the bed, Chelsea closed her eyes and could almost hear the sound of the waves crashing upon the jagged rocks of the cliffs that surrounded Drummore, the wind whistling loudly, howling with the threat of a brewing storm.

High on one of the cliffs, at the end of a winding, narrow pathway, stood Castle Drummore, looming like a dark, frightening shadow above her. The wind swirled around her, biting at her fingers as she held tightly to her small, painted doll, the doll she called Dautie. Damson had given her that doll on her eighth birthday, saying it looked just like her, his little "dautie." Her face was formed from the whitest porcelain, her gown bright pink satin and lace. A mop of dark curls shimmered around her face. Chelsea was never to be found without her.

Above, a flash of lightning cut through the cloud-darkened sky and Chelsea spotted the ship anchored far off from the shore, the ship that was to take her father away. It was tall and ominous, shrouded in the darkness, with its sail fluttering, looking like a raven ready to take flight.

"Now, *dautie*," Damson said as he took her one final time into his arms, "despite what you may believe, I have done no wrong. I have to go away now until I can prove that I am innocent. I love you, and someday, I promise I will come back for you."

How handsome her father had been with his midnight-black hair and shining blue eyes. He kissed her forehead tenderly, gazing at her for a silent moment before setting her down upon the soft sand. He touched the tip of her nose before turning, and Chelsea stood watching as he waded into the water and climbed inside the small boat that was to take him to his ship. She watched until she was unable to see him through her tears, as he rowed farther and farther away.

She cried out his name once and tried to run after him, but her mother, Annora, grasped her by the shoulders, pulling her back from the water's edge. She fought to free herself, kicking and squirming as her mother pulled her along the narrow pathway back toward Drummore, away from her father.

Somewhere along the way she dropped her doll Dautie and when she attempted to go back for her, Annora simply pushed her onward. She never saw her father or the precious porcelain doll he had given her again.

The revolution had taken him away, as it had her brother, Jamie. Why Jamie had taken the Scots' cause she did not understand. She had been too young then. They'd lived in England, at her father's family estate, when news of Jamie's leaving his studies at Oxford reached them. He'd gone to fight for Prince Charlie, they'd said, for her mother's ancestors, the fighting Scots.

Chelsea could still remember the horrible arguments between her parents after Jamie had gone, the newspapers calling her father a Jacobite sympathizer for his son's actions. When her great-uncle Leland had come in the dark of the night that winter to warn of soldiers coming to arrest him, they'd packed up whatever belongings they could, fleeing for the Scottish border and Drummore, her mother's family's keep.

The Jacobites lost their revolution in the end, but not before taking the life of her brother and forcing her father from his home forever.

Tears blurred Chelsea's vision as she stared at the elegant quill strokes on the letter, her mind swimming with the words written so neatly before her.

St. George's Church. Five o'clock.

Chelsea glanced at the wall clock across the room. Half past four. She knew she should not go, the risk was far too great with Gregor so close, but what if this man truly did know something of her father? What if he could somehow send for him? He would be the only one who could prevent her marriage to Gregor, but she had no way of knowing where her father was, much less if he lived under his true name. There was no other choice. She would have to take her chances and meet this stranger named James.

Wiping her eyes with the back of her hand, Chelsea slipped slowly out to the vacant corridor and padded along the flowered carpet, stopping just outside the door to Emma's chambers. Inside, Emma dozed peacefully behind the drawn velvet drapery around her bed, unaware of Chelsea's presence at the door.

She descended the stairs quickly, hesitating as she reached the bottom floor. It was quiet. Peeking in the rooms on either side to assure herself that Rogan had not yet returned, she said a silent prayer that he would remain absent for at least another hour. She did not want to involve him in this. He had already risked his life once for her. She could not allow him to endanger himself again.

Outside the sky was just beginning to dim, the lazy cover of fog already starting to roll in for its nightly shroud. The wind was icy cold, cutting through the wool of her cloak and stinging her cheeks and nose bright red. She would have to hurry.

"Take care, miss!" someone shouted as she emerged from the alleyway. She stepped back just in time to avoid being struck by a passing sedan chair. She quickly asked an old woman selling notions on the street corner for directions to the churchyard. It was near enough to go by foot, if she hurried.

Ahead, in the distance, through dusk's thickening mist, she could just make out the tall spire of St. George's, guiding her like a beacon through the quickly vacating streets. When she arrived, she quickly searched the churchyard for a silver velvet-clad person among the few who wandered about. He was not there. What if she were too late? She glanced to the clock on the tall church steeple. It was just past five o'clock.

Her heart was pounding in anticipation, and Chelsea wandered slowly along the pathway toward the back of the church, the graveled surface crunching under her slippers, her apprehension growing as the minutes ticked by. Where was he? More, who was he? The stragglers around her were quickly disappearing, leaving her to face the stranger, James, alone. Perhaps that was what he was waiting for, until she was alone, defenseless, so there would be no witnesses.

She stopped near a small stone bench surrounded by thick shrubbery and sat down to wait, not knowing what or whom for. She fidgeted nervously. Only five more minutes, then she would leave.

"Miss Estwyck?"

Chelsea started at the sound of the deep, whispering voice behind her. She started to turn.

"No, do not turn around. Remain sitting as you are."

Chelsea sat up straight and stiff, staring toward the church building before her. A small child was playing with a wooden ball in the courtyard, rolling it back and forth before her. She watched the child, her fingers knotting together in her lap.

"I see you received my note."

She nodded, prickles of apprehension running along the nape of her neck.

"I know why you came to London."

Chelsea stiffened. "You do?"

"Your father is well, child. He wants you to know he is innocent of the charges against him."

Her father was alive. Joy leapt in her heart at the reaffirmation of what she'd always believed and at knowing that soon they would be together.

"You mean my mother . . . ?"

"Shhhh. You must not speak. Just listen to what I have to say."

Chelsea swallowed and nodded, waiting for him to continue.

"We are trying to clear his name. He was countermined, made out to be a traitor. Documents were forged bearing his name, documents against the Crown of England. When your brother, Jamie, joined with the Scots, it made matters look all the worse for him. But he is not a traitor and he wants you to know that he will come for you as soon as he can.

"He does not know what happened with your marriage to Gregor Moultrie." The stranger paused. "I thought it best not to tell him. He was against the match from the very beginning, your mother knew that. We can only thank the heavens that it never came to pass."

"But . . ."

"You will be safe here in London until he comes for you. We are watching out for you."

We? Who were we? "But, Gregor . . ."

"Yes, we know he is here in London. You must do everything within your power to keep him away. He has the authority to take you back to Scotland if he so wishes. You mustn't allow him to find you. If you were to marry him, all would be lost. Your father would never be able to return to England. Remember that. You may well never see him again if you do not. His life is in your hands."

Chelsea nodded somberly. She reached into her reticule. "I have your handkerchief."

"No, child. I left it with you for a purpose. If you are ever in danger, leave it in the third pew of this church. I will come for you. But you must remember, you can only use it to summon me once. Go, now, for it grows too dark to ensure your safety on the streets. I will try to contact you when I have more news of your father. Do not tell anyone of our meeting. Your safety and the safety of your father's return depend upon it."

Chelsea stood and started to turn toward the voice, stopping herself before she could. "Wait, please . . ."

A moment of silence. "Yes?"

"Please . . . tell my father I love him and I believe him."

Another moment of silence. "I will, Miss Estwyck. Now go."

Chelsea heard the sound of rustling leaves then heavy footsteps then silence.

"Wait, I am not at the boarding house anymore . . ."

It was too late. Whomever had been there had vanished. Chelsea swallowed nervously, suddenly feeling very alone. How would they reach her when they had more news of her father? Should she leave the handkerchief now? He had said it could be used only once.

The church bells were ringing, pealing out across the city, signaling the time. The time. Chelsea looked to the church tower. Oh, no. It was half past five. The sky had already turned a darkened gray, the fog even now snaking its way through the twisting streets. Soon it would be night. She had to leave. She had to get back to the town house before Rogan returned.

Chelsea rushed away from the church, down the street, back the way she had come, keeping watch around her at every turn, praying to herself that her absence had not been noticed. As she ducked under the opening in the bushes that surrounded the back of Rogan's town house, she felt a surge of confidence. She had made it back before Rogan had returned.

Her cloak caught on a stray twig and it pulled her back. She reached behind and tried to free it, tugging at the fabric. It stubbornly refused to yield. Finally, with one forceful pull and a snap of the twig, it gave way and she started across the garden toward the house.

"May I ask where you have been?"

Chelsea halted at the apparition of Rogan standing before her. He had his hands at the hips of his buff-colored breeches, his shirt open at the top to reveal a rather muscular-looking neck. His face held no expression, but his eyes looked very angry. Her stomach lurched. He had returned and looked far from pleased at having found her clambering through the hedgerow. She wanted to curse aloud her misfortune, but only bit her lip as she tried to frame an excuse for her most compromised position.

Why had he returned at that precise moment? She could not reveal anything that might alert him to where she had been. He would want to meet the stranger, would want to know the nature of their meeting. And it might prevent her father from being able to return. It was far too dangerous with Gregor lurking about. Rogan hadn't asked to be involved in her superfluity of troubles, and she would not knowingly invite more upon him than she already had.

She fell mute, completely forgetting the question he'd asked.

But Rogan did not forget.

"Have you gone suddenly deaf? I asked you where you have been."

Her speech returned as quickly as it had abandoned her. "Oh, Lord Ravenel—you startled me—I did not see you."

"Of course you did not see me. How could you when your attentions were occupied with freeing your cloak from the bushes?" He shifted, crossing his arms over his chest. "Now, I will ask you one more time, where were you?"

Chelsea looked up with all the innocence of a child caught stealing a sweetmeat. "I was here, Lord Ravenel. I was just taking a walk around the garden to clear my head. I felt the need for a breath of air."

She looked away. It was a stupid excuse, she knew that the moment it left her lips, but she could think of no other to offer.

"The garden is over there," he said, pointing at the distinct hedged entrance. "And you are over here. Quite a distance for a garden walk. Now do you want to tell me where you really were?"

"I said I was walking around the gar—"

"I will save you the time and embarrassment of trying to find a plausible excuse, Miss MacKenna. You were not taking a turn in the garden. You were just returning, from where, I do not know, but it must have been quite important for you to risk capture by that fiend again."

"But . . ."

"If you wished to be captured by him, then you could have at least told me and saved me the trouble, because I did not save you from that lout this morning so that you could do something foolish and get yourself caught by him again."

Foolish?

"I did not bring you into my home so that you could run right out and get yourself caught again. And if you expect me to believe that you were walking about the gardens when it is so very obvious that you were not, you are wrong. I do not spend my days standing before knife-wielding fiends, escaping only because of the luck of an errant chamberpot. I saved you because I could not stand by and allow a woman to be attacked."

"But . . ."

"I brought you here to keep you from harm, from the hands of that lout who you seemed to want to avoid so badly. Just what did you expect me to do? Leave you at the nearest street corner, looking like some filthy street urchin, so you could get your fool self cornered again?"

Street urchin? Who was he to call her names? And what right had he to question her? As he went on, extolling his virtues while belittling hers, Chelsea wanted nothing more than to shut him up. But he just went on. He was very full of himself. She thought of pushing him, but decided, with his size, she'd never be able to ground him. She thought of running, but somehow knew he would follow and catch her and harp at her all the more. Instead she took off her shoe and hurled it with all her might and anger at his fat, self-admiring head. It missed its mark completely, and he caught the flying slipper as if it were naught but an offending fly.

Rogan stood there, saying nothing. She thought he might strike her, thought he might throw the shoe back at her. She was surprised when a smile spread across his features a moment later and he crossed his arms, tucking the shoe between them.

She looked at him, frustrated and not at all amused. "Give me back my shoe."

"No."

Chelsea's eyes widened. "I said give me back my shoe!"

"Why? You certainly did not seem to need it so badly a moment ago when you were throwing it at my face."

"But I need it now."

He was looking down at her stocking toes and cocking his head to the side like a puppy. She tried to see what he found so interesting.

"What? What are you looking at?"

"You know, you have large feet for a woman."

Chelsea's mouth fell open. "I do not!"

He held up her shoe as if inspecting it, testing its length against the flat of his hand. "It's even longer than my hand." He looked at her, his mouth curving at the corner. "I always heard it said that a woman's shoes should fit the palm of a man's hands."

"Perhaps if she's ten years old." Chelsea reached for the shoe. "Just give it back."

"I don't think so."

Rogan raised his arm above his head, too high for Chelsea to reach. She didn't care. She pushed at him, her ire growing with each minute she failed to regain her lofty shoe. Maddeningly she couldn't budge him.

"Stop it. Give me my shoe. I—"

She stilled when she suddenly realized Rogan had turned and his face was now inches from her own. He was staring at her quite intently, that idiotic grin still gracing his lips, lips that were so very close now. Chelsea became aware of how they were alone in the garden, no one within earshot. The temperature outside seemed to rise, and somehow she knew he was going to kiss her.

Rogan lowered his head and touched his lips to hers. Chelsea stood very still. She knew she should pull away. It was dangerous not to, but somehow she could not. The only man she'd ever kissed, excepting her father of course, had been Gregor, and this kiss felt so very different, so very warm, soft, and nice. She relaxed and closed her eyes, allowing herself this new experience.

She felt Rogan's arm come down and circle around her, pulling her closer. Still she did not pull away. Nor did she when she felt his tongue glide along her lower lip. She was lost. When his mouth moved over hers, seeking her response, she felt something awaken inside of her. She acted on it without thought. Her own mouth echoed his movements, giving and taking, innocently seeking, filling her with a sense of adventure, free from inhibition.

It was Rogan who pulled away a moment later. Chelsea's breath was short, her heart beating hard, and she looked at him with hooded eyes. Why had he stopped? His breath was warm against her temple when he said a moment later, "You still are not getting your shoe back."

"How dare you . . . !"

Chelsea pushed him away and could not believe it when he turned and left her standing there to stare at his retreating back.

"You pig!"

Before she knew what she was doing, she had taken off her other shoe and hurled it furiously at his back. It bounced off his shoulder without even fazing him, landing in a black puddle, sinking to its tarnished silver buckle. Chelsea was so angry she wanted to scream. She wanted to leap on his back and pummel him with her fists. Rogan just kept walking, ignoring her display behind him. Emitting an angry oath, she started after him, smarting as her shoeless toe scraped against a sharp pebble.

"Ow! Come back here! I want my shoe!"

Rogan did not stop or show any sign of having even heard her clamant plea. She ran after him, circling in front of him to keep him from proceeding any further. Her cheeks burned with anger and humiliation. How dare he kiss her like that then leave her to walk back to the house shoeless? How could she have allowed him to kiss her in the first place?

She wanted to choke him, but inwardly she knew he was not the only one to blame. She'd allowed him to kiss her because she'd wanted him to. She'd wanted him to continue kissing her as well. Her anger was not at him for taking those liberties, but at the way he'd turned and left her there, mocking her with her shoe. She wanted to strike back at him somehow, but knew she would never get her shoe back by doing so. She lowered her eyes as demurely as she could and forced her next words out.

"I am sorry I threw my shoe at you, Lord Ravenel. I did not mean to. It was not well done of me. May I please have it back? Now?"

That cocky half-grin surfaced again. "That was very good. Just the right amount of sweetness and regret, but no, I think I will keep it for the moment."

"Why?" Any sweetness in her voice was gone.

"So that next time you have a mind to," he paused with just the right amount of sarcasm, "*walk about the gardens*, you'll not be so able to sneak off through an opening in the bushes. This way I can keep you here until I am able to take you out."

Chelsea would have stomped her foot except she had no shoe and did not wish to further ruin her only pair of stockings. But she had to do something, anything to respond to him, so she narrowed her eyes, saying simply, "You are no gentleman."

"That, my lady, is without question."

Before she lost what little hold she had left on her temper and pushed him into the puddle along with her other shoe, Chelsea shoved past Rogan, knocking him back from the path, and ran for the house.

Rogan watched her go, skirts flying, stockinged feet running, knowing he had deliberately provoked her. He tightened his fingers around her slipper. At that moment he wanted to throttle her, to wring her neck with his bare hands. No, he wanted to throw her over his knee, fling up her skirts, big feet and all, and paddle her luscious bottom with the shoe he still held.

She'd stood before him, an expression of guilt coloring her face but refusing to admit to where she'd gone, facing him down with more bravery than he'd seen most men display. Yes he wanted to throttle her. He wanted to throttle her for being so stupid as to go out in the city alone. That was precisely how she'd gotten herself into the predicament she now found herself in. How could she be so foolish as to leave the grounds unescorted?

When he'd returned from his aborted marriage proposal to Gwyneth to find Chelsea gone and the lout absent from his usual perch at the gate, Rogan had instantly concluded that Chelsea had been taken. He envisioned her struggling against that fiend, unable to overcome his superior strength, breaking like a porcelain doll between his brutal fingers.

He'd questioned the staff. None of them had seen her leave. It was as if she had disappeared, they'd said, vanished like the fog at daybreak. And when a search of the house had come up empty, but her belongings were still in the chamber she'd been given, he felt certain she had been taken. This made him feel as if he'd failed in some way, failed in his duty to keep her safe. He'd begun to panic, tearing through every room in the house looking for her, shouting her name through each corridor.

He decided to search the gardens as a final thought, and when he'd seen her sneaking so furtively under that hedge opening, he at once felt relieved and furious. How could she have been so stupid as to leave without his protection? What had been so bloody important to be worth the risk of capture again?

He glanced at the shoe he'd refused to return to her. She was right. He was no gentleman. A gentleman would have returned her shoe, profusely begging her pardon all the while. A gentleman wouldn't have kissed her, gaining her response, only to leave her standing alone. If only she knew his reason for pulling away, if only she knew that if he hadn't pulled away when he did, it wouldn't have ended with just that kiss. If he'd meant the kiss to teach her a lesson, he'd ended up punishing himself instead. Even now, just remembering her innocent response, he could feel his blood begin to pound anew.

What was wrong with him? No woman had ever had this effect on him before. He'd always remained cool, keeping his head, but this one made him lose his senses. Hell, he knew what was wrong and it had nothing to do with Chelsea. It had been too long since he'd visited his mistress, too damned long, indeed. A romp with Diana should ease his ruttish urges, but first he had to meet with someone else, to finally learn that which Chelsea refused to tell him.

Come the morning, he planned to know exactly why Chelsea had found it necessary to leave; why she'd refused to tell him where she'd been, and just why the lout had been chasing her down the alleyway before she'd come crashing into his life, leaving havoc in her wake.

A smile crossed his lips and he started for the house after her, tossing her shoe in the air like a child's plaything, remembering the way she'd melted against him when he'd kissed her, remembering the response he'd felt when she kissed him back.

Chapter 5

"They were what?"

Sitting behind the desk in his study, buckskin-encased legs propped upon the burled mahogany desk and a glass, once filled with brandy, now empty, in hand, Rogan heard the words with disbelief.

"They were betrothed," repeated Daniel, holding up his hand to silence Rogan's next words. "But, wait a moment. There is more. Seems on the night before she was to wed him, she disappeared, took the midnight flit without so much as a parting kiss. Odd, though, there was never any hue and cry made for her search. In fact, this spurned betrothed seems to be the only one looking for her. Seems she was telling the truth about not having living relatives to turn to, at least any who are looking for her."

Rogan barely heard the rest of Daniel's words. Two days earlier he'd asked his friend to find out what he could about Chelsea. He had suspected she was lying when she had denied knowing the identity of the man who'd been chasing her, but this? He still could not believe it.

"What else did this—what is his name?"

"Gregor."

"Yes, Gregor—what a primitive name—what else did this Gregor tell you?"

Daniel finished his own brandy and set the glass aside. He shook his head when Rogan motioned to the sideboard as if to ask if he'd like another dram. "That was all I could get out of him, Rogue," he said, "and believe me, that was difficult enough. Spent nearly my entire week's purse trying to get that Scottish beast sotted enough to admit that much. Took an entire bottle of usquebaugh before he'd so much as loosen his tongue."

Rogan fell silent, his thoughts drifting to the woman who slept peacefully in the chamber above him. What could have happened to have made her leave her home and her intended on the eve of her wedding? And why would she lie about knowing who Gregor was? Had she believed Rogan would return her to him if he knew the truth?

He searched his memory, trying to remember what vague responses she'd given when he'd questioned her after she'd literally barged into his life that day. Blast, but he could not recall. All he could remember was the touch of her lips and those dark, haunting eyes wide with fear. His heart softened anew at the memory.

Rogan stood and refilled his glass. He leaned back against the sideboard and took a deep draw, allowing the amber-colored liquid to snake easily down his throat. He ran his finger along the rim of the glass, thoughtful, confused. Perhaps Chelsea had fallen in love with another and had left before she could be trapped in a loveless marriage. But why would she have not run to her lover? Perhaps the man was married.

Somehow knowing he would never find the solution to this mystery called Chelsea that easily, Rogan turned to see Daniel out. He needed time to think—alone.

"Thanks, Dan, I owe you."

"If you want me to try getting more out of him, just ask."

Rogan shook his head. "No. Seems I'll be needing to have a long talk with a certain lady come tomorrow morning."

Rogan closed the door behind Daniel. He turned and started back to his study, spotting a flash of white linen at the top of the stairs. The sound of a door closing and the creak of the floorboard confirmed someone moving overhead.

He frowned. She had been listening. At that moment she was most probably trying to fabricate another story. He downed the remainder of his brandy, setting the glass rather roughly on the polished sideboard. He picked up the sealed letter lying there, the letter he'd written informing Townsend the marriage to Gwyneth would not come to pass. He wished he could see the old cur's face when he read the words informing him of the tarnished virtues of the bride he'd chosen. By no manner of means could Townsend force the match now. It was an impossibility. If there was one thing Rogan knew his father could not abide, it was adultery.

He knew this well. His mother had died for it.

"Perhaps you should marry the girl."

Rogan turned from his place at the window, his brow

drawn in a scowl. He'd been staring out that window, looking at nothing at all, for there was nothing to see but the black midnight sky, contemplating what to do about Chelsea when Diana had posed her ridiculous suggestion.

"Marry her?"

His mistress lifted her head from the ivory damask chaise. "Yes, marry her. Don't you see? It would be the perfect solution. You would have nothing to lose and everything possible to gain. Marrying this girl—Chelsea is it?—pretty name, would snag two fish on one line. It would satisfy your father's demands that you marry, ensuring that Ashbourne would persevere, and you could go on living the life you choose."

Rogan scarcely heard her words, his mouth drawing in a frown at the sight of her lying there. The soft peach satin negligee he'd purchased from Madame Dussault's specifically for her had held to its promise. The filmy silk molded to her lithe body, the lace along its rounded neckline caressing her full breasts. Yes, she was beautiful. She looked as desirable as a virginal girl of seventeen, soft, ripe for the taking, yet the picture she presented before him, her rich chestnut hair spread out around her soft shoulders, had not stirred him. For the first and only time in his adult male life, the sight of this woman, this beautiful and desirable woman who'd been his mistress these past six months, had not brought Rogan's blood to the boiling point. And that bothered him.

At any other time he would be fighting back the urge to pull her into his arms and peel the gown off till she stood naked before him. He knew she would not resist. She had never resisted and had always matched his enthusiasm in bed. Yet he wondered when he took her and she cried out in ecstasy, would he still be haunted by the image of Chelsea's face, as he had when he'd kissed Diana at his arrival this night?

He had come to Diana to forget Chelsea, to forget the past days since she'd invaded his life, and to forget his father's damnable plot to cinch him to a wife. But instead of forgetting her, the sight of Diana had only filled his head with Chelsea more, leaving him feeling oddly incomplete. Even the lovely Diana, with her soft body and accomplished touch, had been unable to coax him. And though he would not admit to it, he knew the reason why.

It had nothing to do with his ability to perform, or lack thereof. He had only to think of Chelsea and the kiss they'd shared and his temperature would soar. His breeches grew tight and his heartbeat leapt in response, all this from one bloody kiss! He didn't even have to be in the same room.

"What is it that has you so vexed about this girl?" Diana suddenly said, breaking his thoughts.

"What do you mean?"

"I know you far better than you think, Rogan Doraunt. There is something about this girl that has you foxed. Now tell me."

Rogan turned, smiling at her perception. Along with being beautiful, this woman was incredibly smart, her golden brown eyes, so clear, so knowing. If only she hadn't married, if only he'd met her ten years earlier, he'd have none of the troubles he had today.

He sat beside her and traced a finger along one shapely thigh. No childbearing marks marred her soft skin, for soon after marrying her husband, the wealthy Earl of Lampley, the lovely Diana found she could never bear children. To Lampley, already father to a brood of ten from his first marriage, all girls except one, Diana's inability to produce another Lampley offspring mattered not. He was utterly enamored of his lovely wife and sought to please her every whim. Yet for all his worldly experience, for all the love he felt for his wife, the earl was as inept a lover as a lad of sixteen and unable to please his young wife in bed.

She never let it be known that he could not satisfy her, for she loved her husband above all else and would never allow him to be hurt by scandal. Instead she'd sought the company of a lover, one who could take her to the heights of passion, yet one who would be discreet and keep her husband's name from the newspapers. She'd found that man in Rogan.

"I cannot place it," Rogan said, more to himself than to her. "There is something about her, something different. She's different. She doesn't dance attendance upon me like all the others looking only for a marriage proposal from a future earl. She doesn't even seem to care what my position in life might be. She sees things differently. She sees me differently. Yesterday, she asked me what I do to make my living. When I told her I did nothing except waste my father's money and ruin innocent girls, do you know what the twit did? She smiled. She just smiled and shook her head and said she was certain I did more than just ruin them, for surely I must do something worthwhile to have them always clamoring after me. No one has told me I was worth more than a bean since my mother died . . ."

He dropped off, suddenly aware of what he'd said.

Diana took her cue to change the subject. "Do you know anything about this girl? Is she gentry or is she just a girl who got herself into trouble?"

"She's a lady. I knew that from the moment I met her. She carries herself like gentry, but I cannot for the life of me figure out who she is or where she comes from. I've asked everyone who would know. She's no family here in London. She refuses to tell me anything. It's almost as if she's trying to protect me from something. But what? I don't know why, it's almost as if she seems to think whatever it is she is hiding might bring me to harm in some way." He shook his head at the realization. "Can you believe it? *Her* protecting *me*. *She's* the one with this two-ton giant dogging her heels. Doesn't she know I could help her?"

Diana gazed at Rogan. She had no fathomable idea what he was talking about. And this puzzled her. She'd never seem him thus. She knew him better than she knew even herself at times. He was stubborn, arrogant at times, yet she'd never known a man to be more concerned with his lover's pleasure. He did not trust easily, sometimes not at all, most probably from being shuffled betwixt a multitude of tutors and schools during his childhood. He'd been utterly devoted to his mother and Diana knew part of the battle with his father was his way of punishing him for her death. But she had never seen him so beset by a woman before. She smiled to herself. He was hooked.

"So marry her, as I said. It would be the perfect arrangement. It would take care of your obligations to your father and would at the same time free her from the two-ton giant."

"And how do I persuade her to agree to this? I rather doubt she'd be so willing to jump into a marriage with one man to escape another."

Diana slanted a brow. "Ah, but if you were to assure her

that the marriage would not change either of your lives, that you would both be free to follow your own"—she reached out and touched his cheek softly—"how should I say?—interests and pursuits—she would have nothing to object to. Do not dwell on the marriage aspect. Make certain she sees the advantages of forever being free from this ogre with no worry of him coming back.

"She sounds a smart girl, which is more than I can say of that Pierpont snip. You need that in a wife. But I would not attempt to force your ideas on her; she seems to have her own mind. You must allow her to make the final decision."

Rogan stood. Diana watched him as he pulled on his coat. Had she paraded before him naked right now, she doubted he would even take notice. No, she realized, Rogan's thoughts were on another, younger, more innocent creature. One who had foxed the man she'd thought never could be foxed. If she were but ten years younger, she had a feeling she would be setting herself for battle against this dark-haired nymph. But she was not ten years younger, so she was left to watching from the wings as this girl took center stage in Rogan's life.

"I'd better go."

Diana followed Rogan to the door and raised up on tiptoe to kiss him softly on the cheek. "Marry the girl and get your affairs and your thoughts back in order. Then come back to me so that we may resume that which we could not this evening."

Rogan headed out the door without responding. He was already submerged in thought, his eyes dark and stubborn, considering her suggestion. He would most probably spend the remainder of the night weighing the advantages and disadvantages against each other over a bottle of his favorite brandy. He would curse his father over and over and wonder if he shouldn't just walk away from it all. But his pride would not allow him that. His pride and his honor for what was just. The same honor which had led him to saving this girl from her jilted betrothed would make him do whatever it took to keep Ashbourne from falling to ruin.

Diana smiled bittersweetly as she closed the door behind him, watching him go, somehow knowing in her heart of hearts this would be the last time she would ever see Rogan as her lover again.

Chelsea's fingers trembled nervously as she heard the footsteps just making their descent on the stairs in the hall outside the dining room. The steps were heavy, unhurried, as if taking one's leisure, quite obviously a man and not some housemaid bringing down the bed linen. He was coming. She began to realize a moment of panic. She could see him in her mind's eye, nonchalantly adjusting the fold of his cuff as he greeted the footman and continued to the dining room. Rogan was coming down the stairs to breakfast, to accuse her of her dishonesty. He was coming to humiliate her before Emma and all the servants. He was coming to throw her out.

She had stayed up most of the night, wondering just what Rogan had learned about her, lying on that bed and staring at the carved ceiling in the moonlight, trying to come to some solution to her ever-growing problems. Her weariness showed in dark circles under her eyes. Hearing his approach coming fast now, she realized she should have left the previous night, before he could throw her out; the idea had come to mind, and she most probably would have acted on it, had she any shoes to carry her. Rogan had yet to return them.

The footsteps came to a halt at the bottom floor. Chelsea took up her cup of chocolate, now cold, and sipped at it. It only left a bitter taste in her mouth. He was coming. He would come and reveal all he knew about her, and he would throw her out.

She had dressed carefully that morning, tying her hair loosely with a white satin ribbon, a few soft tendrils caressing her cheeks. Her gown, made of white sprigged muslin, decorated with delicate lace and tiny pink flowers, fit her intention well. Her mother always told her the gown made her appear an innocent little girl, and innocence was what she was hoping to portray when Rogan confronted her, as she knew he would.

Before he threw her out.

Muffled voices came from the hall, setting her nerves even further on edge. She tried to peer out the door, to see if he was coming to throw her out, but her view was obscured by the liveried footman who stood waiting at the doorway to serve them. She fidgeted, toying with a pearl button at her sleeve, pulling a stray thread that only resulted in loosening the lace at her cuff, then fidgeted more until she thought she would scream from the waiting. Finally he stood in the entryway.

"Ah, good morning, Pip."

It was not Rogan. Chelsea released the breath she had not realized she'd been holding.

This man stood taller than Rogan and strode into the room, looking for all the world like a thin birch tree. He was dressed in a beige silk frock coat and breeches, his legs seeming endlessly long, a white powdered wig covering his head. He wore tiny spectacles at the bridge of his nose, and he smiled as he passed Chelsea, then leaned down and kissed Emma lovingly on the cheek.

"How are you feeling today, my dear?"

Emma smiled adoringly at the man. "Fine, thank you, Fredric, seems my mornings of illness are well behind me now."

"As is, I daresay, your recent affinity for chocolate dipped kippers?"

Emma shot him a churlish, yet, Chelsea suspected, playful stare and turned saying, "Fredric, this is Chelsea, the young woman I told you about. Chelsea, allow me to introduce my husband, Fredric Ellingsford, Earl of Stoughton."

He had the face of a sparrow, alert and keen, his brown eyes twinkling with some hidden amusement. Chelsea found herself wondering what color his hair could be beneath the curled wig and pictured it as a sandy brown.

Fredric smiled at her and circled the table to take her hand in his, soft hands that held hers as if he thought they might break.

"A pleasure to make your acquaintance, Miss, a . . . ?"

"Est—MacKenna," Chelsea responded, wincing as she realized she'd almost revealed her true surname. "Chelsea MacKenna," she repeated.

"Miss MacKenna, you—"

"Good morning, milord."

At the sound of the footman's sudden greeting, conversation ceased and attention, all attention, turned to the doorway and the person who'd just arrived. Chelsea felt her breath catch as Rogan passed by. She wondered how one person's presence could affect so many people at one time. It was as if all thought, all action, hinged on his reverent arrival and as he passed, Chelsea decided it was in his eyes. There was something about them, the way they stared at a person, seeing everything, revealing nothing, glimmering more silver than blue, that created this curious reaction.

He looked even more handsome than the day before, if that were possible, dressed in a fine coat of moss-green velvet trimmed with a black braid and gold buttons. His hair was tied back with a singular black bow, sharpening the contours of his clean-shaven face. His russet-colored breeches fit him well, too well perhaps, molding to his hips and muscled legs and complemented by shiny black riding boots that reached just below his knees.

Chelsea said a silent prayer, hoping he would take pity on her and delay in confronting her about his newfound knowledge of her past, before throwing her out, as she was now certain he would do.

"Good morning to you, Miss MacKenna."

Chelsea wanted to crawl under the table and hide, to avoid the humiliation of his tossing her to the street. But that would be what he expected her to do, to hide her head in the sand to dodge his accusations. He did not know she had listened to the conversation. What right had he to question her? She had never asked him to bring her to his house and shelter her. It was his duty as a gentleman to do that. He wouldn't throw her out. No gentleman would. And he was a gentleman, wasn't he?

"Good morning, Lord Ravenel," she replied, and took another sip of her cold chocolate, meeting his gaze fully before setting her cup in its saucer. Her confidence soared. She would just pretend nothing had happened, that he didn't know Gregor had been her betrothed.

"I trust you slept well last evening?"

Chelsea shifted in her seat at the obvious glimmer she caught in his eyes, her confidence beginning to lag. Was he aware she had overheard the conversation?

"Yes, very well, thank you."

"If you do not object, I should like to discuss a matter of some importance with you after the morning meal."

Her eyes shot up. He *was* going to throw her out. He was going to humiliate her before Emma and Fredric and the servants, then throw her out to the street to face Gregor alone. She looked around. Emma, engrossed in the morning *Gazetteer,* did not seem to take notice of his statement. Fredric was occupied with buttering his crumpet, oblivious to the tension which suddenly surrounded the room.

When she looked back, she found Rogan staring at her, his eyes lit up, as if enjoying her discomfort. Her courage began to soften. What *had* he learned about her?

A silent moment passed, and then another, and another, until, as if he needed no further response, Rogan took up the newspaper and began to scan its pages.

Chelsea's gaze lingered on him, the set of his jaw, the way his broad shoulders filled his jacket. She became entranced by the single lock of mahogany hair that fell over his forehead. She suddenly remembered the way his mouth had felt when they'd kissed her, and her cheeks flushed at the memory. Why was she thinking such thoughts when in a matter of minutes he'd most probably be casting her to the street?

"That is agreeable to you, Miss MacKenna, is it not?"

It took her a moment to recall the question. "Yes, certainly, Lord Ravenel, whatever you wish."

The remainder of the meal passed with light conversation, mostly from Emma, as Chelsea tried to think of what she would say when alone with Rogan. It was inevitable, their meeting, and delaying it would serve no purpose. Her father had always told her to face her problems head on, for trying to avoid them usually made them double.

The waiting was intolerable. Chelsea did not touch her buttered eggs, her stomach too agitated for food.

"Well, I am off," Fredric said finally, standing from the table. "Pip, would you care to stop and see how the renovations are coming on the house?"

Emma's face lit up. "Oh, yes, please?" She glanced at Chelsea. "Chelsea, would you like to come along with us?"

"No, you go along. I will be fine." Though Chelsea wished nothing more than to escape the inevitable meeting with Rogan, she declined. It would save her further humiliation to have them gone when he threw her out, as she knew he would.

She watched them leave, then returned her gaze to Rogan.

He stood, and moved to the sideboard. "Coffee?"

He was going to draw this out even longer.

"No, thank you," she said. Her stomach was churning now, and inwardly she knew adding anything to it would only make her ill.

Rogan returned to his seat, nodding to dismiss the footman across the room.

They were alone. The tall clock against the far wall was ticking loudly, echoing in the infernal silence around them. Chelsea found her toes tapping the floor in time to the clock as she waited for him to begin. Minutes passed, the tension grew. She wanted to scream at him to just get it over with, accuse her of what he knew and have it out, but she just sat there, toes tapping beneath the table in time.

She started when he finally spoke.

"It seems, Miss MacKenna, you have not quite told me the truth."

Chelsea cleared her throat, which had suddenly turned to sand. "I am afraid I do not know what you mean."

"You do not play the ingenue well, so don't insult me with your coquettish games. You know very well what I mean. The question is are you going to admit you know what I mean so we can move on or do I simply call your friend Moultrie in here and ask him for the truth myself?"

Chelsea set her jaw in indignation. "He is not my friend."

"Seems he has a very different opinion of your relationship. Seems he thinks you are to marry. But perhaps we should allow him to tell us."

Rogan moved to stand.

"No!"

He stilled when Chelsea held up her hand to stop him. She purposely softened her tone. "I owe you an apology, my lord. I was not speaking truthfully yesterday."

"That is more like it." Rogan returned to his chair. "You may proceed."

Chelsea fought the urge to run. She had to maintain her calm, keep her head about her. She could not lose her nerve now. She fixed her gaze on him. "As I'm sure you are aware, I do know the man who was chasing me yesterday. In truth, he was once my betrothed."

"That has already been established."

Chelsea went on, her mouth turning down as if she'd tasted a sour grape.

"It is obvious you know as well that his name is Gregor Moultrie. We were to be married a month ago, but I left the night before our wedding was to have taken place. I thought I had eluded him until yesterday when he appeared outside the Andrews boardinghouse, demanding that I return with him to Scotland. I asked him to leave, but he refused. I was afraid. When I saw you standing there, I . . ."

She dropped her gaze to her lap. How could she possibly explain what had possessed her to embrace a total stranger like some street harlot looking for a wealthy gent? She had been trying to escape from Gregor. She had hoped that by Rogan being there, Gregor would not try to take her. She now realized how foolish her actions had been.

"Why?"

Chelsea looked up, her eyes pleading with Rogan not to force her to continue. "Gregor is very forceful and demanding and I do not wish to return with him, I . . ."

"I was not asking why you are afraid, Miss MacKenna. That is plainly obvious. The man is a beast. He belongs in a cage. What I am asking is why you would leave the man you had agreed to marry on the night before your wedding? Did he harm you in some way?"

Chelsea shook her head.

"Did he threaten you?"

Again she shook her head.

"Did you not see him until this night before your wedding, and after seeing his face, ran away in fear for your life?"

As an excuse, it would be plausible, but Chelsea shook her head anyway.

"You did agree to marry this man, didn't you, or were

you forced into the match by someone?"

Like your family whom you claim does not exist, Chelsea finished inwardly. Perhaps she should just tell him the truth, have it out and on the table, and she almost did, except she remembered the words of the stranger, "James," about her father's safety. She could not allow anything to jeopardize his return. She decided against the truth and said simply, "I had second thoughts about the match."

"And that is all?"

Chelsea stared at him. He knew everything. He had to know by the way he was pressing her. But how? Certainly Gregor wouldn't have told him *everything*. "I can only say that circumstances caused me to change my mind."

"Circumstances? And what might they have been?"

She looked at him, loathing him for toying with her so. She felt as she had the day before, standing before him without her shoe on, demanding that he return it while he held it back from her grasp. Only this time it was her pride she was trying to retrieve. "I cannot tell you."

Rogan stood. "I'm afraid, Miss MacKenna, if I am to shelter you in my house, I must know the reasons behind your being here."

How could she possibly tell him her betrothed had preferred another woman to her—worse, her own mother? She would die from the shame of it.

Chelsea watched as Rogan crossed the room from the corner of her eye. "I cannot tell you at this time. I beg your understanding."

"Are you saying you will tell me at some other time?"

She stalled him. "Perhaps."

Rogan stopped before the window, his back to her as he looked outside. They could continue with this verbal fencing for hours. She was not going to reveal anything to him. But why? What was she so afraid of? He knew she was trying to protect him, but he needed to know the truth.

From his place at the window he could see Gregor standing at the end of the drive, watching the house, waiting to take her. There stood what frightened her so, there lay his answer. What had the cur done to make her leave? Had he beat her? The mere thought of that as a possibility made Rogan's fists clench in rage. He'd kill the bloody bounder if he so much as ever laid a hand on her. But what else could it be?

He turned. "I'm afraid it is impossible, Miss MacKenna. We cannot go on living with this man at our doorstep. He is unstable. I would be reluctant to leave you or Emma unattended. Either I, or Fredric, would have to remain here, day and night, to ensure your safety. And, too, this man has some claim to you. You were betrothed, were you not? If you were to be married, were the banns not cried?"

He turned toward her when he did not hear a response.

Chelsea nodded hesitantly.

"And you agreed to marry this man?"

"It was an arrangement made by our families ages ago. I had no choice. I felt I had to honor that agreement."

"But you did willingly exchange a promise of marriage?"

Again Chelsea nodded.

Rogan came to a halt directly behind Chelsea. Her ebony hair tumbled loosely down her back, confined only by a small white ribbon at the nape of her neck. She looked beautiful, so damned beautiful. Something inside him stirred, something he'd not felt for quite some time, something that made him want to reach out and release the tie, loosen her hair around her, and inhale its sweet scent. What was the mystery to this woman?

He turned. "Then, if marriage to this man is so repugnant, your only solution is to marry another."

"What?"

"He could not lay claim to you if you were wed to another, especially with your banns being cried in Scotland. He would have to prove that a promise of marriage had been given before witnesses, and would have to procure those witnesses for the authorities."

Chelsea could not believe what she was hearing.

"And just what are you thinking of doing? Holding a lottery for a prospective husband with the lucky ticket holder winning my hand?"

"Not a bad suggestion, though it would be far better and easier to find someone who is looking for a wife for reasons other than love."

"And just who would want that?" Chelsea asked sharply, wondering if he was mocking her, wishing he would just order her out and have it done with.

Rogan circled the table and leaned his hands upon it.

"I would."

Chapter 6

Chelsea stared at him, disbelieving, stunned and utterly without words.

It took her several moments to regain her composure.

"You? Marry me?"

"Try to contain your elation, Miss MacKenna. That shocked expression leads me to believe wedding me would be tantamount to condemning you to a life in Hades. Am I really that undesirable a choice?"

"No, it's just that . . ." She tried to think of something, anything to explain the reason for the strange rush of feeling that had come over her at his suggestion, a feeling not unlike excitement. "I would never have thought you'd wish to marry me."

Rogan smiled. "Let us just say that at this point in my life, marriage would be most beneficial to me. I grow tired of the puppy dog desperation in the eyes of all the mothers who wish to reward me with their daughters."

"So you would marry me to avoid them?"

"For all purposes we would make it *seem* so."

Now Chelsea was completely confused and it obviously showed on her face.

"Call it a sort of arrangement, if you will, to suit us both. We would go about presenting you as my future bride, which would free me from all those son-in-law seeking mothers, and your overgrown suitor outside would see you no longer have any interest in him and leave."

"Gregor would never leave."

Rogan frowned. This wasn't going at all as he'd hoped. She was finding arguments, valid arguments against every point he made. "Perhaps, but it would protect you from his making any claim on you. By my confirmation that we are to wed, anyone would be hard pressed to believe a man who you deny is your betrothed."

"But we would not truly wed?"

"No. We would simply make everyone, Goliath included, believe we were to wed."

Chelsea could see he had given this idea some thought and she now did likewise. But a pretend bride? Much better than Gregor's unwilling one. Perhaps Rogan was right. It seemed logical. But would it truly work?

"An arrangement?" she repeated.

"Aye, you are in need of a job," Rogan said. "Let us just say I should like to employ you to be my bride."

The way he said it made it sound so indecent. "But I already have a job. As Emma's lady's companion."

"Aye, but Gregor would have nothing to deter him from taking you back to where you came from, now, would he? You show a bold front, Miss MacKenna, but I believe inside you hold a great fear of him, as most anyone would."

Was it that obvious? Chelsea looked to her fingers, which were twisting as if of their own accord before her. Anyone would be frightened of Gregor—except Rogan. He'd stood up to him completely undaunted, facing him down as if he were some misbehaving child. No one had ever done that before. "But what of Emma? She is expecting me to be her lady's companion."

Rogan smiled. She was at the very least considering his suggestion. But why wouldn't she? He was offering her freedom, freedom from Gregor and the past she so carefully guarded. For her to refuse would be foolishness. An earl was certainly nothing to scoff at as a marriage prospect. "I am certain Emma would not mind your change in occupations, given the circumstances."

Rogan wanted to erase the little line that creased between her eyes. He wondered what it would take to coax a smile from her, and bring some light to those dark brooding eyes. He went on, not wanting to give her time to come up with a refusal. "Now, I have given some thought to this and in order for this Moultrie cad to believe this charade of ours, we are going to have to be seen together. The more witnesses we have to our alleged alliance, the better our chances of convincing the authorities, should it come to that."

"Authorities?" Chelsea's face paled.

"Yes. Gregor could, if he thought to, very well exercise his rights to you. And he does still have rights to you. We will only hope we can stave him off. In the meantime, we must do everything we can to assure all of London we are to be married."

Rogan watched Chelsea as she took in his words. He wasn't sure what to expect from her, refusal or agreement, and was not at all surprised when he received neither.

"What are you suggesting?"

"I have the good fortune to be holding an invitation to a social function this evening. A ball at Bedford House, and it promises to be one of the grandest of the season. It will be our coming out, if you will. I will attend this ball with you at my side and we will appear to all as two young lovers about to be married. You will be presented as my betrothed. By the end of the evening, I want no doubt as to the devotion we hold for one another. I do expect some questions from those who know me well, but we must act as if we have planned to wed for quite some time and try to sidestep the questions."

"But I haven't a ball gown to wear."

"Emma, I am sure, can find you something suitable."

Rogan looked at Chelsea. She had been quite calm as he'd issued all these orders, raising only the mildest of objections. He'd expected more of a fight from her. Actually he'd expected outright refusal. But he was not yet finished. He thought back to his meeting with his father's solicitor, Mr. Dubbs, at the first light of dawn that morning. His gouty legs had nearly leapt for joy when he'd been told of Rogan's betrothal plans, exclaiming how Townsend would be pleased as well. And how very little about Chelsea Rogan found he knew when Dubbs had questioned him about her background.

"There is something more, Miss MacKenna. Something which is unfortunately unavoidable. Before we can appear together, I will need to know more about you and your family."

"Why?" Her voice rose noticeably.

"My family is very influential with our social set. There will be many questions as to the sudden appearance of a betrothed at my side. Especially one who is unknown. I understand your reasons for wishing to keep this information to yourself, but I must also be ready to face anyone who might know your family. I will not divulge anything, you needn't worry. But on the off chance that someone recognizes your name, I cannot risk not having the information a bridegroom should have. That is not asking too much, is it?"

Chelsea stared at him, the crease between her eyes deepening. Rogan suddenly felt the urge to kiss her, only this time fully and completely, not with the intent of securing his pistol from his jacket or shutting off her objections as he had in the garden. Perhaps the prospect of playing this charade was not all that unpleasant.

Chelsea straightened in her chair and looked blankly into his eyes. After several moments, she began, her tone matter-of-fact. "My father is a viscount. I told you he was dead, but I lied. I am sorry. As far as I know, my father is living somewhere across the Channel."

She thought of the meeting with the stranger—James—at St. George's, but chose not to mention it. She had to keep Rogan from getting any more involved with her problems. Gregor was dangerous. Rogan could get hurt, or worse, killed. She could not allow that. "I do not know exactly where my father settled, only that his intended destination was Brussels. He has written only once, and that three years ago. He was exiled after the Jacobite Rebellion in 1745. My brother, Jamie, died in the revolt."

She paused. She would not tell him her true family name. Let him think her father had played a traitorous part in the

Scots' revolt and had been exiled. She knew the truth. She knew he was innocent. "The only reason the Crown did not confiscate our home is because my mother still has affiliations with the Court and intervened on our behalf."

"Then your mother is alive?"

"Yes."

"Then certainly you can summon her here as your parent and end this ridiculous betrothal."

"No!" she exclaimed. "My mother must never know where I am. She is the one who sent Gregor after me. She is the one who arranged the marriage and would probably force it if need be. It was a condition of keeping our lands. It was arranged that I would marry Gregor before I turned twenty."

"If it was a condition for keeping your family holdings, then you surely must have had good reason to leave."

She said nothing.

"Miss MacKenna, I must know what it was that caused you to leave Scotland."

Chelsea felt her throat tighten. "I cannot tell you."

"I must know what brought you here."

Chelsea shook her head, knotting her fingers in her lap. Images of Gregor in her mother's bed came to mind and she closed her eyes to shut them away.

"Miss MacKenna . . ."

"No!" Chelsea sprang up. "I cannot tell you! I will not tell you! I do not want to remember." Regretting her hasty words, she covered her mouth with her hand. Before she could reveal any more of the sordid tale, she turned and fled the room, images of her mother and Gregor filling her head.

"Miss MacKenna!"

Chelsea started up the stairs, wanting to escape Rogan, escape his inquiries and the memories they evoked, but her feet became snagged in her skirts and she slipped, falling to her knees. She collapsed on the bottom step, her face buried in her hands as all her frustrations, all the pain and rejection she'd suppressed the past weeks, came pouring out of her in a tidal wave of tears. Why? Why did this nightmare follow her wherever she went, plaguing every day of her life? Why couldn't she just forget?

She did not pull away when she suddenly felt two strong male hands encircle her and lift her gently from the stair. She did not care. Somehow they offered her solace as she wept for what had become of her life, burying her face into the soft moss-colored velvet of Rogan's coat. The smell of him, a woodsy scent, filled her senses. It gave her comfort and she found reassurance in his gentle, but strong arms and held tightly to him never wanting to be returned to the harshness of reality.

Rogan offered her no words, no solutions, only a shoulder to sob on. He wanted to pound the life from Gregor for doing whatever it was he had done to reduce this beautiful girl to this. He cursed himself for pushing her so hard, wanting to force the truth from her, needing to know what she hid so secretively. Her heartfelt tears sent a stab of regret piercing through his heart. His jaw tightened at her anguish and he could only imagine what Gregor had done to cause this.

Several moments passed before Chelsea pulled away from him. She could not look at him, ashamed at her outburst, suddenly angry at herself and at him for forcing her to this. She pushed away from him.

"Miss MacKenna . . ."

No, Rogan did not deserve her anger. He was only trying to help. She stood slowly, her voice hoarse. "If we are to put on the appearance of being in love, do you not think you should at least refer to me by my given name?"

Rogan fidgeted with his cravat for what seemed the tenth time, but no matter how he tried to tie it, it always resulted in the same crooked knot. His nerves were on edge. He didn't know why, but he felt pulled tighter than his Aunt Eustacia's corset strings and he could not get the look on Chelsea's face when she'd been clinging to him in tears out of his head. His insides still twisted at the memory. He felt like a heel. He felt like a consummate cad. Worse, he was a consummate cad. He cursed to himself and turned from the looking glass, giving up on the cravat completely.

"Fredric," he said as he moved into the study, spotting his brother-in-law reaching for a volume high on a shelf, "what is your knowledge of marriage law?"

Fredric turned and peered at him from behind a huge magnifying glass, one eye blinking at him at thrice its normal size. He'd pushed his spectacles to his forehead, giving him the appearance of having four eyes, one of them much larger, of course.

Rogan chuckled at him.

"Can't read the blasted titles way up here," Fredric said, then narrowed his overlarge eye, staring at Rogan quite closely. "Your cravat is crooked."

"Yes, I know. I like it that way. I think all men should go about as such. Now, do you know anything about marriage law?"

"Passing, why do you ask?"

He heard footsteps on the stairs.

"We'll speak of it later. I've something I wish you to look into, if you would, but I haven't the time to go into it just yet."

He turned. Chelsea, wearing a gown of rich midnight blue velvet, and looking more beautiful than he would have ever thought possible, stood in the doorway. She started slowly toward him. Silver lace covered the front of the gown, spilling in layers at her elbows and toes. Her skirts rustled against the carpeting. Her hair was pulled back softly from her face, soft tendrils curled around her fine cheekbones, caressing her slender neck and shoulders in a dark ebony cascade.

"You look stunning."

She looked up at him and smiled. "Your cravat is crooked."

She reached up and, without further word, pulled the crooked tie loose. He watched her as she deftly twisted and turned the lace cravat, her eyes intent upon her task as if the neatness of his tie were of the greatest importance. Her fingers brushed against his throat and he tightened his jaw against the jolt it gave him.

"There," she said, stepping back to survey her work. "Now it's perfect. Father always said a good wife should be able to tie a neat cravat." She smiled at him and it lit up her face with the brilliance of a thousand stars.

"I would like to apologize for my behavior earlier," he said. "I had no right to demand anything of you. I hope you can put it aside and try to enjoy the evening."

Chelsea nodded. "Thank you. I, too, must apologize. I have given you a great burden, one you did not ask to have. Let us just forget this morning and start anew, shall we?"

Rogan felt something within him grow at that moment, something that made him stare into her eyes and lose himself there. He could forget that morning quite easily. If only he could forget his father, forget Gregor. He wondered . . .

He reluctantly tore his gaze away. "Are we ready to leave?"

Chelsea started forward and Rogan noticed that her steps faltered. He took her arm. "Is something wrong, Chelsea?"

She looked up at him and he saw a light shining in her eyes. "Yes, it seems my overgrown feet are too big for your sister's shoes."

Rogan chuckled. "I'll be certain to keep your dancing at a minimum this evening. We'll solve that problem tomorrow with some new shoes from Madame Dussault's."

They reached Bedford a quarter-hour later. The coachman hopped down from his seat and opened the door to allow them out.

"Remember, Chelsea, we must appear to be in love."

"I am ready to proceed with this charade if you are."

Chelsea took Rogan's arm, trying to seem as if she hadn't a care in the world. Once inside, her bravado faltered. She felt as if every eye was upon her. She felt as if all could see through their ruse. She wondered for the millionth time if she was doing the right thing and nodded her head when Rogan introduced her to an aging man named Lord Sydney who looked full of his own importance.

The ballroom was aglow with colors and filled and noisy with the chattering voices of the other guests. They had to stop several times when the crowd became too thick to move. When the aisleway finally cleared, Rogan introduced her to an older lady whose neck sparkled with more diamonds than Chelsea'd ever before seen and whose name escaped her as soon as it was spoken. She noticed the surprised looks on everyone's faces when it was revealed she was Rogan's betrothed. She wondered what they could be thinking of her sudden appearance on his arm, if they would believe the false tale of impending marriage.

"Rogan, I did not think you came to these things unless looking for a night's diversion—oh, who have we here?"

Chelsea felt Rogan tense instantly. A deep line etched its way across his forehead.

"Chelsea, this is my cousin, Beecher Prestwood."

He was what her nursemaid back at Drummore would call a fop, a coxcomb, one more concerned with his dress and appearance than with the state of the world. He looked like a strutting peacock. He was a tall man, dressed in a suit of sky blue silk with purple stockings and bright red heels on his shoes. His hair was pulled back with a large black bow, its ends trailing endlessly downward, his natural hair color hidden beneath a layer of stark white powder.

Beecher pressed a kiss to her palm even before she could offer it, a kiss that was all too familiar in nature, putting her ill-at-ease.

"Always a pleasure to meet a beautiful lady." Beecher smiled, his teeth even and white, his gaze deepening.

As his stare crept openly downward Chelsea felt the sudden desire for a cloak with which to cover herself.

"Beecher, this is Miss Chelsea MacKenna, my betrothed."

Beecher faltered. He seemed about to choke on his response. "Your betrothed?" He laughed an obviously unnatural chuckle that caused Chelsea to take a step closer to Rogan. "What kind of wry jest is this, Rogue?"

Chelsea felt her heart rise to her throat. Oh, God, he was going to expose their lie.

Rogan's next words came very slowly and very precisely. "As I said, Beecher, Miss MacKenna and I are betrothed."

Beecher stared at them, perhaps disbelieving, then after a long moment he nodded slowly to her. "A pleasure, Miss MacKenna."

He excused himself quickly thereafter, almost too quickly, and made his way across the crowded ballroom. He stopped at one point and turned back to look at them for a moment before retreating out the far door. Chelsea noticed the rigid set of Rogan's jaw as he followed his cousin's departure.

"You do not care for him very much, do you?"

"Hmm?"

"Your cousin. I said that you do not seem to care for him very much."

Rogan looked down at her. "What makes you say that?"

"You changed when he came forward. Like you"—she searched for the right word—"did not quite trust him."

"You are very perceptive."

"Why would you not trust him? He is family to you, is he not?"

"Aye but being family does not always make one trustworthy."

Chelsea nodded, understanding more than Rogan could possibly know.

"Now, my dear betrothed, if you keep with that worried expression on your face, everyone will think you are an unwilling bride."

Rogan reached to her and ran his fingertip lightly over her brow. His touch left a sensation more powerful than the deepest caress. It was an intimate touch, one to be expected between lovers, one common between those about to be wed. He stared down at her, his eyes darkening as he trailed the back of his hand softly down the side of her cheek.

It seemed as if the room had suddenly emptied and it was just the two of them standing there. All sound, all movement seemed to vanish. Chelsea swallowed, still looking up at him, uncomfortable under his stare and the sudden closeness between them. She was unused to such intimacy, and though it was not unpleasant, she was still grateful when their exchange was interrupted a moment later.

"Lord Ravenel, how truly pleasurable to see you."

Chelsea turned, ready to meet yet another, and could not help but stare at the vision before her.

The woman who had spoken could only be described as beautiful, carrying her head with an air of assurance and natural grace. She was much younger than the man whose arm she held, with waves of lush brown hair that was only slightly powdered and arranged elegantly atop her regal head. Her gown of lilac silk flattered her lithe figure, complementing the deep plum color of her companion's gold-adorned suit. Though he was advanced in age, Chelsea thought he must have once been very handsome. And he was obviously awed by this woman, for he watched her as she spoke and his expression was filled with adoration.

Rogan smiled warmly, his expression softening as he pressed a kiss to the woman's hand.

"Lord and Lady Lampley, a pleasure as always. May I present Miss Chelsea MacKenna, my betrothed. Chelsea, I present William Malcolm and his wife, Diana, the Earl and Countess of Lampley."

As Chelsea rose from her curtsy, she noticed Lady Lampley's raised brow, the corner of her rouged lips lifting in a knowing smile. "And what a lovely girl she is, too."

She reached out and touched Rogan's arm. "You must be sure to bring her to the fête we are having at Lampley next week. There will be gaming and dancing and much frolic."

Chelsea sensed an instant change in Rogan. He seemed to ease as he listened to this woman, his eyes glinting in the candlelight. She watched him closely, the way the two talked with one another, and suddenly she somehow knew Rogan had been intimate with her. It was something in the way they held each other's eyes, her hand reaching out once again to touch Rogan's sleeve lightly. She wondered if the earl knew. How could he not, when it was so obvious?

"Then we shall see you again soon," the countess said. She smiled warmly at Chelsea. "So nice to meet you, my dear."

After they had excused themselves, gliding away like a king with his queen, Chelsea watched Rogan with interest. His eyes followed the pair as they crossed the room, lingering while they chatted shortly with another couple. He did not break his stare until they were well out of sight.

"She is your mistress, isn't she?"

Rogan glanced down with a look of both amusement and surprise, as if suddenly remembering her. "What?"

"I said she is your mistress. I can tell you have been familiar with her."

Rogan chuckled. "I really do not think it is any of your business."

"Do you love her?"

"No, she is in love with her husband, as well she should be."

"But she beds with you," Chelsea stated as if it were a fact undoubted.

Rogan did not respond.

It was all the confirmation Chelsea needed.

"Does the earl know?"

Rogan could not believe he was having this conversation and wondered how she had been able to guess something that had been hidden from all society and his closest of friends for years. "Do you think he would be standing there talking to me if he did?"

Chelsea shrugged. "I've heard some men are close friends with their wives' paramours. Some even like 'sharing' their wives with them."

"I see, and you have had much experience with married women and their lovers?"

Chelsea giggled. "Ah-hah, I knew she was your mistress."

Rogan couldn't help his smile. "I think we should take you outside to get some air and cool your overheated curiosity." He tugged at his cravat. "I suddenly find it very warm in this room."

Chelsea followed him as he led her through tall french doors onto a wide marble veranda. The knowledge of the countess's position as Rogan's lover set an unconscious frown on her lips. Only when she began to compare him mentally with Gregor and his infidelities did she wonder why she should have such thoughts. Rogan did not owe her any explanation. He was not truly her betrothed. Why the thought of him bedding with that woman should cause her such thoughts troubled her and she pushed them away.

Outside, the moon was hazy, barely peeking through the clouds above, casting long dark shadows on the gray stone walls that surrounded the secluded balcony. The night was cold and windy, whistling through the courtyard below, but Chelsea welcomed the chill and the soothing effect it had. She closed her eyes and breathed deeply, clearing her thoughts and losing herself in the night.

Several couples walked along the railing, their heads bowed close in private conversation. Rogan put his arm around her shoulders and drew her near, steering them toward a deserted corner.

"The breeze should not be that chilling over here."

Chelsea looked up at Rogan. She could barely see the outline of his face in the moonlight, but she knew he was staring at her, the same stare he had given her inside before, when he had touched her face. It set her heart racing.

Distant strains of the orchestra reached their ears, the music lulling, calming her, lowering her guard. Despite the lies, despite the charade they played, Chelsea felt safe with this man beside her. He had saved her from Gregor and certain disaster, without question and without hesitation. She wondered why he would offer to go along with this ruse, why he would risk his place in society to help her. What, perhaps, was he hiding from her?

"Chelsea . . ."

She turned, waiting silently for his next words. He did not speak, but lowered his head and touched his lips softly to hers. Chelsea felt a shiver run through her at the caress of his mouth on hers, tingling and settling deep within her. It filled her with a dull, sweet ache, and she relaxed against him, setting her hands unwittingly against his chest.

She could feel his heart beating readily beneath her palms, the softness of his silk waistcoat, the firm muscles in his chest as he drew her closer to him. She did not protest when he deepened the kiss, his tongue softly entering her mouth.

At the touch of his tongue on hers, she was taken over by a trembling so fierce she was certain Rogan felt it as well. She let her head fall back to accommodate his mouth, felt his hand lightly caress her shoulder. His kiss felt different, soft, gentle, unlike Gregor's demanding and rough ones.

Gregor.

She suddenly remembered a similar night, when she stood nestled behind the bookcase at Castle Drummore. That same night she had found him sprawled atop her mother.

She could not allow this to happen to her again. She tried to pull away, but Rogan held her tightly. She flattened her hands, which had somehow balled themselves into tight fists, and pushed against his chest. Gregor's face rose before her, his dark eyes narrowed at her, filling her with stark fear.

She could not get away. He was coming for her, his hands outstretched, holding her prisoner as she fought against him.

"No, Gregor!"

Somehow she managed to tear away and pulled back. But it was not Gregor who stood before her now.

Rogan released Chelsea instantly. She backed away. She hadn't meant to pull away. How could she possibly explain it had not been him she had been trying to escape? When the image of Gregor's face had surfaced in her mind, all the anger, all the pain he had caused her surfaced with it and she tried to escape it, escape him.

But it was Rogan, not Gregor, who was staring at her now, his eyes darkening with some unknown emotion. He did not speak. She had to say something, anything to break the tense silence that had wound its way around them, but could not find the proper words.

"Why did you do that?" she managed, thinking the question quite stupid the moment it left her lips.

"You needn't look so frightened, Chelsea. I apologize for taking liberties you obviously did not wish me to take. It was not right of me. I was simply trying to play the convincing betrothed."

How could she tell him that she did not mind the liberties he had taken, that she had indeed enjoyed them? "There are none here to convince."

Suddenly she wished she could disappear, leave this place and forget any of the past two months had occurred. As if to remind her she could not erase the present, Rogan came up beside her and rested his hand lightly next to hers.

"Even the most skilled actor must rehearse his lines before a performance."

He was so near she could feel the soft cloth of his coat brush against her arm. Silently he reached out and touched her cheek, sending a rush of feeling whirling through her. She swallowed and looked up at him, afraid to move away.

"I must be able to play the bridegroom well, else how can we expect your friend Gregor to believe we are to marry?"

All previous thought disappeared as Chelsea turned on him, anger flaming in her eyes. "I have already told you, Gregor is not my friend, and I grow tired of your constant use of that word."

"Ah, yes, but the line between love and hatred is so thin, so fine, one would question whether the passion of your hatred for him were not the passion of the other in disguise."

Chelsea wanted to scream aloud Gregor's betrayal, to prove that she felt nothing for him but contempt, yet she could not allow herself to reveal the truth, the shame she wore like a jaded cloak. She could never tell Rogan. Somehow she knew he would go to Gregor to avenge her, and Gregor would kill him without thought. She could never allow that to happen. She would never forgive herself if anything should happen to him because of her. No matter how much she wanted to, she could not tell Rogan the truth. Instead she turned and left without another word.

Chapter 7

Rogan followed Chelsea to where she stood, alone and drawing male attention, atop the steps leading to the dancing area. He knew she was angry. And he knew he'd provoked her intentionally, taunting her into a confrontation, but hearing her call out Gregor's name as he kissed her had doused his desire more effectively than a swim in the icy waters of the Thames in the middle of January.

Two young men, their hearts and their randy ambitions shining in their eyes, rushed forward toward her, bearing down on Chelsea like flies to the feast.

"May I have the honor of this dance, my lady?" one said, a good two feet shorter and wider than the other, his cheeks red from his hasty jaunt across the floor.

"Aye," said the other, shouldering his opponent aside, "she would if she were not already sharing this dance with me."

Rogan stepped forward before Chelsea could reply. "I believe, lads, the lady will share this dance with her betrothed." He could see Chelsea's backbone stiffen at the sound of his voice, her arms tight against her side, one hand clenched in a fist. Were he to hazard a guess, he'd wager that at that moment, she'd like that fist clenched around his throat.

He reached for her elbow, frowning when she flinched away. "Smile, Chelsea," he said, placing his hand at the small of her back. "We wouldn't want everybody saying you were an unwilling bride."

"I, sir," she said lowly enough for only Rogan to hear, "do not require practice."

Across the room, standing amongst a satin-bedecked clump of young ladies, all exclaiming over the bold fashion in which their suitors had held their hands, or worse, fixed their eyes upon their bosoms, Gwyneth Pierpont gnashed her teeth in vexation. Had she ever been so nauseatingly stupid at that age?

A fawn-eyed young girl of no more than sixteen, covered from neck to toe in virginal white and chattering profusely, came up beside her.

". . . and then he said if I would but allow him one kiss from my lips, it would sustain him all the rest of his days."

Gwyneth fluttered her fan to ease the heavy smell of the girl's lily-scented toilet water. Ignorance, that state of numb-minded limbo in which young girls were kept until their wedding nights, that was what caused them to believe such complete flummery. If a girl were told the truth of what a man meant when he asked, "only for the touch of her soft hands," none of them would fall prey to sly-talking fops who promised them undying love and marriage before destroying them completely. *Like Fletcher.*

Gwyneth turned on the girl. "When a man says he would die for a kiss, he's not referring to a kiss from *your* lips."

The fawn-eyed girl returned a look of confusion which developed slowly into an expression of complete bewilderment. Gwyneth gave a chuckle and turned, leaving the girl to stare at the train of her skirts.

She flashed a brilliant smile at a young foppish gentleman strolling by, cocking her head coquettishly to the side, her blue eyes sparking in mischievous invitation. His gaze lingered a little longer on her and she turned away, her skirts rustling with the seductive sway of her hips. She searched the ballroom, scanning each face around her. Her smile faded.

It had been three days since Beecher had visited her bedchamber, three days since he had assured her of his cousin's intent to propose, and Rogan had yet to make an appearance. All day, every day, she waited in her bedchamber, watching for his carriage on the square, jumping each time a servant came by, expecting them at any second to summon her. His father, the earl, had even sent a note all but proposing for his son. Still they had never called for her, a proposal of marriage hadn't been made, and she was left to face the knowing stares of society again.

The crowd that lingered began to disperse, setting their wine and punch glasses aside and moving to the center of the ballroom as the orchestra began playing for the next dance. She spotted the fawn-eyed girl with her suitor, looking at him as if he were going to take a bite of her at any second. She smiled.

"Have you no partner for the rigadoon, Gwyneth?"

Gwyneth hadn't seen her approach. She frowned as Nellwyn St. James stepped forward, a pert beauty with fire-red curls and deep green eyes that complemented the emerald silk gown she wore. Throughout the entire season, the two had been pitted against each other, the numbers of their proposals of marriage compared, the number of dances at each ball tallied. Thus far, both had held out for suitable matches and rumors abounded of the odds on each girl that were being offered in the coffee houses throughout London.

Latest sources revealed that Nellwyn was pulling better odds these days.

Gwyneth turned, trying to appear as if nothing were amiss. "Nellwyn, hello, no, it would seem Rogan was unable to attend this evening. I have declined all the others, of course. Rogan gets terribly jealous if I so much as glance in the direction of another male under the age of fifty."

"Rogan, oh, yes," Nellwyn said, "by the by, I haven't yet heard the announcement of your betrothal. Did you not say at Miranda Grevingham's tea just the other day to expect it within the week? When will those banns be cried? Everyone is sitting on pins just waiting."

" 'Tis only a matter of time," Gwyneth said. With a flick of her wrist, she opened her fan with a flourish, fluttering the delicate ivory and vellum piece before her, her eyes skimming the ballroom area.

"Well, it seems I'll be preceding you to the altar, my dear. Father's just consented to my engagement to Daniel. We wed within the year."

Gwyneth narrowed her eyes. "Daniel Haythorne is without funds."

Nellwyn smiled, undaunted. "Sometimes the wishes of

lovers come before the size of the purse. You still have to bed with them, and much better the lover than the aging purse holder, I say.

"Speaking of lovers," Nellwyn continued, "is that not Rogan standing over there by the balcony door? I guess he was able to attend after all. Who is that with him? Very pretty, isn't she? Such striking features. I do not believe I know her. I wonder who she could be. A distant relative, perhaps?"

She paused with just the right amount of hesitation as Rogan leaned down to whisper something in his companion's ear. "Must be a very close relationship, if they are . . ."

Gwyneth ignored Nellwyn and narrowed her eyes instead on the young woman who stood at Rogan's arm. She did not recognize her, in fact, she felt certain she had never before seen her, but she could see Rogan's arm placed intimately at her waist, his smile warm and charming as he glanced down at her.

Jealousy and outrage filled her in an instant and she would have charged across the room to demand an explanation had Nellwyn not stepped forward.

"And all the *ton* felt certain you were to be next at the wedding altar. Have faith, dear Gwyneth, your day will come."

Gwyneth closed her fan with a forceful snap, eyeing Nellwyn dangerously before turning to make her way across the floor. They would see her day far sooner than they thought.

She smoothed a golden tress behind her ear, took a deep breath and assumed a smile that would charm the hose off a blind man. "Rogan, I wasn't expecting to see you here tonight." She nodded curtly to his companion, looking for some flaw, some disfigured mark on her pale ivory face.

There were none.

She extended her hand to Rogan. She had to be a relative. A distant relative. A cousin from the country, perhaps . . .

"Gwyeneth." Rogan kept his arm draped around Chelsea's waist. "I hadn't planned on attending. We just decided at the last moment to come."

He did not take her offered hand.

Gwyneth stared at him a moment then lowered her hand to her side. Her cheeks burned. She could feel the crowd thicken around her, could see the eyes of the onlookers watching their exchange. She fought to maintain her composure. She assured herself over and over that the girl, that near-perfect-faced girl had to be a relative of his.

Had she not heard he had an aunt in Bristol . . . ?

Gwyneth's voice trembled slightly as she asked, "We?"

She was too young to be his aunt. A cousin, perhaps. Yes, she must be his cousin.

"Yes," Rogan said. "Gwyneth Pierpont, allow me to introduce Miss Chelsea MacKenna."

MacKenna . . . Scottish. A cousin from Scotland.

Gwyneth nodded politely. "A pleasure, Miss MacKenna . . ."

" . . . my betrothed."

She froze, her smile dropping to an expression of utter disbelief. "Your betrothed!"

She spoke slightly louder than she intended. The crowd seemed to double in size. Ladies whispered and nodded to each other from behind their fans. Gentlemen smiled to one another knowingly. A layer of perspiration formed along the back of her neck. Gwyneth suddenly found it difficult to breathe.

She looked to Rogan for an explanation, any explanation, her eyes wide. "You are to marry *her*?" She pointed to Chelsea as if she were something foreign.

"Yes, Gwyneth. Chelsea and I are to wed by spring. We haven't yet made a formal announcement. Our families have to be notified and . . ."

Gwyneth did not hear him. He could have been citing Molière for all she knew and she would not have heard a single word. An image of Fletcher, her dear, beloved Fletcher, rose up before her, taking her back to the day when she had said those same words. *You are to marry her.* How Jeanette, her sister, had grinned when their father made the announcement of her betrothal to Fletcher. Gwyneth had refused to believe it, thinking it some hideous jest. Hysterical, she'd fallen into a sobbing heap at their feet, clinging pitifully to Fletcher's boots as she wailed in denial.

For weeks she listened to the servants whispering outside her door, saying no man married a woman who opened her legs so easily. She could still hear the whispers at the wedding as she stood as bridesmaid to her sister who was marrying the man who should have been marrying her.

They did not know the truth. They did not know how much she truly loved Fletcher, how she had dreamed of being his wife. He told her he loved her, begged her to prove her love for him. At first she had resisted, as all proper young ladies are taught to do. But the more she refused him, the more angry he became and the more frightened she grew that he would find another to wed.

So Gwyneth stopped refusing. And after all his promises

and vows of love, after months of trysts in darkened alleys in the back of his carriage, Fletcher married Jeanette, her dour-faced, proper, older sister, leaving Gwyneth to face the humiliation and the whispers, and the fear when she learned she had become pregnant with his child.

For weeks she had stayed hidden in the safety of her bedchamber, taking every meal there, refusing every social invitation, locked away from reality. The curious had called for her. The scandal had reached the ears of King George himself, and Gwyneth had dropped into the very pit of humiliation.

Until Eula came.

The maid quickly dried her tears, instilling in her the knowledge that she alone had the power to control her destiny. With a small silver hook she ended Gwyneth's pregnancy, feeding her anger at Fletcher's betrayal, teaching her to use her hatred to grow strong. She instructed her young charge of how to use her body, gave her the knowledge and ability to control men as Fletcher had controlled her. She taught her the secrets of discretion, the manners of a lady, and the wiles of the most practiced Parisian whore.

And then, when she had been taught all she needed to know, Gwyneth was ready to face London society again. The rumors had died off. Fletcher and Jeanette retired to the country. The *ton* found another spectacle to whisper about. Gwyneth emerged anew—this time older, wiser, and more in control—and she set her attentions on the one man she wanted, the one man who would restore her respectability in society—Rogan Doraunt, Viscount Ravenel, the future Earl of Ashbourne.

"Miss Pierpont, are you all right?"

Gwyneth started. She narrowed her eyes at the look of

concern in Chelsea's dark eyes. Hatred filled her, a hatred so fierce and so raw that it stretched and wound its way through every limb. She fought back the urge to slap her face, that smooth, ivory face, unmarred by any blemish. She would not cower and slink away amid the knowing smiles and raised eyebrows this time. She refused to be humiliated again. This time she knew exactly what to do. Eula had taught her well and she would use her knowledge to destroy this person.

"It was a pleasure to make your acquaintance, Miss Pierpont," Chelsea said.

Gwyneth lifted her chin and said simply, "Indeed." She turned to Rogan. "My warmest congratulations on your upcoming nuptials, Lord Ravenel."

Without waiting for a reply, she glided back across the ballroom floor, head held high amid the stares and whispers that buzzed around her. The crowd parted, allowing her to exit, massing behind as she disappeared through the double-doored entrance at the other side.

She never looked back.

Early the following morning, calling cards from most everyone who had attended the ball the previous evening began arriving, inviting Chelsea to afternoon teas and soirées too numerous to count for weeks to come.

As Emma and Chelsea sifted through the piles of folded and sealed cards, Rogan began to read through his own personal correspondence across the room. His eyes fell instantly to the one bearing the familiar seal of the Doraunt family.

His father had responded.

He slid his finger beneath the heavy parchment and broke

its seal. The paper smelled of tobacco, the distinct blend that only his father used, suddenly filling the room with his presence. Had he glanced up, Rogan would not have been at all surprised to see Townsend standing there before him, his eyes dark and cold, his tone disapproving as he bellowed to his son.

Lord Ravenel,
I have received your correspondence, and though I regret the consequences, it will not serve to excuse you from your obligations. To ensure your compliance with my wishes, I have added a second codicil to my will. Should you not wed by the thirty-first of March of this year, all funds will immediately revert to Beecher Prestwood. My solicitor has been informed of my wishes and will execute them to the letter. I await the proof of a certificate of marriage. No other proof will be accepted.
The Earl of Ashbourne

The letter was not written in Townsend's scratchy hand. A note followed indicating that his personal secretary, Mr. Billings, had written as dictated, due to the failing condition of his employer.

Rogan thought to Emma's warning about Townsend's declining health. Was this letter true, or was it simply a ploy of his father's to coerce his son to obedience?

He stared at the florid quill strokes that covered the thick parchment. The letter was not addressed to "My Dearest Son," as most fathers would write. It contained no inquiry after his well-being. Instead it informed him, simply and coldly, that if he did not comply with his father's wishes, if he did not marry by the date specified, Ashbourne, his birthright and family estate, would fall to disastrous ruin.

Rogan took a sip of his now tepid coffee. Setting it aside, he twisted at the gold ring on his fifth finger. He could ignore Townsend's demands. The inheritance mattered naught to him. He had acquired enough by his own means to live comfortably for the rest of his life. Yet what of Ashbourne? How could he allow it and everything it stood for to perish?

He could not. And he knew it.

Rogan set the letter aside and looked at Chelsea sitting on the floor, her skirts covered with a blizzard of letters and cards. Behind her the morning sun broke through the window, making her appear as delicate as a fragile flower. She bowed her head attentively and listened to Emma explain which invitations to accept and decline. She smiled, completely unaware of the enchanting figure she presented.

But Rogan was aware. He was all too aware. She was beautiful, and the more he watched her, the more he knew he wanted her. He wanted more of her kisses, more of her sweet body. He had tasted the response in her and wanted more. He wanted her completely and knew he would not be satisfied until he had her.

His mind played over his father's letter as he tried to think of his next move.

March 31.

His time was limited. He would have to act quickly.

"Madame Dussault, it has been so long."

When they entered the spacious shop on New Bond Street, Emma embraced the plump older woman who wore a coiffure as large and as white as the moon on Michaelmas.

"Too long, *ma petite*, too, too long."

Madame, as her most intimate customers called her, wore a brightly colored gown of peach and pale blue brocade satin, her bright eyes glowing as she kissed Emma lightly on each cheek.

"Ah, *ma chère,* you look the *fleur* of the expectant *mère*, so bright and happy. But shame on you, you have not visited me in some months now."

"With my growing waist, I fear you would not have a pattern to fit me."

Madame clucked her tongue. "Nonsense. You are beautiful and we make you a beautiful gown that will accommodate your growing *bébé*."

She then turned to Chelsea, who had been standing at the door watching the exchange. "And who have we here?"

"This, Madame," Emma said, "is Miss Chelsea MacKenna. She is to wed my brother, Rogan. Chelsea, allow me to introduce Madame Lisolette Dussault."

Madame's cheeks grew rounded. "Ah, the young mysterious *fleur* I've heard so much of this morning. So it is you who have captured that rascal rogue's heart?"

Chelsea smiled as Madame Dussault opened her arms to her, giving her a warm embrace. She thought to remind this welcoming woman that not two weeks earlier she had refused Chelsea a seamstress's job, but kept this information to herself, thinking it funny how someone's social status could change how one was viewed by the world.

Madame stepped back, holding Chelsea's arms. "Ah, but you are a rare beauty. Such dark hair, such white skin, and those eyes . . . ah, not like those blond girls who expect me to match their gowns to their lip rouge. We will make you *la belle du Londres. Vraiment!* Already I read of you in the newspapers. Come, *ma chère*, we get you measured, then we make you the most beautiful wedding gown in all of England."

Before Chelsea could protest, Madame Dussault took her by the hand and led her to an airy dressing room at the back of her shop. She took a seat upon an overstuffed fringed settee while Madame disappeared behind the drawn curtain to an antechamber on the other side.

Left alone, Chelsea began to feel uneasy. Her initial role as Emma's companion seemed to have vanished somewhere in the quagmire of lies that seemed to be building with each passing second. That morning, Rogan had suggested she order new gowns fitting the station of the future Lady Ravane. The housekeeper, Mrs. Philby, requested she go over the menus for that week. Even Emma and Fredric were acting as if she truly were going to marry Rogan, introducing her wherever they went as his betrothed. Had they all forgotten this was supposed to be a charade?

Or was it?

"You incompetent little fool!"

Chelsea turned at the sound of the angry voice. Standing before a floor-length mirror, at the other side of the room behind a curtain that was half-open, half-closed, was Gwyneth Pierpont, clad only in her chemise and corset, her blond hair pinned loosely atop her head. Beside her—the obvious object of her contempt—was a frightened young seamstress, clutching a lace-bedecked gown in trembling arms.

"I told you I wanted the peach ribbon. This is orange. Take it back. I do not want it."

"But, milady, you said—"

Gwyneth cracked the girl's cheek sharply with her palm.

The sound of the strike filled the room. "You seem to forget your place. Next time it will cost you your job. Now go!"

The seamstress burst into tears and turned, fleeing the room in a rain of sobs and a flurry of white lace. Gwyneth turned, noticing Chelsea still sitting across the room, and smiled, a chilling smile that set Chelsea's nerves on edge.

"Oh," she paused, "excuse me, I seem to have forgotten your name, Miss . . ."

"MacKenna," Chelsea said in quiet distrust. She didn't know why, she'd only just met her, but something about Gwyneth Pierpont made her think she should watch herself closely.

"Ah, yes, Miss MacKenna. Rogan's betrothed."

Gwyneth turned to regard her reflection in the mirror, gazing at the picture she presented, moving to get a full view of her derriere in the glass. She was beautiful, that Chelsea could not deny, but looked as if she knew it and as if she expected all the world to know it as well.

Gwyneth lifted her chin, running a finger along the line of her jaw and said, without looking from her reflection, "So you are to marry Rogan Doraunt."

Chelsea did not respond, wondering why she would repeat that which she had already stated, somehow knowing Gwyneth had more to say.

"How did the two of you meet?"

Chelsea looked to the doorway, hoping to catch Emma's attention. She answered quickly. "A family acquaintance."

"Family acquaintance, you say? Really? And who might that be? Rogan's mother, the countess?"

Chelsea paused. They had not discussed the particulars

of their supposed meeting. Rogan had not mentioned his mother, but he did speak of his father, or had Emma said their mother lived in the country?

"Yes. The countess knows my mother quite well."

Gwyneth smiled, nodding, then her face fell into a mournful frown. "Then surely your mother was devastated when she heard of Lady Ashbourne's tragic death. Pity she died when Rogan was so very young. You and Rogan must have known each other quite a long time if it was she who introduced you."

Chelsea swallowed. Rogan's mother was dead?

"Sad the way the countess passed, so young. Funny, I cannot recall now how did she pass?"

Before Chelsea could conjure up a response, Madame Dussault burst from behind the curtain.

"Here we are." She carried a small box overflowing with a mêlée of colorful ribbons and laces. The girl Gwyneth had slapped followed a step behind, her face downcast and stained with tears. "Now we get your measurements. *Chère*, you go behind the curtain and Aimie will help you remove your gown."

As Aimie passed, Chelsea noticed the imprint of Gwyneth's hand on her pale cheek. She offered her a consoling smile, wondering if she herself would have been the recipient of Gwyneth's fury had she been accepted for the seamstress's position two weeks earlier.

When they emerged from behind the curtain a short time later, Madame was arranging the same lace and ribbon gown Aimie had fled with over Gwyneth's slim form. Madame turned and smiled.

"Wonderful. Aimie, finish lacing Lady Pierpont's gown while I help Miss MacKenna."

"But, Madame," Gwyneth called, "I would prefer that you assist me."

"Nonsense, Aimie will do it. I am needed to help Miss MacKenna choose her wedding gown pattern."

Madame turned away without further consideration, leading Chelsea by the hand. "Now, I show you the exquisite fashion dolls I just received from Paris."

Gwyneth's eyes widened and she pursed her lips in outrage. Never! She would never take second place to that sniveling milksop! Something wasn't ringing true about this sudden betrothal. Why did the girl not even know Rogan's mother was dead?

She was hiding something, of that Gwyneth was certain. Eula had always told her the best way to ruin someone was to learn their secrets. And she knew just where to begin. . . .

Beecher had not crossed the threshold to Lord Pierpont's study before Gwyneth came running toward him, skirts flying about her feet in a tumult of turquoise satin.

"I want to know who this person is! Where did she come from? How did she meet Rogan?"

Beecher leaned against the door frame running a finger along her shoulder to the froth of lace at her sleeve. "Should we not adjourn to the privacy of your bedchamber, my dear? Your father would not be at all pleased, I'm sure, to find me here."

She waved her hand at him in agitation. "He is out visiting with my mother. Some utterly boring tea. I begged off with a headache. They'll not be back for hours."

She yanked him into the room and closed the door behind them. She even turned the key in the lock as if to keep him from escaping. "Now, are you going to tell me how this person came to ruin my life?"

Beecher drew a cheroot from inside his jacket and struck a match to it, thinking it funny how Gwyneth could always attribute the blame to others for every misfortune in her life.

"Very well, my dear. This *person* is from Scotland."

Gwyneth narrowed her eyes. "I already figured that. MacKenna doesn't have much of a French tone to it. How does Rogan know her? He has no kin in Scotland."

"Precisely. Rogan does not know her. He is just using the little innocent to hoodwink his father so he can delay his imminent marriage."

Gwyneth's expression eased. "I knew it. I knew there was something. But why would this woman agree to this?"

Beecher took a slow drag on the cheroot, exhaling a thin trail of smoke. He watched it curl up toward the carved plaster ceiling allowing Gwyneth to stew just a little longer. A slow smile crossed his lips. "I surely do not know."

Gwyneth was not to be put off. "I think you do know something."

She was no fool, he'd grant her that, watching as she assumed a seductive stance against the bureau. He knew more than he was telling her, and she knew just what it would take to extract it out of him. She glided across the room to him, her silk skirts rustling softly, her face taking on a honeyed expression. She stopped directly before him.

"I think you know something more. And I think you are going to tell me."

Her voice had changed its timbre. His smile deepened. "Perhaps."

She moistened her lips with the tip of her tongue. "Perhaps what?"

"Perhaps, if you can persuade me to."

For the first time he could ever remember, Beecher was the one in control. Gwyneth was in foreign territory, a place where she no longer reigned, but played courtier, a place she did not much like to be. He was curious how far she would go to gain what she wanted.

She took Beecher's hand and pulled him up before her, slowly tracing the outline of his lips with her fingertips. She moved them down over his chin and chest to the fastenings of his breeches. His sex pulsed against the confining silk, straining to be free.

She pressed her palm to it. He drew a sharp breath. She smiled. She moved closer still and wrapped her arms around his neck, pressing her hips against him as her tongue teased his mouth.

"I want you."

With those three words, Gwyneth regained the advantage.

Beecher pulled her against him, ravaging her mouth with his, pushing his tongue deep inside as all thought of Rogan and Chelsea vanished. Gwyneth moved her hips seductively against him. She was driving him to the edge, he could feel his need throbbing against her as she dropped back her head to allow his mouth the column of her neck. His fingers fumbled at the lacings of her bodice, pulling and yanking at the delicate ribbons until, unable to stand the waiting any longer, he ripped the fabric clear to her waist.

His eyes widened at the sight of her bared breasts. With a moan, he buried his face against the soft mounds, squeezing and caressing as he suckled her rose-tinted nipples. He could wait no longer. Sweeping her up into his arms, he carried her across the room, laying her on the soft brocade settee and lifting her skirts to her waist. He quickly unfastened his breeches and freed his hardened sex. He did not even pause to remove them, so great was his need for her.

Gwyneth opened her legs to accept him readily and he dropped to his knees, shoving into her with one savage thrust. She cried out, arching her back as his mouth found her nipple. Beecher groaned aloud, thrusting into her again, then again, each time harder, each time more desperate than the first. Gwyneth wrapped her legs around his waist, the heels of her shoes digging sharply into the flesh of his back. She cried out as his teeth bit softly at her nipple, raising and lowering her hips to meet each thrust he continued to drive madly into her.

She watched his face through lowered lashes, watched as she held him, controlling his desire. He was moaning aloud with every thrust now, his face twisting, contorting, his voice echoing out across the room. She saw his jaw tighten and knew he was nearing his climax. Curling her fingers around the back of the settee, she felt him release his seed into her. His chest was heaving, his forehead beaded with perspiration and he dropped his head onto her breasts, spent and trying to regain his ragged breath.

She allowed him several moments to collect himself. Now he would tell her everything she wanted to know. Threading her fingers through the damp curls at his temple, she softly coaxed him with her touch. "Have I persuaded you?"

"Mmm." He smiled and nodded his head against her, running his tongue across her still-swollen nipple.

A moment passed.

She shifted her weight beneath him, trying to get him to rise. He did not move. Another moment passed. "Beecher?"

"I suppose you would like me to get up now?"

His voice was crisp with irritation.

Gwyneth had to play the game carefully, knowing there was much to gain and everything to lose. "There are servants about, Beecher. They might come in."

"You locked the door. Besides, you did not seem to care a moment ago when you were moaning and bucking beneath me."

She bit back a sharp retort. "Yes, darling, I know but . . ."

"Darling?" He paused. "That is a new one."

He stood, his sex wet and limp. He quickly fastened his breeches and turned from her.

Gwyneth lowered her skirts and tried to secure her bodice. The lacings had been torn through, the delicate fabric rent to her waist. Adjusting it as best she could, she raised her eyes innocently to his. "Well?"

"Well, what?"

"Are you going to tell me what it is you know about this woman or not?"

He raised a smug brow. "Certainly, after you fetch me a brandy."

Gwyneth's eyes narrowed for a moment, then softened. He was deliberately trying her patience, using her desire for information to satisfy his own ego. She stood, refusing to be provoked and lowered her voice. "As you wish."

She crossed the room and uncorked the stopper to her father's best brandy. She poured a liberal amount into a crystal snifter and turned, offering it to Beecher with a sweet smile.

He took it and sipped slowly, moving behind her father's desk. He propped his feet in a leisurely way upon the polished desktop while lighting another cheroot. He took his time in speaking.

"Seems this woman has a betrothed in Scotland from whom she is fleeing. She has agreed to Rogan's plan for this supposed union to try to keep the other man at bay."

"And where is this betrothed?"

"Usually camped outside the Doraunt gates. Seems the man wants her back."

Gwyneth thought for a moment. "Can you bring him to me?"

"Most probably. Why?"

"Let us just say I would like to help this man get back what is rightfully his. A gesture of goodwill."

Beecher chuckled, knowing Gwyneth never did anything for the sake of others. "I'll see if I can convince him to come by this evening. Around ten?"

Gwyneth nodded, already formulating a plan.

Beecher stood and started for the door.

"Wait a moment."

He stopped.

"There is something more you are not telling me."

He turned, smiling at her perceptiveness. "Well, I did learn something more. Something even dear Daniel failed to tell cousin Rogan about our false bride."

"Which is?" Gwyneth's eyes lit up eagerly.

"She lied to him about her name. It is not MacKenna."

"It is not?"

"No. Her name is Chelsea Estwyck, only living child of Damson Estwyck, Viscount Drummore."

Gwyneth recognized the name, but could not place it.

She searched her memory. "Viscount Drummore . . ."

"Aye, the same Viscount Drummore your father crusaded against to have arrested and who was exiled for his part in the Forty-five. A traitor to the throne and all England."

Gwyneth touched a thoughtful fingertip to her chin. "And Rogan has no knowledge of this you say?"

"Not that I am aware of. Why?"

Secrets. More to use against that woman, more to crush her with, more to destroy her. She smiled. "If her father was exiled, then who has provided for her all these years?"

"Her mother, the Viscountess Drummore and former Annora Cannamore of Scotland."

Two hours later, alone in her bedchamber, bathed and changed into a fresh muslin gown, Gwyneth sat at her carved rosewood writing table, quill in hand. Perhaps she should tell Rogan this woman had deceived him, had lied to him about who she truly was. She could use her father's treason against Chelsea and expose her for the fraud she was.

Yet what if Rogan did not care? What if he was truly only using this woman to fool his father?

She changed her course of thought, remembering the former betrothed. If Chelsea had run away, he might be able to appeal to the authorities and force her to return with him to Scotland. Even more, Chelsea's mother could force her to return. . . .

Taking a single sheet of parchment from her desk drawer, Gwyneth dipped the quill into the silver inkwell, thinking a moment before setting her hand in motion.

To My Lady Drummore . . .

Chapter 8

Rogan dropped the curtain back in place and moved from the wide bay window as the clock in the hall outside his study chimed the nine o'clock hour. He glanced to the doorway, noticing the vacant stairwell.

Where the devil was she? For thirty minutes he had been standing at that window, watching the steady procession of carriages filing through Grosvenor Square on their way to Lampley and the fête being held there that evening, waiting for Chelsea to come down from her chamber so they could leave as well. Thinking back now, he realized, he had not seen sight of her since early that morning at breakfast and then she'd only stayed long enough for a quick cup of chocolate and a buttered scone which she'd left half-eaten.

Emma had assured him when she and Fredric left for Lampley themselves over an hour earlier that Chelsea knew of the fête and would be down to leave by eight to avoid the crowd. And it was now nine. What was taking her so damned long?

He thought back to the past several evenings, Chelsea's ready excuses as to why they could not make an appearance among the *ton*, her constant avoidance of committing to any social event. Why was she not keeping to her part of the arrangement?

He thought to the past few days he'd spent in her company. How her face had grown still with the intense concentration of a child when she had played the spinet for him the previous night. She had played as if she were performing before hundreds, her hands moving fluidly over the ivory keys. He remembered how she had debated with him over the meaning of a senseless little poem she'd read in one of Emma's books, acting as if it were the most important thing in the world to her.

Everything she did, she did with passion. And everything he said, she listened to with rapt attention, disagreeing with him and stating her views as no other woman would ever dare do. Whereas most women would be bored with a discussion of ships and cargo and the best price for lumber from the northern regions, she took in everything he said and offered him a suggestion or two of merit.

Chelsea was not one to spend her days concerned only with the latest color in fashion or the newest coiffure. She seemed to find some worth in him, some reason for his being on earth. Perhaps, he should consider Diana's suggestion after all . . .

The clock chimed the passing of another quarter-hour. Rogan downed the rest of his drink and crossed to the hall. He glanced to the top of the stairs. No candlelight shone through the blackness above to indicate that Chelsea was at all close to being ready. He could not even hear her moving overhead.

He slowly started to climb the stairs. When he reached the top riser, he stared down the corridor toward Chelsea's door. A dim glow of candlelight streaked out from beneath the closed door.

"Chelsea?"

Silence.

Thoughts of Gregor came unwittingly to mind. *What if . . . ?*

His step quickened. He stopped at the door. He could hear no sound of movement from inside. "Chelsea, are you in there?"

"Yes." She spoke softly. He barely heard her.

He wasted no time, flinging the door open wide.

"What the . . . ?"

She sat on the bed curled among a cloud of thick pillows, her feet tucked beneath her like a child. She wore a soft dressing gown of pale ivory silk that fastened to her chin with a row of tiny pearl buttons, her dark hair braided loosely and draped over one shoulder. Soft loosened tendrils swept over her neck and shoulders as she leaned on one elbow and peered at the book lying on the mattress.

She looked more lovely than he could have imagined possible, lovely enough to stare at for hours—but she was not dressed to attend a fête.

"What the devil is wrong, Chelsea? Why aren't you dressed?"

She did not look up when he crossed the threshold and entered her chamber.

"Chelsea, did you hear me? Why aren't you dressed?"

She frowned in annoyance, still reading her book. "Because I'm not going."

"You're what?"

She shifted then and looked up at him directly. "I said I am not going this evening."

Rogan crossed his arms across his chest, his brow rising in amused interest. For the past three nights, since the ball at Bedford, she had found a different excuse to avoid any social situation. She'd begged off with a head cold that miraculously cured in the space of three hours. Then she'd turned her ankle getting out of a hack, the resulting limp having healed by the following morning. And the last, and definitely most inventive, had been the "strange lightheadedness" she'd experienced after eating the poached salmon at dinner the previous evening.

Cook had been beset with worry. Rogan had just been beset.

"So you are not going to Lampley?" he asked again as if it had been a bluff.

She did not reply.

"What excuse is it this time, Chelsea? A fit of the fever? The vapors, perhaps? Or did you break a fingernail?"

Chelsea narrowed her eyes at him.

Rogan narrowed his eyes back. "Well, which is it?"

"None of them."

"Good," Rogan said, stepping closer to her, "then I guess I can expect you downstairs within, say, the next quarter-hour?"

She did not move.

"Chelsea . . ."

"Rogan, I already told you, I am not going. If you

choose not to believe me then you have nobody to blame but yourself."

He gave her a long, level look. "Oh, yes, you are going."

He came to the foot of the bed and stood there, waiting. Chelsea stared at him but did not budge. If he expected her to jump to her feet to do his bidding, he was sorely mistaken. Instead she flipped a page and turned her attention to the book she had been reading or rather trying to read, attempting to ignore his officious presence.

She had been staring at that same page, and the same line on that page, for well over an hour. She knew Rogan was waiting for her, assuming she was getting ready for the fête, but something within her refused to go. It was the way she had been questioned, nay interrogated, by Gwyneth Pierpont at Madame Dussault's. In the space of three minutes, that woman had refuted their scheme with ease. What was to stop someone else from doing the same? Why should she have to be on constant display, game for anyone who wished to delve deeper into her life? *Like Gwyneth Pierpont . . .*

Rogan stared at her. She scanned the page, completely ignoring him. His patience began to wane. "Chelsea . . ."

She cocked her head at him. "Yes?"

She was mocking him.

"Are you going to get up from that bed and get dressed for the fête?"

"No."

She was pushing him.

"Might I ask why not?"

"Because I do not wish to," she said sharply. "Is that not explanation enough? I am not some puppy you can command at will. Why must I continue with this idiotic charade when all of London has accepted me as your betrothed?"

She peered back down at the book, flipping another page and added, "Besides, I haven't a thing to wear."

"Is that so." Rogan turned from the bed and crossed the room. He did not say another word, but walked very calmly to the tall rosewood armoire, pulling the double doors open wide. Silently, he began searching through the gowns hanging there, yanking them from inside one by one.

"What are you doing?" Chelsea jumped from the bed and ran to him in a flurry of ivory silk. "How dare you touch my things!"

He turned to regard her with amused interest. "Your things? On the contrary, my lady, *my* things. Purchased with *my* coin." He tugged at the billowy sleeve of her dressing gown. "Even this is mine."

When she could not respond to his obvious statement, Rogan resumed his search, taking two more gowns from inside and discarding them to the floor.

Chelsea gasped and pulled at his coat sleeve, yelling now, "Stop it! You're wrinkling all my—all *the* clothing. It will take hours to re-press them. I told you I haven't anything to wear. Why can you not take my word? The remaining gowns I ordered from Madame Dussault will not be ready for at least another week. She only made these so quickly because she knew I was in desperate need."

Rogan stopped then, his eyes falling to the back of the armoire and the last gown, a crimson and ivory satin confection, hidden behind the rest. He removed it, holding it out in front of him.

"This will do nicely."

Chelsea's eyes grew wide and she shook her head. "No—I cannot wear that!"

Rogan tossed the gown across the bed. "Yes, you can and you will."

"I will not wear that dress, Rogan."

"You will if I tell you to."

"No, I will not!"

"Why not?"

"Because."

"For what reason?"

"I cannot say."

Rogan exhaled loudly, weary of their bout of verbal fencing. "Chelsea, I am in no mood for your games. Now, you have known about this evening for three days. You never once said anything about not wishing to attend. We are going to the fête and you will wear that gown even if I have to dress you myself." He advanced, ready to see his threat through.

"No." Chelsea held out her hands to keep him at bay, shaking her head while she backed across the room.

Why? Why did he have to find *that* dress? It was her wedding gown, a gown made of the colors she'd chosen, the gown she was to have worn when she married Gregor. She'd taken it with her only because she'd hoped to sell it for extra coin. She couldn't wear it. She could never wear it. Every stitch, every carefully placed bow and seed pearl reminded her of Gregor and the night she'd found him in her mother's bed.

She nearly tripped when she met with the bed behind her. She clamored upon the mattress, still holding her hands in front of her to keep Rogan back.

He stopped at the foot of the bed, smiling. "You cannot run any further, my lady, unless you plan to leap out the window, which I do not believe you stupid enough to do.

So which will it be? Do you put the dress on yourself, or do I do it for you?"

He could not be serious. Surely he was not serious. No gentleman would do such a thing—yet, she reminded herself, Rogan was no gentleman. Although he had the title and manner of noble birth when called for, there was a wild, unrestrained side to him that only she seemed to see. She found his name quite fitting for the gentleman rogue. Still she did not take his threat seriously.

"I will not wear that dress." She raised her chin and looked at him straight.

Rogan shrugged. "All right. But remember, I gave you the choice."

Perhaps she should have taken him seriously. Perhaps she should have listened. He gave her no time to reconsider when he reached forward and wrapped his arms around her legs, buckling her knees and pulling her down to the mattress beneath him.

She tried to push him away. "Get off of me!"

Rogan chuckled, easily straddling her. "You had your chance. You chose not to cooperate. Now we will do things my way."

He grabbed her wrists and jerked them over her head. She twisted from side to side, unable to break free. The more she struggled, the more he laughed at her, and the more furious she became.

"Let me go, Rogan, or I'll scream!"

Rogan grinned, lowering his head until it was but inches from hers. Oh, God, he was going to kiss her, and the thought sent a tremor racing through her. She stilled and held her breath, waiting . . .

He whispered, his breath touching her lips. "Scream all

you wish, my lady, there are none here to heed you. The servants have been dismissed for the evening and Fredric and Emma left over an hour ago. It is just you and I, in your chamber, on your bed—alone."

Chelsea struggled anew, bucking off the bed. Rogan was swift, giving her no time to fight. Even as she shrieked at him, he was pulling at the buttons on her dressing gown. When they proved too difficult to unfasten, he simply grabbed the delicate fabric and ripped it apart.

Now she did scream. "Stop it! What do you think you are doing?"

Rogan pushed her back to the mattress and fell atop her, pinning her to the bed once again. He was heavy against her; though she was not uncomfortable, still lying there in such a position was far from her liking.

He leaned on his elbow above her, scanning the length of her. He'd managed to remove her dressing gown, rather its shredded remains, and the sight of her clad in a lacy chemise and stays, her breasts heaving beneath the taut fabric, made his blood hot. He reached out and traced a finger along the line of her collarbone to the hollow of her throat. Her struggles ceased. He could see her pulse drumming wildly, the heat of her skin warm against him as she flushed a deep crimson beneath his touch.

"Get off of me this moment," she ordered through clenched teeth.

Rogan shifted his weight to his side, supporting his chin with his hand. "Brave words for a lady in your very compromised position." He smiled devilishly. "At least I can thank you for wearing your underclothes. I always was better at unlacing those things than at lacing them."

She narrowed her eyes. "Of that I have no doubt."

Chelsea tried to rise again, but fell back just as quickly. When she tried to turn away, Rogan snaked out his arm and curled it around her middle just below her breasts.

"Going somewhere, my lady?"

She gasped as he pulled her back against him. Her breasts were crushed against his chest, his leg hooked over her thighs. A sly grin spread across his lips. She felt a shiver run through her at the closeness between them and tried to push him away.

"No, my lady, I am afraid we are not quite finished. There is still the matter of your apparel; or should I say the lack thereof? Now, despite the fact that I would thoroughly enjoy keeping with you in this position for the remainder of the evening, I will only ask you once more. Are you going to quit this foolishness and get dressed so we can leave?"

Chelsea itched to slap him. She itched to kick him in the shin as hard as she possibly could. "I haven't a maid to help me."

His smile deepened. "I will be your maid."

"I think not!"

"Then you will have to dress yourself. If you promise to obey me, I'll release you and let you finish dressing on your own."

She thought for a moment. There really was no choice. She had no doubt now he would do whatever he threatened and she could no more run from him dressed in only her smallclothes than she could sprout wings to fly away. She nodded silently.

"Good girl."

The way he spoke to her as if she were a puppy made her bite her lip in anger, but she kept her mouth clamped shut. She just wanted him gone.

She felt his hold on her waist slacken and watched him rise slowly from the bed. His shirt was hanging out from his breeches, his hair rumpled from their struggle, but still her heartbeat quickened at the sight of him.

He stood back and watched her carefully. Like an obedient child, Chelsea stood, ignoring the humiliation of standing before him in her shift, just wanting him to leave, and quickly.

As she stood before him, her breasts nearly spilling from her rumpled chemise, her hair free from its braid and tumbling over her shoulders in waves of midnight silk, Rogan felt his desire surge. She looked more beautiful than the most carefully coiffed noblewoman at court. Her eyes, demurely hidden beneath her thick lashes, held the anger he knew she was trying so hard to subdue. Try as she might, she could not hide the stubborn lift of her chin, the toss of her head as she raised her eyes to him.

At that moment he wanted nothing more than to throw her on the bed—Lampley be damned—and ease the wretched tension that pounded within him. He wanted her. His blood began to boil at the thought of her naked and twisting wildly beneath him and he couldn't help but wonder if she would react similarly when he took her.

He forced his eyes away. "Would you like me to get the gown for you?"

Chelsea nodded. She watched as Rogan bent to retrieve the gown from where it had fallen on the floor. She wanted to hit him, knock him over on his face, but at the same time she wanted to be back in his arms. What was wrong with her? She had to get away from this man.

She walked to the door. She pulled it open and stood waiting for him to leave. "I wish you to go."

Rogan moved up beside her, leaving hardly a space between them. Chelsea turned away. He reached out and pulled her back against him. Her buttocks were pressed against his hips and she could feel something through the thin fabric of her shift, something hard, something . . . Oh, God.

"Are you certain you wish me gone?"

His warm breath sent a tremble along the nape of her neck. His hand began to caress the underside of her breast lightly. She felt him press his hips against her. A shudder coursed through her, nearly buckling her knees, spreading liquid fire deep within her. She sagged against him. What was she doing? Had she no control, no will to fight him?

Chelsea turned her head to offer what little protest she could and found her mouth covered by his, her senses possessed as he pulled her against him. This was madness, but she cared not. All sense, all clear thought seemed to disappear as his tongue traced her lips, entering her mouth to crumble her final, weak defense. She felt afire, alive with a burning, aching need unlike anything she'd ever felt before. A tremble raced through her, possessing her, spurring her onward as she wrapped her arms around his neck, giving in to the imperious need that burned its way through her.

She was so soft, so yielding. Rogan knew he could seduce her, take her now. Suddenly he'd never wanted anything more in his life, and he knew she would haunt him until the day he possessed her. But he could not. He nearly groaned aloud as he pulled away.

"Though I want nothing more than to continue this with you, we really must go. I would wish it all to perdition to stay."

Chelsea stared at him breathlessly, her lips still moist

from his kiss. He was vile. He was a beast. She looked away in disgust at herself.

"Can I trust you to finish dressing or must I remain?"

Chelsea nodded, keeping her head down. Her body still tingled from his touch, her skin burning wherever he'd touched her, and she'd welcomed it. She didn't know or understand herself any longer.

"I'll take that as your wish for me to leave you. I will be waiting downstairs. Twenty minutes, Chelsea, then I will return if you are not ready to leave."

When he'd finally gone, Chelsea's knees collapsed under her and she dropped to the bed. What had she done? Standing nearly naked in his arms, she'd allowed him to kiss her. She'd wanted him to do more. She'd wanted him to touch her. She could only thank the heavens he'd left when he had.

She glanced to the clock. Nearly five minutes had passed since Rogan had left. Snatching the gown from the bed, she moved quickly across the room, sweeping back her hair as she took a seat at the dressing table.

Rogan waited outside, listening. His insides still clenched from the touch of her soft body, the sweet taste of her lips. God, he wanted her, wanted her more than he'd ever wanted a woman before. And he could have taken her there on the bed, could have finally eased the blasted tightening in his loins.

But his honor would not allow it.

He almost laughed aloud. He, who had slept with the wives of his father's friends and colleagues. He, who could have any number of a dozen noblewomen and had. He could not allow himself to take this woman, because of some code of honor instilled in his head since birth. Chelsea had given even when she hadn't wanted to yield to him. She was an innocent, her kiss told him that. Yet he had tasted her passion, felt her body tremble against his, and knew a fire simmered within her, a fire he so wanted to unleash.

Exactly twenty minutes later, and not a moment sooner, Chelsea came down the stairs, cloaked and ready to leave. She stopped in front of Rogan, looking as if she wanted nothing more than to strangle him.

"Thank you for agreeing to accompany me tonight."

If this was his attempt at an armistice, it was sorely lacking.

"Perhaps you will one day realize the difference between agreement and coercion," she said matter-of-factly, and pushed past him out the door.

She said as little as possible and kept as much distance as she could between them during the coach ride to Lampley. She was angry, angry with Rogan and angry with herself for allowing the situation between them to have gotten so out of her control. She thought back to the episode in her bedchamber, how powerless she had been at his slightest touch. Had she no control over her own body, no will to refuse him?

What she had felt for Gregor had not been like this. It could never have been like this. His kisses had never filled her to her very soul. His touch had never set her body aflame. This inability to resist Rogan, the heat that burned within her when he so much as glanced her way, filled her with a feeling so real she could not believe it true, but at the same time, it frightened her to her very depths.

She knew now she could not remain in his house any longer. If she did, it would mean certain ruin. She could get herself with child, Rogan's child. No, she would have to leave, that night. She would go to the stupid fête with him, but when they returned, when he was asleep and no one was about, she would take her belongings and leave.

"The gown is stunning," Rogan said, handing their cloaks to the waiting footman as he led her toward the ballroom.

Though Chelsea hated to admit it, she knew what he said was true.

The upper bodice was fashioned of crimson velvet, so rich, so dark that at times, in the dim light, it appeared nearly black. A crimson overskirt caught up polonaise-style with the most delicate pearls and brilliant rosettes draped back softly over layers of soft ivory silk underskirts that fell in a shimmering cascade to her toes. Hundreds of seed pearls and bright glimmering brilliants embellished the silver and gold embroidered stomacher, sparkling like stars beneath the lights of the crystal-adorned chandeliers above. Any bride would be proud to wear it. But she was no longer a bride.

They made their way slowly through the crowd, stopping occasionally to greet an acquaintance or two before crossing the supper parlor to the gaming salon beyond. Inside it was hot and crowded and cloaked with a thick cloud of smoke as the men smoked their cheroots and pipes freely.

Two older gentlemen, sitting beside the entrance and puffing on long clay pipes, debated over whose tailor was the more skilled while somewhere across the room, a wine glass shattered on the floor. Laughter and conversation filled the room so that Chelsea could barely hear Rogan when he asked if she wished some refreshment.

She shrugged and turned as Rogan left, fluttering her

fan and walking slowly about to ease the stagnant air. Dampness beaded at her temple despite the fan and she searched the room for a window that might provide relief from the heat.

As she passed a secluded table to her right, she nearly gasped aloud at the sight of an inebriated youth standing upon his chair and urinating into a chamber pot on the floor. He missed his target to soil the fine Turkish rug while cheers urging him to fill the porcelain vessel to its rim rose from those seated around. When he finished, he took a sweeping bow before his audience, nearly toppling himself as his breeches fell to his knees.

"Unfortunately gentility is checked at the door," Rogan said, coming up behind her. He handed her a goblet of ratafia and led her from the debacle.

He stopped just inside the doorway. "Chelsea, I want to apologize for my behavior this evening. It was not well done of me. I was no gentleman. I was an idiot. If I promise not to behave like a complete cad, can we call it a truce and try to enjoy the evening?"

Chelsea could see the sincerity in his eyes. Inwardly she had to admit that she was as much at fault for what had transpired as he. And what did it matter? She would be leaving soon anyway. She might as well make the time that remained pleasant. "Yes, thank you, I should like that very much."

Just then, a laughing, drunken woman swept her glass of wine from her hand while her equally inebriated partner buried his face in her low décolletage. The dark red wine barely missed staining Chelsea's skirts.

"Let's move out of here."

Chelsea followed Rogan through the chaotic assemblage

of crowded tables. They walked through to another salon, this one set off for more private conversation and other, simpler amusements. After pausing for a moment to watch a comical puppeteer, Rogan led Chelsea to a red velvet curtain which was drawn on a small antechamber off the main salon. A painted sign hung crookedly over the darkened entryway indicating it was a place where fortunes were told.

"Come," Rogan said, pulling her toward it, "perhaps the tarot cards will foretell what the future holds."

"I do not think . . ."

Rogan dragged her inside. It took a moment for her eyes to adjust to the scant lighting. She peered across the room. Sitting with but a single candle for light was a figure bent over a small wooden table. Closer inspection revealed a slightly fleshy woman, strikingly attired in purple and gold, with heavy gold earrings dangling from her ears. Her skin was olive-toned and set off by thick black hair shot through with silver that hung loosely around her shoulders.

" 'Tis a Gypsy," Chelsea whispered. "I remember once, when I was a young girl, a wandering band of Gypsies stopped at Drummore seeking shelter from a brewing storm. My father allowed them in to bed in the woodshed for the night. In appreciation the Gypsies performed for the residents of Drummore, dancing and singing sad songs about a girl who had lost her lover to the sea."

Rogan urged her forward into the small circle of light given off by the candle.

"Ah, good evening, my dear. Have you come to have your future told?"

The Gypsy had a foreign accent that Chelsea did not recognize. She started to back away.

"No, I'm sorry."

"Come, come, you take a seat here at my table. I will not hurt you."

Chelsea stared at the seat. This was foolishness. She was not the least bit superstitious and would never believe the answer to her problems could be found in a deck of tarot cards.

"Come," the Gypsy repeated, holding out her hand. Her dark eyes sparkled mysteriously in the dim candlelight.

Chelsea turned back toward the opening in the curtain, looking for Rogan in the dim light. He was gone. She looked back. The Gypsy reached out toward her.

"It is all right, my sweet. Come."

Without knowing why, Chelsea stepped forward.

"Such soft hands . . . tell me, my dear, why are you so troubled?"

Chelsea's eyes widened. "How do you know I am troubled?"

The Gypsy chuckled softly. "Why, it is written all over your face, my dear. Your eyes, such dark, sad eyes. They betray you. I have learned the language of the eyes. One can never hide what is in their eyes. Ah, it must be love. Only love could make a beautiful woman such as you so troubled."

Chelsea glanced down at the table.

"Yes, it is as I thought. Perhaps that handsome gentleman who brought you to me?"

Chelsea remained silent.

"You do not wish to tell me? Come, then, we shall let the cards tell us."

The Gypsy shuffled a deck of tall, brightly colored cards, dealing several face up before her on the smoothly polished table. She took Chelsea's hand and focused her attention on the cards lying before her.

She pointed toward the first card in the set.

"Fortitude, my child. You will face many obstacles in your life's path. At times, it may seem as if your world is crumbling around you, but if you listen to your heart, really listen to your heart, you will triumph in the end." She looked to Chelsea.

Chelsea remained silent, skeptical of the prophecy the Gypsy seemed to find in the card's images.

The Gypsy moved on, motioning toward the next card.

"Ah . . ." she said, smiling, "you must make a choice between two. Lovers, perhaps?"

Chelsea looked at her. She thought of Rogan and Gregor, but that was not a choice to be made.

"You will make the right choice," the woman assured her, nodding again.

Chelsea started to rise, wanting to end the silly venture, but the Gypsy's words stopped her.

"Someone has deceived you."

"How did you know . . . ?" She looked to the card. It held an image of the moon, full and bright against a black sky. She glanced to the Gypsy in wonderment. "Yes . . ."

"The card tells me someone very close to your heart has hurt you deeply. Someone you love. Someone you trusted. Yet despite your love, you cannot trust this person for they will betray you again."

Chelsea returned to her seat. The Gypsy moved to the next card.

"I see that someone who is far will return. Someone very close to you."

Her father?

The Gypsy shook her head as if reading her thoughts. "Yet it is not who you would think."

Chelsea mulled over the Gypsy's words, watching her reach for the next and final card. It held an image of a skeleton draped in black and holding a scepter amid a barren field. Beneath the skeleton, the words *La Mort* were painted in bright, bloody red. The color drained from her face. She needed no explanation of the card or its meaning.

Death.

Chelsea pushed back her chair, knocking it to the floor in her haste. She wanted to forget the reading, telling herself it was nothing but foolish nonsense. The Gypsy reached out and grabbed her wrist, her gold bracelets chinking together loudly.

"Release me, please, I wish to leave."

"Wait, my lady, please. We always take one more card, for luck."

Chelsea stilled, unsure of whether to flee or remain. The Gypsy released her wrist. Warily she watched as the woman took the first card from the top of the remaining deck. She knew the urge to leave, to forget she'd ever seen the cards, but something, some strange, invisible hand was holding her back. It was nonsense, she repeated over and over, superstitious blather. No one could see into the future.

The Gypsy turned the last card over, placing it directly before Chelsea on the table. Her eyes lit up and she smiled.

"Ah, the Knight of Cups. He is good, my lady. He is your protector. He will save you not once, but twice from one who wishes to cause you harm. This is the man who will be your champion. This is the man who will be your life's love."

Chelsea started to say that she doubted such an emotion even existed, but turned to leave. The Gypsy continued talking, her voice following Chelsea as she backed from the room.

"He is not yet your lover, but shall one day be. This is the man you must choose of the two. Not the other. The other seeks to harm you and those you love. This is the man of your destiny."

Chapter 9

Chelsea emerged from behind the curtain, her mind still filled with the fortune-teller's words.

This is the man of your destiny.

She stopped beside a tall marble statue, remembering the Gypsy's warning that she beware of others trying to hurt her. She began searching the many faces around her for Rogan, but the image of the death card stayed with her like a dark cloud. She thought of the danger she had placed Rogan in just by knowing her. Too allow him to be any more involved would be certain disaster. Somehow she did not think she could live with herself if something were to happen to him because of her. She already planned to leave that night; the Gypsy's prophecy only supported that decision.

"Hoping the cards might foretell what marriage will hold for you?"

Chelsea had not seen Gwyneth approach. She did not reply. She looked down to where Gwyneth held her forearm with her long slim fingers. She stepped away, pulling her arm free. "Thank you, but I do not think it is any of your concern."

Gwyneth advanced, leaning against the wall to bar Chelsea from leaving, eyeing her with the interest that a cat would show a mouse. "Oh, but it is my concern. You see Rogan and I have been," she smiled, "*acquainted* for quite some time. I do not wish to see him hurt."

The tiny hairs on the back of Chelsea's neck bristled. "You needn't worry. I would never hurt Rogan. He is my betrothed."

She started to push past, but Gwyneth took her arm again. "Betrothed. What a funny little word. Seems you have had more than your fair share of those in your life."

Chelsea narrowed her eyes. "I do not know what you are talking about."

"Oh, I think you do. I think you know very well what I am talking about. You can cease with the pretense. *Miss Estwyck.* I know about your little game, and if you don't watch yourself, I will make certain all of London knows as well. In fact, if I were you, I'd show a clean pair of heels and get out before it is too late."

Chelsea pulled her arm free. "Well, you are not me, so your advice is for naught. I'll take my chances."

She shoved past Gwyneth, knocking her back against the wall. She did not look back.

Gwyneth smiled to herself as she watched Chelsea go, pleased with her accomplishment and pleased with the effect her words had. She thought back to the previous evening. It had been so very easy to seduce Gregor. He'd needed to prove his manhood after Chelsea's desertion. He proved it on her. He'd been more skilled a lover than she had at first expected and it hadn't taken much for her to climax at his hands. His rod did not need coaxing, his fingers knew well how to bring pleasure, and together they'd matched passions on the dirt floor of the Pierpont stables.

He'd been no gentle lover. He'd taken her roughly, thrusting deep within her, punishing her for Chelsea's rejection until she'd cried out from a mixture of pain and pleasure. The bruises that colored the insides of her thighs were worth the end result. And after he'd sated his desire, regaining his male confidence, it had been just as easy to convince Gregor he could take Chelsea, take her by law, and return to Scotland with his prize in tow. It was his due, Gwyneth had told him, it would be the only way to restore his honor and his respect among his people. He had to take her for if he did not, everyone would think him the fool.

Gwyneth quickly learned that Gregor did not take kindly to anyone suggesting he might lack intelligence. She played on that weakness, using it to bend him to her will. The thought of Chelsea's pale perfect skin bruised purple and black from his rough handling made her smile deepen with delight. Soon everything would be back to the way it had been, soon she would be Rogan's wife and Chelsea would be gone forever.

All the letters she'd written to Townsend under the anonymous name of "Lady Talmidge" informing him of his son's fabricated scandalous affairs. All the carefully placed warnings to noble fathers warning to keep Rogan far away from their daughters. It had all worked before, and it would serve again, as soon as Chelsea was gone.

* * *

Chelsea's pulse was pounding when she rushed into the gaming salon. She scanned the tables for Rogan. She wanted to leave. She wanted to leave now. She wanted to get as far away from that wicked woman as possible. How had Gwyneth learned about Gregor? About her true name? And what else did she know? Soon all of London would know the truth, that Rogan and Chelsea were not truly betrothed, that they were playing a ruse, and Gregor would come for her and take her. She had to leave before that could ever happen. She had to find Rogan and make an excuse to leave, any excuse, to get away. She never should have come here tonight.

She found him standing in a smoky corner of the gaming salon. His back was to her as he spoke with Fredric. They were deep in conversation, a rather heated one at that, and did not even notice her approach from behind.

"I'm telling you, Rogue, you've got to make a decision quickly. Her time is running out. Soon you will be unable to—" Fredric paused, noticing her over Rogan's shoulder. "Oh, good evening, Chelsea. You look absolutely ravishing."

"Thank you, Fredric." She turned to Rogan. "Would you mind overmuch if we left? I am not feeling all that well. It must be the heat and the smoke and all."

"She is looking a little flushed," Fredric said. "Perhaps it would be best if you take her home and keep her there. Why don't you find her something cool to drink and I'll see about retrieving your cloaks."

Rogan and Fredric exchanged a silent glance that left Chelsea wondering its meaning. Fredric excused himself and turned. He froze. "I do not believe I will be able to retrieve your cloaks after all."

"Gregor!" Chelsea gasped.

He stood in the double-doored entrance to the ballroom, flanked by at least a dozen men and looking more evil than the Devil himself.

Rogan took Chelsea by the hand and started in the other direction.

"There she is!"

It was too late. The soldiers surged through the crowd, knocking some aside, trampling others. A woman screamed. The soldiers drew their weapons.

"Come!" Rogan started running, pulling Chelsea behind.

"Halt, Lord Ravenel!"

A shot rang out and pierced the ceiling above, sending small bits of plaster falling to the crowd below. Another scream cried out amid the growing confusion.

Rogan hurried toward the balcony, grabbing the door handle and twisting it hard. It was locked. Cold fear gripped Chelsea's heart. They were trapped.

"Rogan . . ."

"We're not caught yet."

He urged her back from the door and lifted his foot, kicking at it with a mighty blow. The wood splintered and it flew open, a blast of cold night air blowing inside. Rogan took her hand. The wind whistled around them, lifting Chelsea's skirts as they raced across the shadowed balcony.

Rogan released her at the railing. "Stay here. Do not move until I tell you."

Chelsea was trembling both with fear and the winter cold. She wrapped her arms around herself. "Please, Rogan, don't leave me. He will take me. He and my mother will make me marry him and they will—"

He pressed his fingers to her lips. "Shh. Don't give up, Chelsea. We're not caught yet."

He bent down and pulled her against him for a kiss, filling her with his warmth, giving her some of his strength. He pulled away and before Chelsea could blink, swung his leg over the ledge and disappeared into the darkness below.

She heard a dull thud as he hit the ground.

"Rogan?" she said, her voice frantic.

"Climb over. I'll catch you."

She could not see the ground. She could see nothing beyond the carved stone railing. "I cannot see you."

"There she is!"

At the sound of the soldiers so close behind, Chelsea lifted her skirts and slid to the edge of the railing. She peered below, searching for Rogan.

"Jump," she heard him call from below.

She moved out a little farther. Her feet dangled over the edge of the balcony and she inched her way even more. She gasped as she nearly lost her footing. Her fingers clutched at the damp stone railing.

A hand grasped her shoulder, taking hold of her sleeve.

"I've got you, lass!"

Chelsea screamed and shoved off the balcony's edge, leaving Gregor to hold the sleeve of her gown. She closed her eyes and prayed she would not die as she fell into the darkness.

A moment later she landed safely in Rogan's arms.

"After them!"

Heavy footsteps pounded a hasty retreat on the balcony above.

Rogan lowered Chelsea gently to her feet. "Can you run?"

Chelsea looked up, but could only see his silhouette. She was so frightened, she could not speak. She managed a nod.

"Good. If all goes well, Fredric should have a horse waiting for us at the side of the house."

As they ran across the courtyard, Chelsea had to clutch Rogan's sleeve to keep from falling to her knees. She could feel her hair coming loose from its pins, tumbling down her back as the wind whipped it about behind her. Her chest heaved, the icy night air searing her lungs. She thought back to another time, another day, when she was running from Gregor down a deserted alleyway with this man beside her.

There would be no chamber pot to save them this time.

When they reached the horse, Rogan lifted her swiftly into the saddle, her legs dangling over the side, then swung up behind her, taking the reins.

"Hold tight, my sweet."

He tightened his arms around her waist and kicked the horse into a gallop. They were off, racing as wildly as the wind around them. The horse's hooves clattered on the cobblestoned drive as they sped recklessly away.

A single shot fired behind them. Chelsea cried out.

"Shhh," Rogan said against her temple, "they cannot see to aim. They are merely trying to frighten us."

How could he be so calm, so sure, when at any moment they could be killed? Chelsea closed her eyes against the thought, clutching the saddle pommel with both hands as they raced into the night, the Gypsy's words echoing through her mind.

He will save you not once, but twice. . . .

* * *

Rogan pulled the horse to a halt at a small, deserted courtyard lit by a single lantern hanging atop a tall post. They had ridden for what seemed hours through a twisting and turning maze of alleyways until no threat remained of the soldiers having followed. Chelsea slid from the saddle, her toes numb from the cold beneath the dampness of her slippers. She rubbed her arms with her hands to warm them.

"Where are we?"

Rogan took off his jacket and placed it over her shoulders. "At the Fleet."

"But isn't that a—"

"Yes, the Fleet is a prison for debtors. We are not at the prison itself, but at an inn nearby."

Chelsea spotted a drunkard relieving himself at the side of a building while a doxy, her dress open to reveal large fleshy breasts, called down to him from a window two floors up. She stepped closer to Rogan's side.

"Shouldn't we have kept riding out of the city? Why would we stop here?"

"To get married."

Chelsea looked at him in utter astonishment. "What?"

"This is the closest place, short of galloping all the way to Gretna Green."

She was still reeling from his first announcement. "Married?"

"Listen to me, Chelsea." Rogan took her by the shoulders, his voice a rough whisper. "We have no choice. We have to wed right now. I had some suspicions and I had Fredric do some checking. He found that my suspicions were correct. By law, Gregor can take you back to Scotland and force you to marry him."

"How?"

"By your promise to marry him, you are bound to him, legally and unquestionably. The only way to break that tie and to prevent your marriage to him is for you to wed another, truly wed another. I had thought he would leave by now, give it up, but obviously I misjudged him. Nor, judging from this evening's events, will he stand idly by and do nothing. Obviously he has learned that he can take you and means to do just that. We cannot go on running. I could try to take you out of the country, but sooner or later they will find us and there will be naught I can do to help you."

Chelsea could not believe what she was hearing. "But marriages take time. Surely the authorities would understand."

"Yes, they may, which, in turn, will give Gregor more time to prove you were betrothed to him first. You would at least be required to explain your reasons for wishing the engagement broken."

Rogan did not need to reason further. An ashen pall fell over Chelsea at the mention of what had prompted her to leave Scotland. The shame of having to explain that her betrothed had preferred her mother over her, that he had found her so unsightly . . . she couldn't bear the thought of having the sordid facts revealed.

"But how can we marry now? We've no license. No banns have been cried."

"Marriage law is viewed differently here at the Fleet. All you need is the weight of the coin in the cleric's hand and near anything is possible. With a few shillings more, I may even be able to persuade him to predate the certificate of marriage to indicate we were wed two weeks ago."

"But we had not even met two weeks ago!"

"A formality which no one need know. It certainly would help to convince the authorities that Gregor is nothing but a spurned lover seeking revenge. Anyone can say they are going to marry. It is the proof of a marriage certificate we need. And with that proof, who do you think they will believe? Gregor has no material proof, only his word against yours. The authorities will have to believe us and you will finally be free from him."

"Free from Gregor, but married to you!"

Rogan stared at her, silently willing her to agree. His reasons for the marriage—his father and the damned estate—nothing of it seemed to matter at that moment as much as keeping her safe from Gregor. He couldn't understand these feelings he had. No woman had ever mattered to him, making him want to protect and shelter her the way Chelsea did. Even now, with her dark eyes shimmering in the dim light around them, her hair tumbling wildly about her pale shoulders, she had never looked more beautiful to him.

Chelsea considered Rogan's words. No matter how she viewed the situation, what arguments she brought against marrying him, what he said was true. She was not foolish enough to believe that he did what he did out of love for her. The very existence of the emotion was at best doubtful anyway. She thought of her choices—of returning to Scotland to her mother and marrying Gregor. If she did this, she would never see her father again, would be condemning him to a lifetime of exile, and would be left to a life of knowing her husband had bedded with her own mother.

"Why would you do this? Why would you want to marry me? We both are well aware of what I would be gaining, or rather ridding myself of by this union, but you know nothing of me. I could be something else, someone other than what you believe me to be. I could be a thief waiting only to rob you of your riches. You could have most any noblewoman you choose, one who could trace her lineage back to any number of respected kings and queens, one who would bring you an ample dowry. I bring you nothing. I have nothing. No family, no wealth, no title or lands. What would you be receiving for giving me your name?"

Rogan did not know what to say. His purposes—no matter that he would be helping her to avoid Gregor, seemed suddenly reprehensible. Perhaps he should have told her the truth long ago, when he first suggested the idea of their make-believe betrothal. Perhaps he should have explained about his father's will. Perhaps she would have understood.

But perhaps not.

"Let us just say that I have my reasons and you have yours. I do not question your reasons for wanting to avoid marriage to Gregor, so allow me the same. The reasons are of no matter. If it suits us both so well, why question them?"

Rogan looked to Chelsea for her reply. She did not appear convinced. He went on, playing his final trump. "What if I promised you your freedom?"

"My freedom?"

"Yes. Once this is over and Gregor is gone and your life is yours again, what if I vowed not to stop you from trying to leave, should you wish it. I will even give you a settlement of, say, five hundred pounds to begin your life anew."

Chelsea suddenly thought of Gregor. She could no more marry him now than sprout wings and fly away. She knew what she must do, what she had to do in order to save her father. And herself. She had no one else to look out for her now, only herself.

She raised her chin and pushed a stray tress of hair from her cheek. "Where must we go?"

The irony was all Chelsea could think of as the cleric, whom she learned was called Mr. Goodfellow, read hurriedly through the passage in his worn black Bible. He wore no robes. There were no flowers or grand sunshine streaming through the windows of a chapel. Only his torn shirt stained with the remnants of his dinner and a single candle to aid him in reading. She stared at the frayed red ribbon hanging from inside the book as Mr. Goodfellow droned on, his voice a monotone, the words he spoke meaning nothing to him.

All she could think was the irony of marrying one man to escape marriage to another. The irony of marrying a man of whom she had no knowledge and for whom she had no love. The irony of marrying that man in the dress she was to have worn when she married the other.

"Miss . . ."

Chelsea glanced down at the rows of seed pearls and brilliants, the dull shimmer of the fine ivory silk and satin now splattered with mud, one sleeve hanging to her elbow, the other completely gone, and wondered somehow if the Fates were laughing at her.

"Miss?"

She looked up as Mr. Goodfellow's voice rose.

"Miss?" he repeated a third time, and she suddenly realized he was asking her name.

"Miss Chelsea Mac—" Rogan began.

"Estwyck."

Chelsea glanced to Rogan. His eyes took on a look of confusion. She was trying to set her life aright, trying to make the proper decisions. She could not do so living a lie any longer.

"My name is Chelsea Estwyck, daughter of Viscount Drummore of Castle Drummore in Scotland."

She glanced to Rogan to see what his reaction would be. He looked at her in silence, his silver-blue eyes sparkling in the candlelight. The corner of his mouth rose in a half smile, and he looked to Mr. Goodfellow and nodded for him to continue.

"Doth thou taketh this man to be thine husband?"

After she had given her assent and Rogan his, Mr. Goodfellow asked Rogan for the marriage ring. Chelsea started to tell him there was no ring, but Rogan broke in.

"Here . . ."

He removed the gold band he wore on his fifth finger. It was too large, sliding easily over her finger so that she had to fist her hand to keep it from falling off.

Mr. Goodfellow pronounced them man and wife and Chelsea turned, wanting nothing more than to leave quickly. She was stunned when Rogan suddenly pulled her to him for a kiss.

They were married.

She did not speak as Rogan paid Mr. Goodfellow, tossing in a few extra coins for him to pre-date the certificate. She did not comprehend the words written before her as she hurriedly scribbled her name across the bottom of the soiled and wrinkled parchment. Even as they walked outside, she still did not utter a sound, somehow thinking it all a dream.

They stood in the courtyard, man and wife now, forever bound. Chelsea could suddenly think of nothing to say to this man who was now her husband. Wind ruffled the edge of her tattered skirts, chilling her and frightening her with icy uncertainty.

"Chelsea, are you all right?"

She nodded, though inside, her stomach churned.

Rogan left her to retrieve their mount. Chelsea looked down at the too-large ring on her finger. It glimmered dully in the muted lamplight. She was now a wife. Rogan's wife. She twisted the ring around her slim finger, inspecting its scratched and worn surface, then closed her fist and stared up at the moon. The wind gusted up, driving an icy breeze against her, stinging her cheeks and bare shoulders. She heard a clap of thunder above them; the skies seemed to split and a chilling rain began to fall down upon her face, like tears of a crying maiden.

Chapter 10

"We're home, Chelsea."

Home? Chelsea opened her eyes to the lights of the Doraunt town house burning ahead. Rogan had allowed the horse to pick its way over the cobbles slowly, and she'd fallen asleep, lulled by the gentle rocking motion of the horse and the warmth of Rogan's arms around her.

And now they were home. Rogan was her husband. The events of the past three hours came back to her in a tidal wave.

It had stopped raining while she'd slept. The wind had died down, leaving an eerily silent calm in its place. She looked down at her gown, its rich crimson velvet soaked from the rain, hanging heavily on her, her hair wet and clinging to her shoulders and neck. She must make quite a lovely bride.

Several uniformed figures waited at the front of the

house. They quickly took a defensive stance as the horse stopped before the gate.

"Lord Ravenel?"

Unwrapping his arms, Rogan swung his leg over the horse's back to dismount. Chelsea shivered, more from his leaving her than from the cold.

"A bit late for a social call, is it not, gentlemen?" he said, grasping Chelsea's waist as she slid from the saddle after him. He smiled down at her as if to say everything would be all right.

One of the soldiers, a scrawny youth with straw-like hair and a pointed face, stepped forward. He narrowed his eyes at Chelsea. "Be you Miss Estwyck?"

Chelsea looked to Rogan uncertainly.

He nodded.

The soldier reached forward and grabbed her by the arm. "Ye're to come with me. I'm to return you to your rightful betrothed." He pulled her roughly with him.

Chelsea's feet stayed rooted to the ground. She looked to the soldier and said in a voice quite calm, "Unhand me."

The soldier tightened his grip and yanked her forward. "I said I'm returning you to who you belong with."

Chelsea was too tired to struggle. "I belong to no one."

"She belongs to me!"

Gregor suddenly emerged from the shadows. He stepped up beside the soldier, towering over him by a good two feet. Chelsea just looked at him as if he weren't real.

"Thought you'd never see me again, didn't you, lass?"

She didn't reply. He reached for her.

"I wouldn't if I were you, Moultrie."

Rogan stepped between them, drawing his pistol from inside his coat.

Gregor's lips curled in a snarl. "You going to shoot all these soldiers, too, *coulie*?"

"Smith, what is going on here?"

An older man who, judging from the cleanliness and quality of his uniform, was obviously in a position of some authority stepped from inside the house. Rogan's valet, Moller, stood behind him, a branch of candles in hand, looking much like a worried parent. "Is everything in order, my lord?"

Rogan nodded.

"Smith—" repeated the captain.

"I was just tryin' to apprehend the lady likes you ordered," said the straw-haired youth.

The captain looked to Chelsea. "You are Miss Estwyck?"

Chelsea started to nod, but Rogan broke in.

"No, Captain, she is not Miss Estwyck. Not anymore at any rate. She is Chelsea Doraunt, Lady Ravenel, and my wife."

"What!" Gregor bellowed.

The captain's face turned red. "This woman is not married!"

"I'm afraid you've been given false information, Captain. Allow me." Rogan reached inside his coat and removed the marriage certificate. He handed it to the captain.

Inwardly Chelsea prayed that the ink was dry.

The captain read the document. "But . . ."

"He's lying," Gregor roared. "She's mine! She was mine long before she ever knew him!"

"Now, Mr. Moultrie," the captain said, "it appears as if Lord Ravenel is telling the truth. He does have a certificate of marriage. Have you any proof that this woman is betrothed to you?"

Gregor did not respond.

"I am afraid then that you have no right to her. She is now the property of Lord Ravenel."

Property? "I am no one's—"

Rogan took her arm, pushing her along. "Quiet."

"But . . ."

Gregor stepped before them, blocking their way to the stairs, eyes black with rage. "You'll regret your actions. I'm going to make you sorry you stuck your *coulie* nose into my affairs."

"I look forward to it," Rogan said, and led Chelsea past him into the house.

Rogan slowly opened the door to Chelsea's bedchamber, staring at her sleeping form in the blue-tinged moonlight that shone through her chamber window.

One hand flung carelessly across her forehead, she lay on her back among a nest of downy pillows, her hair curling about her face in waves of ebony silk.

He stepped inside, closing the door without a sound, and removed his dressing robe, dropping it to the floor. With the smooth silence of a panther, he lifted the sheet and slid his naked form underneath. The mattress sagged beneath him as he positioned himself carefully upon the bed. He leaned on his elbow and stared down at her.

God, but she was beautiful. Dark, thick lashes rested softly on her pale cheek. He reached out to smooth back a stray tendril of her hair, relishing in the silky softness of her skin. A surge of desire ran through him. He wanted her. Wanted her more than he'd ever wanted before. And he could have her now. She was his wife.

She stirred then, turning slightly, and parted her lips.

Deep red and full, he could not keep from lowering his head to brush them with his own.

Chelsea opened her eyes, blinking in confusion.

Rogan's face smiled down at her. "Hello, wife."

"What are you doing?" Her voice was husky with sleep.

"Joining my wife in bed."

It hadn't been a dream. Chelsea sat bolt upright, pulling the covers to her chin and off Rogan as she scrambled to the far side of the bed. Her eyes went saucer-wide when she saw him in the moonlight.

"You're naked—"

Rogan did not move to cover himself. "Yes, I am. And I was rather hoping you would be, too."

Chelsea was stunned. Her mouth gaped open at the sight of his bare body. He was magnificent, glowing in the moonlight, not a spare pound of flesh anywhere to be seen. Sleek and taut, from his broad shoulders to the lines of his muscular chest, he seemed sculpted from stone. Her eyes traveled down over his shoulders and chest to the flat plane of his stomach, lower still to the dark hair that thatched his abdomen to . . . a sound not unlike a gasp sounded from her throat.

"I am glad you are so pleased. Now, perhaps you will allow me the same perusal of your person."

He reached to her, taking her by the shoulders and pulling her against him. Her nightrail had ridden up and she could feel the rasp of the stiff hair on his legs against her thighs, the heat of his flesh sending a sudden tremble swirling through her.

"No!" She pulled away, fleeing the bed and taking the bedcovers with her. Rogan remained sitting, unashamed of his nakedness.

"Have you no modesty? No decency? Can you not cover yourself?" she gasped. Her eyes strayed to his manhood, standing stiff and erect. She could feel the blood rising to her face. "What do you think you are doing?"

"Sharing my wife's bed. Not an odd thing to do on one's wedding night."

"It is when—when . . ."

She could offer no argument. They were married, and married people slept together.

He chuckled at her loss of words. "You see, it is not such an odd thing."

"This whole marriage is odd."

Chelsea stared at him, but her eyes could not avoid looking down at . . . she forced her eyes up to his face again. He was grinning at her like some satisfied cat. She looked away, focusing on the glowing orange embers in the hearth.

"Well, are you going to stand there all night staring at the fire or are you going to come to bed?"

Chelsea pursed her lips irritably. "I am thinking."

"As am I, though I doubt our thoughts are running in the same direction. I was just wondering what you'd look like without that blanket clutched to your chin and without that schoolgirl's nightrail, your body naked and—"

"Must you be so bold? Can you not leave me in peace to sleep alone?"

Rogan's grin faded. "What is wrong, Chelsea? We are wed. It is certainly permissible, and expected, that we should sleep in the same bed."

This was true. But when she'd agreed to marry him, she hadn't even thought of *that*. Not that *that* was such an undesirable thing. His sudden appearance in the bedchamber had just startled her.

"I think I know why you are behaving like a frightened schoolgirl."

Chelsea looked at him. How could he know? "You do?"

"Yes, it is obvious. I am a fool not to have known from the beginning. I apologize for being so insensitive."

Chelsea eased her guard. "Thank you."

"Of course you would be modest about speaking of such things, but I am your husband now, Chelsea, and you can talk to me about anything . . ."

Chelsea nodded. He did understand. He was wonderful.

" . . . so we will just have to delay our consummation until after your monthly flow."

"My what?"

"Your monthly flow. That is what women call it, isn't it. Do not be embarrassed, Chelsea. I am perfectly knowledgeable in these areas. We will wait until after your time."

Chelsea couldn't believe she was at all having this conversation, much less standing and talking before a magnificently naked man she barely knew who was now her husband. What in heaven's name had she done?

Rogan stood. "I will even sleep in my own bed so that you will feel more comfortable."

He kissed her forehead.

Chelsea just stared.

"Good night, Chelsea. I shall see you in the morning."

He turned and walked slowly, completely naked, out of the room. Chelsea watched him go. Her mouth was partly open, half from shock, half from being at a loss for words. She should have told him he'd been mistaken, that it was not her monthly time. She should have been honest and explained why she'd leapt out of the bed when she'd woken to find him kissing her. She started to call him back, but stopped herself.

Perhaps it was best to allow him to think that she was having her monthly and could not bed with him, giving her more time to accustom herself to the idea of being married to him. She remembered the sight of him lying naked on her bed. Her stomach still tingled at the memory. She moved back to the bed, curling up in a ball at the edge. One thing was for certain. Being married was definitely going to be different.

Chelsea woke early the next morning, jarred from sleep by a loud thud.

"Careful with those trunks, boy, if you damage any of Lady Emma's things, I'll have your hide!"

Crash!

"You clumsy whelp! Come back here!"

Chelsea crossed her room to the door, nearly colliding with a pair of youths who were lugging an oversized trunk down the corridor.

"Pardon, milady," one of the boys said, tipping his crooked hat and smiling a crooked grin.

Behind them was yet another pair of boys, their arms laden with a small settee.

"Hetta," Chelsea called to the head housekeeper, Mrs. Philby, "what is going on here?"

The woman stepped into the corridor, holding a delicate vase in one hand, one of Emma's best gowns draped across her other arm. "Good morning, my lady. So pleased to see you up and well. Many congratulations on your marriage to Lord Ravenel."

Chelsea nodded. "Thank you. Where are these boys taking all these things?"

"Oh, yes, Lord Fredric and Lady Emma are moving to their new house today."

"Moving? I thought the renovations weren't to be finished for weeks."

Hetta shook her head. "Lord Fredric paid the workers extra to get it done sooner for Lady Emma."

The sound of shattering glass erupted behind them.

Hetta spun about, scolding one of the boys who had dropped a fine porcelain plate. Chelsea turned just as Hetta was boxing his ears, and closed her bedchamber door.

She sagged against the door. Moving? Emma couldn't leave. She would have no one to talk to, no one to confide in. She would be alone with Rogan.

Grabbing her dressing gown, Chelsea quickly pulled it on and moved to the door, weaving her way through the trunks and boxes that lined the corridor to Emma's chambers. Inside, at least a dozen young men were busy packing and carrying things. Emma was nowhere to be seen.

Chelsea took the steps quickly downstairs. As she passed the dining salon, she spotted Emma sitting at the table, scanning a page of the morning paper as she sipped her breakfast tea.

"Emma, is it true? Are you really leaving?"

Emma set down her cup and smiled. "Yes. That sweet sneak Fredric has had the men working day and night to complete the renovations and they finally finished the house yesterday. He wanted to surprise me."

"But you cannot leave. If you do . . ."

Chelsea heard the rustle of papers behind her and turned just as Rogan was rising from his chair. "If she leaves, what, my dear?"

He was handsomely dressed in a suit of burgundy velvet and black, his hair pulled back neatly with a black tie. He smiled and his eyes seemed to hold her aloft. "You really could have dressed before coming down, my dear. We would have held breakfast for you."

Chelsea looked down and her cheeks flamed in embarrassment. She was still in her dressing gown. Without looking, she knew her hair must be a tangled mess. Suddenly she felt every bit the fool.

"Well, I am off to the shipyards today, my dear," Rogan said. "I'll be back for supper. Emma, if you are gone when I return, good fortune in your new home. We'll expect a dinner invite within two weeks." He kissed Chelsea's forehead and turned from the room, whistling a merry tune as he left. Minutes later he left the house.

Chelsea stared at the empty doorway, dropping to the seat beside Emma. "What will I do without you?"

Emma chuckled. "You are married now, Chelsea. You certainly do not need me here as a chaperon any longer. By the by, I never did congratulate you properly. I am so happy we are sisters now. I know it will be strange at first, but believe me, it will be much more pleasant for you and Rogan without Fredric and me bothering you. Besides, I am so happy to be moving into my own house now. We've waited such a long time."

Chelsea could see the excitement in Emma's face and regretted her selfish reasons for wanting to keep her there. "You are right. I hope you will be happy there. I will miss you."

"It is not like I am moving to the country, Chelsea. We are only a short distance away. You may visit whenever you like and you can help me decorate every room."

"Pip, are you ready to go?" Fredric poked his head in the doorway.

Emma rose from her chair. "Oh, yes, is everything packed already?"

"Hetta's taking care of it."

Chelsea watched as Emma quickly donned her cloak and turned. "Good luck to you, Chelsea. I know you and Rogan will be very happy here. I remember when Fredric and I first married. All we wanted was to be alone." She gave her a quick hug, then turned and left.

They were gone before Chelsea could say Godspeed.

"They're what?" Gwyneth's pale face colored bright red to her hairline at Beecher's words.

"They are married, my dear."

"How could they be? It is inconceivable. There were no banns cried. Surely they could not run off to Gretna Green and back in the space of a night."

Beecher took her arm, leading her down the secluded garden path to a small bench beneath a flowering primrose vine. "No, they were married on the Fleet last night after jumping off the Lampley balcony to escape the soldiers and that beast of a betrothed. They had it done in the back room of some seedy tavern down there. I am no more pleased with the news than you are, my dear, but there is naught either of us can do to change it. It is already done."

Gwyneth was oblivious to his words. Her face pinched with rage, she stared at a single yellow flower that trailed beside her. She snapped the flower from the vine, ripping its petals viciously from its stem. At that moment, Beecher sensed that that flower must represent Chelsea.

It would take days for Gwyneth to regain a pleasant

disposition, and he no more wished to suffer her wrath than to step over hot coals with his feet bare. He had plans of his own to put into action, plans for his cousin and his newly-wedded wife, plans to gain finally what was rightfully his.

He stood. "Well, I'll be off then. Just thought I'd bring you the happy news. If you need me, you know where to find me."

"Yes, yes," Gwyneth said, dismissing him with the wave of her hand. She did not even see him leave.

Gwyneth remained sitting, staring at the crushed petals and bare stem on her skirts for several moments after he'd gone. Raw fury swelled in her throat, threatening to choke her. He'd married her. Rogan had married that little nitwit and now Gregor would have no way of taking her back. She could not allow this to happen. There had to be some other way to rid herself of that bothersome snip. There had to be. . . .

"Eula?" she called out sweetly.

A rustle of leaves. "Yes, my pet?"

Gwyneth rose and followed the voice to a small alcove hidden beyond the bench. She found her dear maid watering a potted plant, her hair, a nondescript shade of brown, pulled back tightly, making her face look pinched and severe.

Eula lay the watering can aside, wiping her work-roughened hands along her crisp white apron.

"You heard?"

Eula nodded without looking at her. "Mmm . . ."

"What will we do?"

Eula looked at her, the pupils of her odd golden-colored eyes darkening. "What is it you want, my pet?"

"Rogan Doraunt."

The maid nodded knowingly. "And what is it that stands in your way?"

"His wife."

"Then we must make the his wife disappear." A smile touched her thin colorless lips as she inclined her head slightly. She lowered the pot she had been watering, pushing it under a patch of golden sunlight that filtered down through the trees. "Perhaps another letter to the mother?"

"Telling her they have married?"

"No, my pet."

Gwyneth looked into Eula's eyes. "What then?"

"Tell her the girl plans to wed someone else, that she must make haste to stop the match." Eula looked at her then, the lines of her weathered face deepening with her smile. "She will come, my pet, and she will take your trouble away."

Chelsea woke early with the dawn to find Rogan's bed empty, the bedclothes still neatly turned down, the candle at his bedside table burned to a stump.

He had not returned all night. And she hadn't seen him much in the past several days. Always off for some meeting, out till all hours. Business, he claimed, but what sort of business did one conduct in the early morning hours? She didn't wish to sound like some nagging peahen, but since their wedding night, she hadn't seen Rogan more than in passing, and then only for a quick peck on the cheek as he headed out the door.

She wandered down the stairs to take her morning chocolate and rolls in the dining room. She stopped when the door to Rogan's study opened and Diana Malcolm started out, turning just inside the doorway. Chelsea drew back to the shadows.

"Twelve o'clock tomorrow night is agreeable to me. Charles will be in Dorset at the Lampley country estate, so we can meet at the flat if you like. No, do not get up, darling, I shall see myself out. You get yourself off to your bed and try to get some rest."

Diana turned and grabbed her cloak from the hook on the wall by the door. Chelsea watched her leave. Her heart rose to her throat, pulsing there. Rogan had been with her, his mistress, all night? She didn't want to believe it.

She started down the stairs slowly. Before she reached the bottom step, Rogan came out of his study, wearing the same clothes he'd worn the previous day. Chelsea stopped atop the last stair.

"Good morning, Chelsea."

He did not even attempt to hide the fact that his mistress had been leaving his study, calling him "darling" and arranging to meet him again the following night.

"I was just coming to wake you for breakfast. I have just enough time before I must go . . ."

"I will not have it, Rogan."

He smiled. "You will not have breakfast? Well, perhaps you'll sit with me while I have mine."

Chelsea swallowed hard. "I saw her leaving, Rogan. I know you did not sleep in your bed all night. I will not have you continuing your relationship with her. I just cannot take it."

"You were speaking of Diana."

Why was he acting as if it were nothing?

"Of course I am speaking of her. I know she is your mistress, but I am now your wife. I can tolerate just about anything—drinking, cursing, even gaming—but this is one thing I cannot live with."

Tears were pooling in her eyes, but she blinked them away.

Rogan's smile faded. "Is that why you ran away from Gregor?"

"Yes."

Rogan came forward and took her hand. "Let me assure you right now that I no longer have a mistress, Diana or anyone else. You have my word."

Chelsea stared into his eyes. She believed him.

"Now will you reconsider joining me for breakfast? I hate to eat alone."

He led her into the dining room, pushing in her chair gently. He poured her a cup of chocolate before taking his seat beside her. "Oh, yes, before I forget. Do not have a place set for me at dinner this evening. I've a business meeting and will be out late."

Chelsea nearly choked on her chocolate.

Standing before her cheval glass, Chelsea scrutinized her reflection, pulling the brim of the three-cornered hat she'd pilfered from Rogan's chambers down to shield her face. His heavy velvet jacket hung loosely on her small shoulders, brushing past her knees, her hands hidden beneath the wide velvet cuff. The breeches she'd borrowed from the stableboy, Will, fit her snugly, too snugly, perhaps, so that she was thankful for the shield of the coat.

She couldn't believe she was doing this. She must be mad, but when Rogan had all but confirmed he would be keeping his meeting with Diana, her inner voice, that same inner voice that had told her to leave Drummore after finding

Gregor with her mother, this time clucked its tongue. All men were faithless, the voice had told her. But he'd given her his word. She couldn't accuse him without knowing for certain.

She heard a door open in the hall outside her chamber. She waited as Rogan's footsteps drew near, and wondered if she should latch the door. He stopped. Her heart began to pound. She held her breath, listening, waiting . . .

"Anne?" Rogan called to the maid.

"Yes, my lord?"

"Is Lady Ravenel still asleep?"

"Yes, my lord. She had the devil of a headache and took a cup of Cook's tea with her to bed. She asked not to be disturbed. Do you want I should wake her for you, my lord?"

He paused. "No, let her rest. I will see her on the morrow. Good evening, Anne."

"Good evening, my lord."

Chelsea waited for several minutes to be certain he had gone, then opened her chamber door slowly. Carrying Will's worn leather boots under her arm, she moved silently to the stairs, descending two, then stopping at the third. She could see shadows moving at the foot of the stairs and drew back when Rogan came into view, followed by his ever-present valet, Moller. They stopped at the door.

"I'll return in the morning, Moller. Keep the door locked and post Krune at the front after I leave."

"Aye, sir. Where shall I tell my lady you are, should she ask?"

Rogan pulled on his cloak. "Do not. I doubt she'll ask, but if she should, tell her you do not know."

Chelsea frowned at his reply. When Rogan left and Moller

had disappeared to the study, she quickly skimmed the stairs and slipped out the back entrance.

"My lady! Over here!"

She followed Will's voice, pulling on his oversized boots. She met him by the stables. Beside him stood her mount, saddled and ready to ride.

"Thank you, Will. Can you give me a leg up?"

The lad, Krune's son and no more than sixteen, with a freckle-covered face and stringlike hair the color of mud, looked nervous as he moved to lift her. He started for her waist, then her legs, then stepped back, unsure of where to place his hands.

"Oh, here," Chelsea said, "bend down on your knees."

When he did, she placed her booted foot atop his thigh, then pushed herself up from his back, swinging her leg over the saddle. She gathered the reins from him.

"My lady, what if my lord is angry when he finds out I helped you?"

"He shan't be, Will. If he should find out, I will take the blame." She patted his arm reassuringly. "Now, in which direction did he go?"

"Southward toward Charles Street."

"Good," she pulled the horse around, "thank you again."

She flashed him a grateful smile and set her heels to the horse's sides, trotting toward the opening of Grosvenor Square.

Chelsea pulled the horse back when she saw Rogan climb into a hackney coach at the corner. She followed him for about a quarter hour to a small, secluded courtyard off the Strand. Tethering her mount to a post, she watched him from the shadows as he stepped down from the hack and walked to a darkened house nearby. He pulled a key from his coat pocket and opened the door, disappearing inside.

Chelsea started after him. As she crept toward the window, her heart racing anxiously, she was suddenly reminded of a similar night, the night she'd followed Gregor through Castle Drummore and found him in her mother's bed. She hesitated. She did not wish to find what she had that night. She did not want to see Rogan with Diana. Somehow she did not believe she could take the pain.

She turned to leave.

"What're ye doin' 'ere, boy?"

Two huge arms the size of tree trunks clasped around her upper body and lifted her from the ground.

"Let me go!"

Chelsea lashed out, kicking to get free, but her captor merely chuckled and shook her till her teeth rattled. "Stop yer fightin', lad."

He slung her under one huge arm like a sack of market potatoes and carried her thus down a darkened alley, her head spinning from his shaking. Before she realized what was happening, he had opened a door and had shoved her inside.

" 'Ere, milord, found this boy sneaking around outside."

Chelsea nearly dropped when she saw Rogan rise from behind the desk across the room. She lowered her head to hide her face behind the brim of the hat.

Chapter 11

"Thank you, John. You may leave us."

Chelsea watched the giant, John, move to the door and open it just an inch. She readied herself to run, waiting for him to push it wider.

"Are ye sure you don' want me to stay and teach the boy a lesson?"

"No, you may leave this one's lessons to me."

Before she could take a step to run, the mammoth man had gone. She wondered how someone so large could move so quickly, but did not have the opportunity to reflect further as Rogan snatched the hat from her head.

She gasped.

"Very interesting attire, my dear."

"How did you know it was me?"

Rogan chuckled. "Did you not think I would recognize my own coat?"

He tugged at the gold braid on the collar. "Come, Chelsea,

most young boys do not wear such finery."

He walked around behind her, scanning her up and down, his eyes lit with amusement. A slow grin curved his lips as he came around to face her. She crossed her arms across her chest when his gaze moved there and lingered.

"Now, I know those are not my breeches. Dare I ask what man you charmed them off?"

Chelsea glared at him from the corner of her eye. "You should not question that which you do not practice, my lord."

He chuckled at her. "Is that what this is all about? You thought I was having an illicit tryst with Diana and followed me here dressed like some runaway stripling to assure it? What did you plan to do if you found her here? Call her out to the dueling field?"

Before she could respond, he stepped closer to her, his eyes turning a dark, steely gray. "I gave you my word, Chelsea." His smile faded. "Take off the jacket."

She did not move, her eyes meeting his directly.

"Chelsea, the jacket."

She stood still. She would not allow him to belittle her by bullying her.

"Must we go through this again? You did not win the last time, nor will you emerge the victor now. I will always be stronger and thus, I will always win." He took her by the wrists and pulled her arms down to her sides. She did not fight him, but remained standing still as stone. Slowly he slid his hands beneath the coat, pushing it back over her shoulders. It fell to the floor. Rogan sucked in his breath at the way the breeches encased her hips, fighting to control his growing desire. Her full breasts strained against the fabric of the shirt, his shirt. He felt himself harden at the sight of her in his clothing.

"Very nice."

Chelsea stood very still as he moved around behind her and untied the black ribbon that held her hair. She did not even flinch when he spread the dark waves loosely over her shoulders, his fingers grazing her neck, caressing her skin. He smiled when he saw her tighten her jaw against her reaction.

"I should be angry with you for going out dressed like this in the middle of the night. You could have been attacked. It was not done well of you. Did I not give you my word I no longer had a mistress?"

Chelsea did not respond. She felt a fool.

He came around her to face her again, his eyes on hers. "Have I ever given you cause not to trust my word?"

"Perhaps I just wondered why you would want to spend your nights with someone else and not your wife."

For a moment, Rogan actually looked taken aback. He nodded thoughtfully. "Are you telling me your monthly flow has stopped?"

She looked at him straight. "It never started."

Rogan raised a brow. "So when I came to you that night, you lied to me to keep me from taking you."

"I didn't lie."

"No, you just did not think to inform me that my assumption was incorrect."

"I just wasn't ready. I hadn't thought about that . . ."

"But you are ready now?"

Chelsea stared at him. "Yes."

Rogan's response was swift and sudden. He reached out to her, grasping her about the waist and pulled her against him, his mouth possessing hers with a fierceness he'd never before shown. Chelsea's body trembled in response. His tongue plunged into her mouth, sapping any resistance and replacing it with the heat of wanting, the fiery tension of need. He released her for only a moment to sweep her into his arms. He carried her down a dark hallway, kicking the door wide and crossing the room in two strides to lay her gently upon the bed.

Rogan stood over her and slowly unfastened his shirt. He lifted it over his head and tossed it across the room. His chest gleamed in the moonlight, lean and defined. He was beautiful. Chelsea's heart began to pound.

He lit a small candle at the bedside table, encircling them with its golden halo of light.

"Look at me, Chelsea."

He leaned down toward her, releasing the first fastening of the shirt she wore. She raised her fingers to assist him in loosening the others, but he pushed them away.

"No, allow me."

Rogan took her hand and kissed each finger. He continued with the unfastening of her shirt, each tie loosening slowly. Chelsea's breath grew short, her breasts rising and falling as the fabric opened a little more each time. When he reached the last fastening just below her breasts, he pushed the light cambric aside, his eyes darkening markedly.

"Beautiful . . ."

Chelsea took in a breath and held it as his hand encircled one firm breast. A wave of feeling so intense sung through her and she closed her eyes, releasing a gasp when his thumb stroked her nipple. It swelled to erection under his touch.

"Do you like the way that feels, Chelsea?"

She could not deny it. She closed her eyes, dropping her head back and lost herself to the sensations.

"Open your eyes. I want you to see how much I want you."

Chelsea watched him in curious silence as he lowered his head to take her nipple in his mouth. A surge of white-hot passion overcame her and her hands unwittingly flew to his head as she arched her back against the sensations, unable to curb her body's reaction to his touch.

"Yes . . ." Rogan murmured against her, "that's it." Slowly he lifted her and slid the shirt over her head.

As she lay back on the bed, Chelsea shivered, more from her reaction than from the cold, and lay back upon the bed.

Rogan ran the flat of his hand over her belly and slowly unfastened the buttons along her breeches.

"Someday you must tell me where you found these. They do become you. Perhaps we should have more made up for you." He pulled them down over her hips and tossed them to the floor. He moved back to study her.

His stare was so intense. No man had ever seen her naked before. Chelsea moved her hands to shield herself.

"Do not cover yourself from me, Chelsea. I am your husband. I will not harm you."

Chelsea slowly lowered her hands to her sides.

Rogan thought he'd never before seen a more perfect woman. Her skin was like silk, milky white, her ebony hair curling about her shoulders like a soft, silky cape. She moistened her lips with her tongue then and he felt his sex begin to throb. His eyes fell to the dark triangle of curls at the joining of her legs. He lowered himself over her and slid his hand up along her leg from her ankle to her knee, sliding it back down and taking her stocking with him. He tossed it to the floor, then, still holding her foot, pressed a kiss to her toes.

He did the same to the other leg, and then, when she was completely naked, he moved up beside her, leaning on his elbow while he devoured her with his eyes.

He took her hand and pressed it against his breeches. "Do you feel how much I want you, Chelsea?"

Chelsea stared at him mutely, blinking in the candlelight. She suddenly knew longing for the first time and wondered at it, lost in the spell of desire, unable to speak.

Rogan rose from the bed, and for a moment she thought he was going to leave. Instead he stood before her and unfastened his breeches. She looked away.

"Look at me, Chelsea. I want you to see what you do to my body."

She looked back to him and her eyes widened when she saw his staff standing rigid from him. She swallowed. What had she done? She knew what he would do, how he would come inside her. She glanced at him again. He would rip her in two.

"Don't look so frightened, my lady," he said, reading her thoughts clearly. "I may look intimidating, but your body will accommodate me."

Rogan rose over her. Chelsea suddenly felt afraid. Did he mean to take her now? So quickly?

"Here, little one, sit with me."

He patted the mattress and she reluctantly obeyed, expecting him to leap upon her at any moment. Her back to him, he set his hands gently on her shoulders and began to massage her tense muscles. Fear and tension seemed to evaporate with each stroke of his hands, and she relaxed under his gentle touch. Her head fell back against his shoulder. When she felt his lips graze her neck, she melted against him, a tingle running down along her spine.

His hands moved down her back to her hips, then slid around to her front. His mouth nipped lightly at her shoulder. She felt a chill from his moist mouth and closed her eyes, his hands moving upward along her belly, caressing gently, softly.

His hand cupped her breast and a tremble raced through her, spreading liquid heat deep inside of her. A strange, urgent feeling seemed to rise within her, and without realizing it, she raised her arms above her head, clasping them behind Rogan's neck, wanting more.

She had never felt such heat, such burning, all-consuming desire. She dropped back to the bed as Rogan cradled her in his arm, moving around to face her. His mouth covered her breast. She cried out at the sensations she felt, her fingers squeezing into the sheet as he suckled at her breast. God, she did not want it to end. She was floating now, rising higher than the clouds, borne on the wings of her own desire.

Instinctively she pressed her hips against his, seeking to ease the tight knot of heated tension that filled her. It only grew, expanding, consuming her with need. She felt his hand part her legs, his mouth moving up to hers. She shivered when she felt his tongue glide over her lips.

"Open your mouth, Chelsea."

She parted her lips slightly. As his tongue slid inside her mouth she felt his fingers touch her at her most private spot, sending a shock wave through her.

She tensed.

Rogan stilled but did not remove his hand. "Relax, Chelsea."

His finger moved over her then, pushing slightly inside, circling softly. He parted her thighs a little more and covered her mouth with his as his finger delved deeper and found her center. A fierce fever coursed through her and she raised her hips against his touch, wanting more, needing all. His mouth took hers with a driving hunger, his finger moving over her deftly, and the tension inside her began to build, growing hotter, more intense with each movement of his hand.

Her fingers wound themselves through his hair and she tightened the muscles in her legs, seeking release from the burning, aching need. She felt a wetness between her legs and the sensations increased, growing stronger and stronger as she strained toward something, what she did not know. She was gasping now, struggling against the movement of his hand, her body taking over. Her head fell back and Rogan kissed a trail down to her breasts while his hand continued its rhythmic assault. She nearly cried out loud, climbing higher and higher still, rising to the heavens.

The blood was pounding so loudly in her ears, she could hear it. She felt certain Rogan could hear it as well. Over and over it drummed, louder and louder until . . .

"Rogan? Are you here?"

There was a pounding at the door.

Rogan raised his mouth from hers. "Damn . . ."

Chelsea did not understand. She was lost in the netherworld of her own desire, floating down at first, then plummeting back to reality.

The voice grew louder, closer now. She heard footsteps

echoing in the hall. Rogan pulled the bedclothes over them as a lone figure entered the room.

"Rogue, you've got to come quickly. I—" Beecher halted when he saw them on the bed.

Chelsea lowered her eyes, flushing hotly.

"My apologies, madam," he muttered, then entered the room without the least embarrassment. "Rogan, you've got to return to the town house directly. Your father has just arrived from Ashbourne and wants to see you."

"This? This ragamuffin is what you married?"

Rogan did not respond to his father's question, knowing if he did, Townsend would ignore him anyway. It did not matter what Chelsea looked like. He could have married the daughter of King George himself, could have received a queen's ransom of a dowry, and still it would not matter. Townsend would have found something to object to, some small imagined flaw, and all because Rogan had chosen her, and not he.

When he'd written the letter to his father to inform him of his marriage to Chelsea, he'd never expected him to travel the two days journey to London to confirm it. He'd expected his father to reply in his usual unfeeling manner that Rogan had fulfilled his obligations and Ashbourne would be safe. That was, after all, what he had wanted. A wife for his son. His will had said only that Rogan must marry by March 31. He'd never stipulated that the wife be of his choosing.

Still, with Chelsea standing before him now, dressed in Will's too-small breeches and Rogan's too-large coat, her hair haphazardly tied and wild about her head, it did not make matters look any better. If only his father had not come to London this night. If only he'd not been waiting for them at the entrance hall when they'd arrived. If only . . .

"Have you lost your mind? She's dressed like a man, for God's sake!"

Yes, she was dressed like a man, a sight that still brought Rogan's blood to boiling each time he looked at her. Knowing how close he'd come to having her made it all the worse. They should be naked on the bed right now, wrapped in each other's arms and legs, not standing before his father in the entrance hall of the town house where the servants hinged on every word.

Rogan looked to his father. The look of disgust that had crossed his face when first told that Chelsea had married his only son still lingered. He wondered what his father would say if he knew the reason Chelsea had donned a man's clothing, if he were told that only moments before his son had been giving her the most pleasure she'd ever before felt. He would become apoplectic.

Townsend glared at Rogan then, his eyes dark, his face filled with obvious disapproval. "*This* is your idea of a future countess?"

Chelsea flinched as if she'd been struck, withdrawing at her father-in-law's insults. Rogan could remain silent no longer. This had gone on long enough.

"Yes, sir, she is my idea of a countess and very well suited for it."

"Suited, ha!"

"Her father is a viscount."

Townsend did not speak further, his frown deepening the lines around his pinched mouth. He came before Chelsea then, peering at her face quite closely.

"Well, she's no marks from the pox, I'll grant her that, and her nose is not overlarge."

Chelsea's eyes regained some of their spark. "I am so pleased I meet with His Lordship's approval. Would you care to see my teeth? They are all my own, you know."

Rogan smothered a chuckle.

Townsend's face grew still. Finally, he drew back from the offensive. "Cheeky snip, isn't she?" He turned, as if to say he'd seen his fill. "She has a deep voice for a girl—and big feet. Does she go about dressed like this often?"

Chelsea could but stare.

Rogan stepped forward. "I think it best we adjourn to the study and allow Chelsea to remove herself to her chamber so she may change into more suitable clothing."

"A good idea." Townsend waved a hand and started down the hall. "I've sent word to Emma and Fredric to be here in an hour for a late supper. See to it she is ready by then."

Chelsea wanted to scream at this officious man for speaking about her as if she weren't there. She had never felt more humiliated in her life. She felt every inch the fool. She wished she could leave. She wished to be anywhere but there before him, standing while he inspected her as if she were some broodmare he wished to purchase.

When they arrived at the town house, she tried to rush to her chambers to change, but Rogan's father, the Earl of Ashbourne, stood waiting for them at the door. He was taller than she had expected, his hair, which from its thinness she guessed was not a wig, was alabaster white and pulled back tightly. And he had the darkest, coldest eyes she'd ever seen. There was no warmth, no feeling in them when he spoke to his son. She suddenly pitied Rogan his childhood.

When Chelsea returned a half-hour later, she felt better prepared to deal with her father-in-law. She wore a very feminine gown of pale blue silk, the sleeves slashed atop a white, puffy chemise and the overskirt drawn back to reveal a delicate gossamer petticoat. A matching ribbon was threaded through her hair, which was freshly brushed and tumbling down her back in loose, thick curls.

She found them waiting for her in the dining room. Townsend looked at her, but said nothing. Chelsea figured that was as near an approval as she was going to receive. Emma and Fredric were already in attendance, as was Beecher, who seated himself at Chelsea's left. Rogan took the seat beside her at the head of the table, leaving Townsend to the seat directly across. She placed her napkin in her lap, trying to ignore his direct stare.

Beecher leaned toward her. "So sorry to have interrupted you earlier," he said, low enough for only Chelsea to hear. "Perhaps all ladies should discard their skirts for breeches if they become them as attractively as they do you."

Chelsea flushed, watching him with all the interest a meadow mouse would a snake. Although he was Rogan's cousin and now her family as well, she still did not trust him and she sensed he did not find her a welcome addition to the Doraunt clan.

She nodded to the footman to begin the meal. As plate after plate was brought out and uncovered, she wondered how Cook could have prepared such a repast in so short a time. Tender salt beef steamed on a bed of baby potatoes with tender asparagus swimming in a delicate white sauce.

A platter of jugged hare with tender carrots and peas completed the display, a queen's pudding served with clotted cream reserved for dessert.

Chelsea took a bite of the hare, nearly choking when Townsend suddenly barked at her.

"My son says your father is a viscount."

He stared at her as if awaiting a response.

"Yes, he is," she said politely. She took a sip of her wine to wash down the hare which had suddenly clotted in her throat.

"I do not believe I was ever told your family name."

The way he made statements as if they were questions unsettled her. She looked up to him. "My family name was Estwyck."

Townsend took a bite of salt beef, chewing it reflectively. "Estwyck. That does have a familiar ring to it." He paused to swallow. "I believe I remember an Estwyck. Once sat on the House of Lords. He was found guilty some years back of treason in the Forty-five rebellion with those filthy Jacobites."

"That would have been Damson Estwyck," Chelsea said, smarting at his statement about her father. "Damson Estwyck, my father."

Townsend sputtered. His eyes grew two sizes wide and his face turned bright red. He gasped and coughed. Chelsea thought for a moment he had gotten a piece of salt beef stuck in his throat and nearly got up to whack him on the back until he roared at her a moment later.

"Your father! Do you mean to say my son has married a traitor's daughter?"

Chelsea rose from her seat. "He was not a traitor!"

Now Townsend did choke on his salt beef and began hacking and gagging, clutching his throat as his face became as red as a beet.

"Father!" Emma said.

Fredric rushed to his side and began pounding him hard on the back with his fist. After a few well-placed whacks, he succeeded in dislodging it and Townsend took in great gulps of air until his face returned to its normal color. He launched on Chelsea again.

"Your father deserved to be hanged! He was a traitor! He deserved to be drawn and quartered!"

Chelsea was screaming now. "My father is not a traitor! He is innocent!"

Emma was sobbing, with Fredric at her side trying to calm her, while Townsend and Chelsea screeched at each other from across the table. Beecher smiled, watching the performance with glee lit in his eyes.

Rogan sat back in his chair, watching the display with a mixture of both amusement and disbelief. He took a deep swallow of his burgundy wine. This was a comedy, but not a Shakespearean comedy of errors. No, this was a comedy of horrors.

"No grandson of mine is going to have traitor blood in him! I demand that this marriage be annulled! I demand that you leave this house at once!"

"Then you'll have no grandson at all!"

"Get out! Get out at once! I want you gone by morning, you Scottish—"

Rogan stood, splayed his fingers on the table and yelled. "That is enough!"

Every voice grew silent and every face turned to stare at him.

He lowered his voice. "I will not have you insulting my wife in my own house."

Townsend, who had been staring at Chelsea with an expression of sheer mortification, turned on his son in shock.

"Insulting your wife? It is an insult to me that you would wed the Scot's strumpet. You know good and well how I feel about those heathen Highlanders. And now to find out that she is of a family of traitors. I want her out by morning and—"

"Enough!" Rogan roared. "Let me remind you, sir, this is *my* house. We are not at Ashbourne now. I am master here. Chelsea is my wife and will be so for the rest of my life. Your grandchildren will come from her womb, her Scottish womb, and if she wants to name our first son after Bonnie Prince Charlie himself, then she may do so with my blessing. I will not have you insulting her or her family again. You will keep a civil tongue. If you do not like the choices I have made, then you are free to leave."

Townsend did not say anything for what seemed like a very long time. He just stared at Rogan as if unable to believe he was his son.

Everyone was silent. Chelsea did not know what to do or say. She felt responsible for everything. She didn't know what had come over her. She was usually very tolerant. Insults usually bounced off her like sand. But when he'd called her father all those horrible names, saying he deserved to die, she'd lost all thought of tolerance in an instant.

"This is your decision then?" Townsend said.

Rogan nodded, his face holding no expression.

Without saying another word, Townsend turned and left the room, asking Moller to fetch him a coach.

No one moved or said a word. Emma was sniffling when Townsend came again to the doorway with his cloak in hand. She rushed across the room to him.

"No, Father, please do not go. Rogan did not mean that you should leave."

Townsend looked to his son. "Did you mean that I should leave?"

"If you cannot behave with at least the modicum of control and refrain from insulting my wife or her family . . ."

Townsend looked to Emma. "Then I must go. I will not stay in the same house as a traitor, especially a Scottish traitor. Your brother has made his choice. He will have to live with that choice. I will have my coachman retrieve my things." He turned to leave.

Emma looked to Rogan. "Rogan, stop him. You cannot let him go. It is the middle of the night, for heaven's sake. It is cold and wet outside."

Rogan did not speak. He just stared at the empty doorway where his father had stood. When would it end? He'd done what his father had wanted, he'd married and by the end of March, and still it was not enough. It was never enough. Townsend would always disapprove of Rogan, regardless, and nothing would ever change that. He had been living his entire life, doing what his father did not want him to do, not what he himself would have chosen. Every decision, every path in life he took, had been the opposite of what Townsend would have wanted. And why? To punish him? He'd only ended up punishing himself in the end.

The following morning dawned warm and bright, a presage of spring, and Rogan offered to take Chelsea riding in Hyde Park in hopes of forgetting the grim events of the previous evening.

He did not know where his father had gone, if he'd stayed with Emma and Fredric or had left for Ashbourne that moment. He had sent a footman early that morning before dawn to retrieve his belongings.

Rogan knew why Townsend hated the Scots as he did. It was precisely the reason he'd avoided telling him anything about Chelsea's background. Yet Townsend had learned of it despite his efforts and he'd most probably write some new condition in his will to keep Rogan from inheriting, and thereby he would ruin Ashbourne in the end.

Rogan did not care anymore. If Townsend did allow Ashbourne to crumble, so be it. It would be felled by his hand and not by Rogan's. Rogan had made his choice, a "Hobson's choice" Fredric would have called it. It was the choice he'd had to make, one he'd make again, if need be. He had spent the night cudgeling his brains over it all and he'd finally come to a decision in the wee hours of the morning. He would no longer live his life for his father, making every move just to provoke him. He would begin living his life for himself, would move toward the future he wanted.

When he thought of the future he pictured Chelsea beside him, and that had surprised him. He pictured her belly growing large with his child, pictured her with children scampering at her feet. He was not fool enough to think what he felt for her was love. He was incapable of such an emotion—incapable, or perhaps afraid? What he did know was honor and he would protect her to the best of his ability, even against his own father.

"Thank you, Rogan," Chelsea said as they dismounted

and left their mounts with the stable lad, Will. "I so enjoyed our ride."

Rogan smiled at her. She'd not said one word about his father or the things he'd said to her, and he was grateful for that. Most women he knew would have gone on and on about the whole thing. He did not blame her for coming to her father's defense. Even the most meek-mannered of persons could not have kept their tongue at such an uncalled-for affront. Had it been Rogan Townsend he had been offending, it would have been very difficult to keep from slamming his fist in his father's face. And he did not doubt Chelsea would have risen just as quickly to his own defense.

When they entered the town house Moller met them at the door. His expression, usually staid and unemotional, changed markedly at the sight of them.

"My lord . . ."

Rogan removed his cloak and handed it to the valet. "Yes, Moller—"

"My lord . . ."

"Chelsea, if you do not mind, I've some papers to look over in my study," Rogan said, turning away from them both.

Moller looked to Chelsea nervously. "A word please, my lord." His frown deepened at Rogan's retreating back. "It is your father, my lord. Something has occurred."

Rogan halted. He did not turn for several long moments. When he did, his face was set, his eyes hard and dark. "What? Is he back again to create another spectacle or has he gone to his solicitor to change . . ." His eyes flitted to Chelsea and his words dropped off. "Yes, Moller, what is it?"

Moller eyed Chelsea again before speaking, his hands twisting nervously. She had never seen him so upset. "A messenger came around while you were out. I am afraid, my lord, your father, the earl, has died."

Chelsea lifted a hand to her mouth in shock. Rogan's father had just been there. How could he be dead? She looked to Rogan. His expression remained unchanged, giving no indication that he at all heard what Moller told him.

"Thank you, Moller," he said finally. He turned and started back down the hallway to his study, closing the door behind him.

Chapter 12

Rogan did not emerge until late that evening. Chelsea had his place set for dinner, not quite expecting him to come. She smiled when he came in and took his seat at the head of the table. He did not speak, but just stared off, sipping his wine in silent thought.

"Has Emma been informed?" he asked suddenly when Chelsea had nearly finished her meal. She looked up from her supper plate. He hadn't taken more than a bite of the tender roast duckling and buttered potatoes Cook had prepared for him.

Chelsea set down her fork and knife. "Yes. I sent Moller to her."

The slight inclination of his head was the only indication that he had even heard her.

Chelsea watched him as he fell back into thought. She cleared her throat once in an attempt to gain his attention, but failed. Finally she spoke.

"Shall I instruct the house staff to pack your things?"

Rogan looked at her over the rim of his wineglass. "Why? Am I going somewhere?"

Chelsea frowned in confusion. "Your father . . ."

"Yes?"

"His burial at Ashbourne. Do you not wish to attend?"

Rogan set the glass down. "Not particularly. We had no regard for each other while he was alive. Why should things change now that he is dead?"

His response chilled her. "But he is your father, Rogan."

"*Was* my father, and only in name, certainly not in the true sense of the word. He was my sire. He provided the seed to create me. That is all. Had I a choice, I would have preferred another. You saw yourself what little regard we had for one another. I have written to his solicitor asking him to spare no expense in arranging matters. I will travel to Ashbourne when time permits in a month or two to assume my duties. The house staff there has run that estate well enough without me before now. I am certain they will continue to do so in my absence."

Chelsea stared at him, unable to believe his cold words.

Rogan took another sip of wine. "Take heart, my dear. My father's passing is all the better for us both. You have acquired a new title; you are now the Countess of Ashbourne, and I"—he lifted his goblet in toast to his words—"I have finally inherited my freedom."

Chelsea caught a glimpse of Rogan's coattails as he passed her chamber door. The sound of a door closing confirmed his intent to retire for the evening.

Since his father's death, and for three nights afterward,

Rogan slept in his own bedchamber alone. He did not go out at night as he had before. He rarely spoke to her and when he did, it was only in passing. He spent every minute holed up in his study, no candle to light the room, rarely eating more than three bites of the meals she sent to him, staring off at the fire with a look of emptiness in his eyes.

She thought of the flagons of brandy that were emptying all too quickly these past days. At first she'd thought to allow Rogan his grief, give him this time alone to come to terms with his father's passing, but his demeanor seemed to worsen more each day. Yesterday, he snapped at her when she asked for his opinion on an invitation they'd received. This morning she heard him bark at the housemaid who brought him his breakfast because his coffee was cold, threatening to dismiss her if she brought it to him cold again.

Chelsea had consoled the frightened girl, assuring her she was a wonderful maid and would always have a position with them, but inside, she knew she had to do something to help Rogan. If he did not eat or see daylight soon, he would—she did not know what would happen. She did not want to think of the possibilities, she only knew she had to do something about it immediately.

She stood back and regarded her reflection in the looking glass. She had dressed carefully that evening, pulling her hair back with a wide white satin ribbon at the nape of her neck, soft loosened tendrils caressing her cheeks and forehead. Rogan had once told her he liked her hair that way. Her ivory silk nightrail, just arrived from Madame Dussault's, was decorated with seed pearls and blond mignonette lace, its full sleeves tapering down her wrist to a point. Smoothing a curl back from her forehead, she started for Rogan's chamber.

Chelsea raised her hand, hesitated, then knocked softly. She was not surprised when he did not respond. She tried the door handle, twisting it open.

"Rogan?" She pushed the door inward.

Inside, the room was cloaked in shadows and it took her eyes several moments to adjust to the faint light given off by the fire which barely burned in the hearth. Then she saw him. He sat in a large wingback chair before the tall windows facing the back garden, staring out at the night sky. She stoked the fire to flame and added another log before she proceeded across the room toward him.

Chelsea stopped beside the huge chair he filled. He held a goblet of brandy propped against the arm of the chair. The bottle on the small table beside him was half-filled.

"May I?" she said, motioning to the chair opposite him.

When he did not respond, she sat upon it anyway.

"I will not be very interesting company," he said, his voice a deep rumble from lack of sleep.

Chelsea curled her legs beneath her. "Allow me to be the judge of that."

They sat in silence for several minutes. Chelsea studied Rogan's profile in the firelight, his face shaded with two days' growth of beard, his hair coming loose from its tie. He had removed his cravat and had unfastened the top buttons of his shirt, which was wrinkled and hanging out of his breeches. His sleeves were rolled to his elbows. She could see the slow steady beat of his heart at his throat as he tipped his head back and drained the brandy in his glass.

He reached for the bottle. She covered it with her hand. He looked up at her when his hand touched warm skin and not the cold glass he'd expected.

"Allow me," she said, lifting the bottle.

He inclined his head.

Chelsea tipped the flagon to the rim of the goblet, allowing it to fill only halfway. She knew if he had poured, he would have filled the glass completely and would have drunk it till it was empty. She did not wish him to drown his feelings in spirits any longer.

Rogan turned his attention back to the window.

"Emma and Fredric left for Ashbourne this morning," Chelsea said after a moment.

"Hmm."

"You have received quite a lot of condolences, even one from Kensington."

"He was well acquainted with our King," Rogan said. He turned toward her and she thought she detected a slight spark somewhere deep in his blank blue-gray stare. "Chelsea, I have no wish to discuss my father any longer. It is done and I wish only to forget it." He turned back to the window.

"Will you, Rogan? Will you forget, or will you continue to punish yourself over the guilt you feel that you were somehow responsible for his death?"

Rogan turned on her, his eyes glinting in the firelight, but she spoke again, cutting off his response.

"No, you listen to me now. I should be the one to feel responsible. It was because of me that he left that night. If you had never married me, none of this would have happened and your father would most probably be alive today."

Rogan snarled and threw the goblet to the floor, shattering it at her feet. His voice thundered at her. Chelsea flinched only slightly.

"I am the one who ordered him out. You heard what Moller said. The coach skidded on a patch of ice and plummeted to the bottom of the ravine. It was not his health that did him in. It was me."

He turned away, snarling.

Chelsea refused to cower. She stood and grabbed his sleeve. "Rogan, look at me, I want to show you something."

She held out the package she'd found earlier that day. It was rectangular and heavy and had been the only item left behind after the footman came to retrieve Townsend's things.

Rogan took the package from her. On its top was a card that read "To my son." He swallowed hard. He knew what the package contained. He had been waiting for it all his life. Slowly he untied the red corded drawstring that held it and removed the top of the box. Inside, wrapped in aged black velvet lay the dragoon pistol, the pistol that had been handed down to each Doraunt heir since his great-grandfather, Silas, the pistol that had hung on the wall above all the portraits of the Doraunt men that Rogan had stared at for hours as a boy. Its carved steel barrel glimmered in the firelight as he pulled it from inside.

"It is beautiful," Chelsea said, staring at the intricate engravings that covered it.

"Yes, it is. It was my great-grandfather's when he served as a dragoon in the cavalry. See this tiny switch under the trigger? When the switch is up, the gun will not fire, even if it is loaded. My great-grandfather had it fashioned that way so if the enemy were ever to take it from him, they could not use it to kill him." He smiled, placing the pistol back in its case.

"Do you not see, Rogan. Your father did care for you. He brought this pistol here for you. That was why he came to London. Not to give his approval of me as your wife."

Rogan shook his head. "He did not care for me, Chelsea. Don't you understand? He never cared for me. He only came to see the woman I married."

"He left the dragoon's pistol for you."

"No."

"Why would the footman leave just this box when he collected your father's belongings? Why do you refuse to believe he cared?"

"Because believing he did not is easier than wondering if he truly did."

He looked around then, searching for his crutch these past days. Spotting the shattered goblet on the floor, he growled and reached for the flagon on the table.

"No!" Chelsea said, swiping it away.

She threw the bottle from his reach, the amber liquid spilling out in a wide arc across the carpet as it flew across the room.

"Numbing your senses will not make it go away!"

Rogan paced, his boots crunching on the broken pieces of glass. He looked disoriented, raking a hand through his hair in frustration. "I have to work. I have to get out of here." He turned. "I am going to the shipyards."

"No!" Chelsea ran in front of him, blocking his way to the door. "Running away is not going to make it disappear either. You have to face this thing, Rogan, before it kills you. I cannot allow you to ignore it any longer. You are not leaving."

"Who the hell are you to tell me what I can or cannot do?"

"I am your wife!"

Chapter 13

Rogan's eyes widened, and with an animal growl, he seized Chelsea by her shoulders and pulled her hard against him. She opened her mouth to protest, but his own descended upon hers, his tongue plunging into her mouth, punishing her.

She relaxed against him. If he had expected her to struggle, he was mistaken. Sharp needles of pain shot along her upper arm from the grip with which he held her, but she did not raise her hands to fight him. Even his anger was better than the absence of emotion he had been showing the past days. He needed to care, to feel again. She would make him feel.

She inched her hands up along his chest. She could feel his heart drumming against her palms beneath the starched fabric of his shirt. She opened willingly to him, becoming pliant in his arms as she reached up and touched the side of his face.

At her soft touch, Rogan loosened his hold. Chelsea curved her hands around to the back of his neck as his mouth moved downward, leaving her mouth, searing a path of heat along the soft column of her throat. A shiver touched her deep inside and Chelsea let her head fall back over his arm as Rogan pushed the fabric of her nightrail aside, burying his face in her bare breasts.

Currents of desire shot through her, stretching outward through every limb as he ran his tongue softly over her nipples, teasing them to erection. He urged her back to the bed, lowering her gently onto the soft mattress as his mouth continued its relentless assault on her flesh.

"Oh, Rogan . . ."

Rogan raised his head to look down at her in the firelight. Their eyes met. For a long moment, neither spoke. They needed no words to convey their feelings to each other. Chelsea saw something shining in his eyes, a glint of silver-blue passion unlike anything she had ever seen before. It seemed to add to the fire already running rampant through her and she reached up to him, lightly caressing his cheek with the back of her hand.

Her touch seemed to soothe him and he closed his eyes before he reclaimed her lips, this time tenderly, touching, tasting. She returned the kiss with ardency, thrilling in the taste of him, the velvet feel of his mouth on hers, losing herself to the glorious feelings he was creating within her.

Sensations swirled through her as his fingers edged their way downward and began to unfasten the many tiny pearl buttons that lined the front of her nightrail. He fumbled at the intricate closures, and in ardent desperation, yanked the delicate lace apart, scattering the tiny buttons along the hardwood floor. And then, as gently as he might handle a babe, he lifted her up and into his arms, slipping the negligee over her naked form.

Rogan sat back and stared at her in the firelight, her skin glowing warmly, her dark eyes beckoning him to her. God, but she was lovely. Her hair had come loose from its ribbon tie and was settling wildly about her bare shoulders, splaying across the white pillow in an ebony silken drape. He stood slowly and removed his shirt, his eyes never leaving her.

He discarded his shirt to the floor and knelt on the bed, sliding his hands beneath her and lifting Chelsea into his arms. He clutched her tightly to him as if afraid to let her go. The heat of her against his chest sent a shock of feeling bolting through him. He buried his face in her hair and breathed in its sweet essence, reveling in the familiar floral scent that clung to her soft skin.

God, he wanted her, wanted to claim her for his own. And he would have her. Nothing mattered at that moment more than having this woman. His heart beat wildly, his body throbbed with need, and he wanted to take her then and there, but he held back, knowing the need to pleasure her first.

Chelsea watched him through half-parted eyes as Rogan lowered his head to her breast. A tremor of pleasure so intense she nearly cried out loud rocked her body, sending her senses reeling. She arched her back against his sucking mouth, desperately wanting, seeking release from the hot liquid tension building steadily within her. She felt his hand slide down along her stomach, leaving in its wake a trail of fire. She felt a burning deep in her stomach.

She felt his finger slide downward, brushing against the curls between her legs, parting her woman's flesh. The fire inside her leapt in response. "Rogan . . ."

She raised her hips upward, quivering as his hand moved lower. Sensations gripped her when he touched her in her most private place, causing her to gasp out loud, her mouth falling open with a pleasured sigh.

His head moved lower still, kissing down over her belly. He parted her thighs, sliding between them and when she felt his mouth on her there, she bucked beneath him at the intensity of the sensation.

"Chelsea . . ."

And then his tongue touched her there and she had never known such intense hot feeling. It enveloped her completely, taking her soaring upward to the skies. Slowly, rhythmically, he found her center and began to move his mouth, soft and gentle, stroking over her, coaxing her response.

Chelsea began to lose herself, her body alive with each movement of his mouth. It stoked an even greater fire in her, its dancing flames fanning outward through her, burning with the heat of growing desire. It consumed her, melting her. She felt a tightening deep inside that seemed to grow with each stroke of his mouth. Stronger and stronger it grew as his movements increased and he deepened the pressure, taking Chelsea higher and higher still.

Her legs tensed instinctively, as if seeking a release from his constant touch. But she did not want it to end. She never wanted it to end. She wanted to die from the pleasure of it. Her breath came in short gasps now and she clenched her fingers into the bedsheets, straining against him, lifting her hips as she climbed higher and higher toward her climax.

His hands cupped her buttocks and he lifted her to him, deepening the intense pressure of his mouth. Blood was pounding in her ears, her body throbbing as she began to writhe beneath his touch. She begged him for release from the sweet anguish she was in. She clenched her teeth tightly, a moan escaping her, her legs trembling with need until she thought she would cry out from the sheer pleasure of it.

And then she did cry out and her eyes flew open with the wonder of it as she was suddenly and abruptly released from the sweet tension. An outburst of sensations showered over her, shaking her to her very core, taking her to the heavens and back. It left her breathless and unaware of her surroundings, panting as Rogan lowered her to the bed again. His mouth left her then and he pulled her against him, wrapping her in the splendor of his arms and holding her there in his warm embrace as waves of feeling continued to rock her weakened body. He held her until the sensations ebbed, the pleasure subsiding, filling her with a glowing feeling of completion, of warm wholeness unlike anything she'd ever before experienced.

Rogan released her and she fell back onto the bed, quivering in the aftermath of this glorious experience. She saw Rogan rise up before her. She watched him through lowered lashes, unable to move or speak, still floating in the wonder of her climax.

He moved between her still-trembling legs, her body and mind miles apart, far from any cognizant thought. She felt something press slightly at the moist entry between her legs and Rogan slowly raised her buttocks, his hands gently squeezing her soft flesh as he pushed himself slightly forward into her.

God, she was so tight around him, Rogan felt he would burst from the brilliant sensation of her body stretching to hold him. Passion gripped him as he pushed deeper still, driving him near mad with desire. He hesitated when he touched her maidenhead and drew back slightly, not wanting her pleasure to end, knowing the pain that was to come. He rose up on his arms and with one quick thrust bounded forward, covering her mouth with his to stifle her pained cry.

A sharp pain ripped through Chelsea as Rogan came fully inside of her, taking her innocence with one quick stroke. She squeezed her eyes shut, reveling in the feel of him inside of her. He filled her completely. He lay still for a moment, his hands gripping her hips tightly to him as he waited for her pain to subside. Then he began to move, slowly at first, pulling back then pushing slowly inside, each time filling her, delving deeper and deeper. The pain softened to a dull throb and the sensations that had possessed her before seemed to mass again as his body began to move faster. His hands were squeezing her hips, spreading her legs wider, and Chelsea felt her hips rise on their own to meet each thrust he delivered.

Possessed by need and driven by passion, Rogan began to thrust faster, his breathing labored and uneven, as he fought to hold his own pleasure for want of hers. She was so hot, so tight around him, he could not control the movement of his body as it compulsively thrust forward into her. She was rising to meet him; she must be near, but he could feel his own release coming quickly, rising up, burning inside, pounding through his entire body, until he could hold it back no longer.

"Oh, God, Chelsea . . ."

Rogan thrust forward, his face clenching as spasm after spasm rocked his body. He drew back slightly, thrusting forward again, and she could feel him empty his seed fully inside of her. He held her there for a long moment, his fingers clutching her hips against him, his face buried against her soft shoulder. His shoulders rose and fell as he fought to regain his ragged breath. He groaned aloud, spent and exhausted, easing her back and laying his head upon her breast.

Chelsea did not move for what seemed a very long time. She marveled in the feel of him upon her, covering her, holding her. The weight of his body was not uncomfortable on her. She welcomed it, the touch of him, the feel of his arms still so tightly around her. She felt a throbbing between her legs where he lay sheathed within her still, filling her, making her complete. She ran a fingertip lightly through the dampened hair at his forehead as her senses returned from the impassioned heights he'd sent them flying to.

Never had she dreamed it would be so between a man and woman. Never would she have imagined the completeness and the warmth. She never wanted it to end.

Rogan's back rose and fell slowly now, his breathing growing even, and Chelsea knew he had fallen asleep. Exhaustion from the past days had finally claimed him. Cradling his head against her breast, she settled back against the pillows and closed her eyes, resting her cheek against his temple, the warmth of their wondrous lovemaking lulling her to sleep.

The drapes snapped back and daylight streaked through the windowpanes, showering the room with light and waking Chelsea in an instant. She shifted and rose slowly from the nest of pillows that surrounded her, squinting against the blinding light to see who had invaded her chamber at such an ungodly hour.

"Oh." The maid, Anne, bowed her mobcap-covered head, dropping a quick curtsy. "I am so sorry, milady. My lord was already awake. It is nearly noon. I did not think anyone was in this room. I'd no idea you'd be sleeping in here."

Sleeping where? Chelsea glanced around her, recognizing the royal blue and gold wall coverings, the dark mahogany bed. She was in Rogan's room. In Rogan's bed. She closed her eyes, flinging her arm across her forehead, and lay back on the pillows as memories of the previous night filled her head. His hands touching her, his body joining with hers, making her feel . . .

Chelsea opened her eyes at the nervous clearing of the maid's throat.

"It is all right, Anne. It is getting late. I should have been awake hours ago. I will take tea and cakes in my chambers, please."

Anne dropped another curtsy before hurrying from the room to see to her mistress's task. No doubt word of the countess's sleeping arrangements would be spreading throughout the household in moments, contradicting the rumors that the newly-married lord and lady did not share a bed.

Chelsea pushed back the thick coverlet and sat upright, moving to the edge of the mattress. She hesitated at the slight soreness between her legs. She retrieved her wrap from its place at the foot of the bed, realizing Rogan must have placed it there after it had been tossed on the floor the previous night. She stood slowly, her eyes straying to the sheets, the splotches of blood, bright red against the white fabric. She was no longer a virgin. Her body tingled at the thought as she remembered the fierce need with which Rogan had taken her, the tenderness he'd shown hours later when he'd woken her again in the middle of the night to take her a second time. She pulled the counterpane over the stained sheet, and started from the room.

"A bath, please, Anne," Chelsea said as she entered her own chambers a moment later.

She stopped before the corner looking glass and peered at her reflection. Her hair was tangled around her neck and shoulders, curling wildly at her forehead. Her lips were red and swollen from his kisses. But she did not really look any different. Her eyes were the same color and her face hadn't changed its shape overnight. Looking at her, no one would notice any difference. Still, she felt very *different.* She couldn't quite name it, but spending the night in her husband's bed had not at all been what she'd expected.

Nighttime whispers of schoolgirls could never describe what she and Rogan had shared, the closeness between them, the tenderness of joining together to become one. She never knew completeness more than when she had taken Rogan in her body and could feel him filling her inside. He had been so very gentle when taking her maidenhood, almost as if wanting to take her pain upon himself. And the pain hadn't lasted. The only reminder of it was the sight of her virgin's blood on his sheets this morning, and that was a mere footnote to the wondrous experience they'd shared together.

Chelsea turned from her reflection and took a small bite of the sweet rolls set on a tray near her dressing table. She ran a brush through her hair as two houseboys brought in the oval copper tub and deposited it before the hearth. Anne came in then and emptied pitchers of steaming water into the tub until it was half-filled, then added several drops of lavender water before turning from the room and closing the door behind her.

Chelsea lingered in the bath, allowing the steamy water to soothe her while her mind wandered back, remembering each touch, each caress from the previous night. She closed her eyes and leaned her head against the rim of the tub, still awed by what had happened between them, still wrapped in the silken splendor. If they were married for the rest of her life, would it always be thus, the closeness, the wonder? Would it feel the same years from now when he took her?

She realized then that she'd just considered the possibility of remaining Rogan's wife forever. She smiled. And what of a child? What if at that moment a tiny life was growing inside her? She closed her fist tightly around the too-large, yarn-strung band of gold on her finger that marked her as Rogan's wife, and settled back amongst the cloud of fragrant suds that covered the water's surface.

So lost was she in her thoughts, Chelsea did not hear her chamber door open. Nor did she hear it close a second later. She did not even hear his footsteps as he moved across the floor toward her. Still, she lay there, languishing in the bathwater, her hair pulled atop her head, that same smile touching her lips.

Rogan leaned against the bedpost and watched her at her bath. He wondered at the smile that curved her lovely lips, what she could be thinking to have caused that alluring smile, and found himself staring at the small dimple that touched the corner of her left cheek.

He'd never seen her smile like this before and suddenly he never thought her more beautiful. Her breasts rose just above the surface of the bathwater, her nipples wet and inviting. He felt his desire surge. He completely forgot all reason for coming to her chamber, for wanting to make certain she was not sore from their coupling, to ease her fears when she saw her virgin's blood on his sheets that morning. Seeing her there, with her cheeks flushed from the hot bath and her breasts, those delicious breasts, beckoning him to taste them, he felt himself harden anew with a lust unchecked.

"What are you doing here?"

He had not seen her open her eyes, so intent was he on her lovely breasts. She covered them now with her hands, pulling her knees over them as well, the languid smile vanishing.

"Good morning, my dear."

"Rogan! I am taking my bath!"

Rogan smiled a devilish grin. "Yes, I can see that. I was just enjoying it quite well."

It had been so different the night before in the darkness with the two of them unclothed, wrapped in each other's arms. Now, in the stark daylight, she suddenly felt modest before him.

He was not moving.

Chelsea's eyes grew wide when she realized he did not plan to leave. She looked for the towel Anne had left for her, but it was on the bed, too far for her to reach from where she sat. "Will you leave me to my privacy, please?"

His grin deepened. "Oh, I please, but not to leave you."

Rogan grabbed the towel she had been searching for and stepped forward. He opened it before her. "Would my lady care for her towel?"

"Yes."

"Well, then, you may come and get it."

"Can you not allow me even the smallest amount of modesty?"

Rogan took another step forward. "You certainly didn't seem to mind my seeing you last night while you were screaming with pleasure." His eyes sparkled in the sunlight. "Of course, it was a modest scream." Chelsea stared at him. He took a step forward.

"Wait!" Chelsea held out one hand while still trying to cover herself with the other. "Do not take another step."

Rogan raised a brow. "You mean another step like this one?" He moved closer.

Chelsea grabbed the sponge beside her, flinging it at him and hitting him square in the shoulder. It bounced off him and rolled along the floor, leaving a dark, wet stain on the sleeve of his jacket.

"Look what you've done," he said, taking another step. "My clothes are all wet. Now I, too, will have to take a bath. Perhaps you'll allow me to join you."

He began to unfasten his breeches, and before he got to the second button, Chelsea sprang from the tub and bolted naked across the room, grabbing her dressing robe and pulling it around her. "I don't know what happened to me last night," she said breathlessly. "That wasn't me. It was someone else."

"Oh, it was you all right, and you were enjoying it quite a lot."

"No, I wasn't."

Rogan started toward her. "Now, Chelsea, can you truly deny it?"

Chelsea backed against the bed. She could not. Even now, her body was trembling. All he had to do was look at her and she melted.

"We are husband and wife. Nothing should embarrass you with me."

Chelsea sighed. "Well I am new to this marriage thing. You will have to give me a little time to accustom myself to it. Now will you please leave?"

Rogan looked at her. Her hair was falling down about her, her skin glistening with the bathwater. "Are you even aware that your dressing gown is clinging to your legs and breasts in a most provocative manner?"

She picked up a scent bottle, readying herself to throw it.

"All right, all right. I will leave you to dress, but only because Emma awaits you downstairs in the parlor. She and Fredric just returned from Ashbourne. I thought perhaps you could cheer her. I only came up here so you would not think me a heartless cad to leave you after last night."

"You are a heartless cad."

"Be that as it may, I will be leaving for the shipyards and will probably be gone until late. I have a meeting with an associate this evening, so do not wait up for me."

Another late night meeting with—? Chelsea pushed the thought away.

"Might I have a kiss from my wife before I go?"

"No!"

Rogan assumed a wounded look.

Always he mocked her. She raised the bottle of scent in her hand. "I've already fallen for your trickery. I'm not fool enough to do it again. Now go!"

Rogan shrugged. "Well, then, until later, my love."

He turned and was gone in seconds, leaving Chelsea to smile at the place left vacant by him.

* * *

Chelsea found Emma in the parlor propped upon the settee with a bowl of candied cherries, reading a volume of Shakespeare's sonnets. It had only been days since she'd last seen her, but her belly seemed to have doubled in size. She must be carrying a boy, Chelsea thought, a rather large brawny boy.

Emma looked up as Chelsea entered the room. "Good morning, Chelsea. You look lovely. I was wondering what was keeping you. I hope I did not call too early." She rose to meet her, or rather tried to rise, her corpulent belly hindering her progress. Chelsea gave her a hand and pulled her upright.

"Thank you. Someday, when you are in the same condition, I will return the favor. I also wish to thank you for whatever you did for my brother. Rogan looks so much better this morning. I don't know what you did to cheer him, but it worked, whatever it was."

Chelsea glanced away and smiled, knowing full well what it was that had cheered him.

"I have been worried about him," Emma said, her tone suddenly turning serious. "I want you to understand. I see you have already made a difference, but you need to know the truth. Rogan and my father were never close. They were as distant as two ships on either side of a vast ocean. My father was never satisfied with anything Rogan did. No matter how he tried, Rogan could never live up to what my father expected. It was almost as if by refusing to give his approval, my father believed Rogan would continue to strive to do more. But it only served to work against him. Rogan ended up doing the exact opposite of what my father wished. They were always arguing. And then, after my mother's death, their relationship worsened. It never was quite the same after that."

Chelsea remembered Gwyneth questioning her about Rogan's mother that day at Madame Dussault's. "Rogan has never spoken of your mother. In fact, I did not know she had died."

Emma frowned. "I do not even know how she passed. I was away then, visiting relatives. Rogan had come home from his schooling to pass the summer months with my parents. She died just before he was to return. They had already buried her by the time I reached Ashbourne, and no one would discuss what had happened. They said it was a riding accident, but I do not believe it. My mother was the best horsewoman I've ever seen. The house staff just shook their heads to my questions. It was almost as if they were afraid to talk. Only Rogan and my father truly knew how she died, and they refused to discuss it. I can see it haunts Rogan to this day. He blamed my father for it. He wouldn't tell me what happened that summer, but he was never the same after that. It was as if something in him died with her."

Chelsea awoke instantly as two hands turned her and eased her onto her back. She had no idea what time it was; her bedchamber was dark, nor, as she felt Rogan's mouth nibbling at her earlobe, did she care.

"I want you, Chelsea." His voice was a hoarse whisper. "I want to feel you around me, holding me inside of you."

She could see his silhouette looming above her in the moonlight. He lowered his head and kissed her, his hands insistently pulling her nightrail over her hips, bunching it at her waist.

"Will you let me take you, Chelsea?"

She could not see his face. She whispered. "Yes."

His urgency was great and she could feel his member pulsing against her thigh even as his fingers gently probed her moist entry. He slid his finger inside of her and she sucked in her breath at the taut sensation it brought to her. He drew her hips upward then and covered her with his body, his mouth taking hers as he sheathed his length inside of her, filling her completely.

His fingers delved between them as he moved inside her, probing her, finding her center, bringing her alive with desire. His fingers teased her aching flesh as he began driving into her with hard, quick thrusts, stroking her sensitive flesh with intense purpose.

Chelsea cried out when she was taken by her climax, showered with a burst of vivid sensations that made her feel alive. He drew her hands above her head, his body thrusting now, plunging deeper and deeper still as he fought to reach his own passion's height.

Rogan drove forward and he cried out, his body stiffening, and he emptied his release deep inside of her. He held her tightly to him, his fingers digging into her shoulders, his face buried against her neck as he drew a ragged breath, exhaling deeply.

"I am sorry for yelling at you last night," he said to her in the darkness a moment later. He moved to her side. Laying on his back, he reached for her and cradled her head against his chest.

Chelsea splayed her fingers over the firm muscles of his chest, her yarn-wound gold wedding ring glimmering at her in the moonlight. She thought of all Emma had told her about how greatly their mother's untimely death had affected Rogan so, causing his deep-seated ill feelings toward his father.

"I understand."

Rogan was silent now. His fingers strayed to Chelsea's temple, and he smoothed her hair back softly with the lightest touch of a feather.

"Rogan?"

"Hmm . . ." He nuzzled her forehead.

Chelsea hesitated. "Tell me about your mother."

He tensed, the gentle ministrations of his fingers ceasing instantly. She fully expected him to refuse and did not even know why she asked him. It had been so peaceful between them. Why had she ruined it with her overanxious curiosity? She started to tell him to forget the question when he spoke a moment later.

"She was beautiful and young, younger than my father, too young, perhaps."

He dropped off and Chelsea knew his thoughts were straying, back to a time when he had been a child, when the mother he loved had been alive.

"She had the reddest hair you'd ever seen, flaming red they called it, and she was impetuous and winsome, with a temper to match the color of her hair. She loved to do what all young girls did, to laugh and gossip and enjoy court life. She was an accomplished flirt and it was said that she even caught the eye of the king's son. Her marriage to my father was arranged by her parents to curb her wayward ways. She was only sixteen and my father forty when they wed."

Chelsea nodded, her head against his chest, thinking he had finished. She was surprised when he went on.

"My father got her with child very soon after they were married. She had barely turned seventeen when I was born.

She had fulfilled her duty to him, and she was rewarded for it, by being sent to the country to live at Ashbourne while my father remained in London. My mother hated to be alone. She was still very young and very much alive. She loved to dance and wanted to attend court, but my father refused to allow her to return, probably for fear she'd become the new king's mistress. He would visit her every three or four months, and when he did, she would plead with him to allow her to return. He always refused.

"Seven years later, on a blizzardy night, Emma was born, the result of one of his quarterly visits. My father did not come to see his daughter until her first birthday. My mother was so lonely, and when he finally did come to Ashbourne, she begged him to let her come to London, but her pleas fell on deaf ears."

Rogan paused again as if collecting his thoughts.

"And then, she met the brother of a neighboring landholder, a young, handsome sort who showered my mother with the attention she was so starved for. He was captivated by her the minute he laid eyes on her. Who wouldn't be? It was impossible not to be. They said her eyes lit up any room she entered and her laughter sounded like the chimes of heaven.

"Her suitor was bold in his pursuit, but she resisted him for two years. Then one day, when my father had neglected her once again, she gave in to her impulses. She'd given up any hope of my father ever loving her and reached out to the one who offered what she needed. The affair lasted three years before my father learned of it, but by then my mother was pregnant with her lover's child."

Chelsea spoke up. "Do you know who he was?"

"No, only that he was a Scot, which is why my father reacted to you the way he did. He hired a group of sea rovers to kidnap my mother's lover and bring him to Ashbourne, where he forced my mother to watch as they beat him senseless. Then my father delivered him, broken and unconscious, to a press gang in Bristol, who forced him into service in His Majesty's Navy. My mother would never see him again.

"To punish her for her unfaithfulness, my father locked her away in the north tower at Ashbourne. She begged to be released, pleading for his forgiveness, but he refused."

Rogan paused and Chelsea felt his chest tighten.

"I can remember hearing her cries, calling his name, then calling for anyone to please let her out. I would try to go to her and speak to her from the other side of the door, but he ordered me away.

"And then one day her cries stopped. I told him something was wrong, but he insisted it was just a trick to get him to open the door. Late one night I stole the keys from his desk and went to the tower door.

"And when I opened the door, I found my mother hanging from the ceiling by a noose she had fashioned from her own petticoats."

His voice dropped off, and his breathing became uneven.

Chelsea's heart went out to him, and a tear rolled down her cheek for the sorrow he had lived. She reached up and lightly touched the side of his face. "I am sorry I made you relive such a painful memory."

"It is all right. It helps, you know, to talk of it. I never have before now. After she died, I found her diary in her room, hidden far back in her dresser drawer. I read every page and learned everything she felt, the hell she had lived through. I wanted to kill my father, Chelsea. I never told Emma the truth. She hadn't been there to see it and I did not want her to feel the pain, to hate him as I did. I did not want her to know what kind of a monster our father really was."

Chelsea took Rogan's hand and squeezed it tightly. She wanted to comfort him, to ease the pain he'd felt all these years. Her heart swelled as she realized he had shared this most private memory with her. How difficult it must have been for him to speak of it, reliving his mother's tragic death once again.

"That ring you wear was hers."

A tremble came over Chelsea at knowing he had given her his mother's ring.

She stayed awake for a long time after he had fallen asleep, listening to his even breathing, wishing she could somehow erase his pain, until she was certain he finally slept. She thought of what had brought her to this man, of all they had shared in their short time together. She felt his pain, his sorrow at the loss of his mother, his hurt at his father's rejection of him and suddenly Chelsea realized she loved him.

She did not know when it had happened, and it mattered naught, for her heart was suddenly filled with love for him. And then she remembered the Gypsy's prophecy.

Rogan was the Knight of Cups, the one who had saved her not once, but twice, from harm's way.

Rogan was the man of her destiny.

When Chelsea rose the next morning, awake and feeling very much alive, she had come to a decision, a decision she'd pondered all through the night, mulling it over thoroughly in her mind. She would tell Rogan everything, of her reasons for leaving Scotland, about her father's exile, and about the stranger called James, who was seeking to clear his name.

By telling her about his mother's death, a thing not even his sister truly knew, Rogan had shown her trust without condition, faith in her without expectation of anything in return.

And now she owed Rogan the truth about herself.

Although she loved him, she hesitated to reveal her feelings for him, uncertain if he returned her love, afraid he might not. She knew now what she felt for Gregor all those years had not been love. It had never been love. It had never rocked her with its passion, warming her with its trust and filling her with a sense of well-being unlike anything she had ever felt before. With Rogan she felt as if she belonged, as if she had a purpose, and there would be no more lies, no more deception, only the truth. Her heart surged with a warmth and joy she had thought never to know again.

Chelsea dressed hurriedly, choosing a gown of rosewood-colored silk edged with delicate blond lace. She did not take time to dress her hair, leaving it loose and flowing down her back in a soft array of curls and waves. As she made her way down the stairs, her heart began to drum in expectation.

At the bottom of the stairwell, Chelsea heard the murmur of voices coming from Rogan's study. She paused just outside the door, peering in so as not to disturb him with his guest.

"I am certain she will be most pleased," Rogan said. He was seated at his desk, his fingers steepled before him as he leaned back casually in his chair. His visitor sat opposite him, obscured from Chelsea's view by the high-backed chair in front of his desk.

He noticed her at the door. He smiled and crossed the room to join her. "Chelsea, come, we have a guest I think you'll want to see."

He took her hand and led her inside. Chelsea assumed a graceful smile in preparation for the introduction. His guest rose slowly from the chair.

And then she froze dead, her smile vanishing as her mother, Annora, turned to face her.

Chapter 14

"My dear Chelsea, how very lovely you look. I have missed you so very much these past months."

Chelsea could but stare as Annora moved forward to embrace her. She stood still as stone when she pulled away.

"What is wrong? You look at me as if I've sprouted horns upon my head!"

And well she could have, with a forked tail to match, as stunned as Chelsea was to see her. She should have expected her to come, and had, though many weeks ago, long before she'd married Rogan, long before she'd fallen in love with him. But now, seeing her there, flesh and blood, standing in her husband's study, she couldn't believe it true. She did not want to believe it true. She wished it were a nightmare and she would wake to open her eyes and find her gone. She wished anything but for her mother to be standing there, swathed in layers of lemon yellow silk, acting as if nothing had happened between them.

Annora took her hand. "Come, let me see you."

"Mother . . ." Chelsea stepped back warily.

Annora looked stricken. "What sort of greeting is that for a mother who hasn't seen her dear daughter in nearly three months?" She extended her hand. "Come, now, cease this nonsense and give your mother a kiss."

Chelsea took her hand automatically, though reluctantly, watching Annora as if expecting her to take a bite of her. She pressed her lips quickly to her mother's powdered cheek, the cloying scent of her violet perfume invading her senses, making her feel all of seven years old again.

As a child, she'd been permitted to see her mother only when Annora wished it, and then only to preen over her or to put her on display before visiting relatives and friends. Their visits together never lasted long. No more than an hour or two. Dressed in her best gown, Chelsea would curtsy and kiss her mother's cheek as she just had, reciting a phrase of poetry, the obedient, well-mannered child. She never spoke out of turn. She never dared gainsay her mother. She practiced the spinet and spent hours stitching needlework, the expected accomplishments of a genteel young lady, preparing herself for her fated role in life, the dutiful and serene wife of Gregor Moultrie.

And then, as clearly as if it had been only yesterday, Chelsea saw her mother as she had last seen her, naked and sprawled beneath Gregor's body.

She pulled away.

"Why have you come here?"

The sharpness in her voice was not lost upon Annora.

She glanced nervously to Rogan and said, "I am here to see my daughter get married, of course. It isn't every day one's only child weds. Shame on you for not writing to tell me. To hear from strangers . . ." She shook her head and her gold ear bobs chinked from the motion. "And then to find I am too late. How sad I was to hear from your handsome husband that I already missed your wedding."

Annora smiled then, turning her gaze toward Rogan. Chelsea felt the chilly finger of foreboding trace along her spine. She started for the door as if to show Annora out. "Yes, we have already wed. Unfortunately there was not enough time to write, so I am afraid your journey was for naught."

Annora did not move to follow. Chelsea was a fool to have thought she would leave now that she was there, in London, in Rogan's house. Still, she could hope.

"Well, we must celebrate regardless. We will have a big party. A grand ball. The grandest yet. I still have many friends here in London, despite Damson's scandal and . . ."

Chelsea tightened her fingers around the door handle at the mention of her father. She wanted to inform her mother that she knew the truth, that Damson was innocent, but bit back the words and said only, "That will not be necessary, Mother."

Annora narrowed her eyes slightly, but enough for Chelsea to notice her irritation. "I cannot leave after just arriving."

Before Chelsea could utter the retort that waited on her lips, Rogan broke in.

"You do not have to leave. You may stay here with us and spend time with Chelsea while you are in London. Stay as long as you wish. I will have Moller send someone for your things."

Chelsea gaped.

Annora smiled.

"Oh, I couldn't. Truly. You are newly wed and you certainly do not need your mother-in-law around."

"Nonsense, I insist you stay."

"Splendid." Annora turned away with a swish of her skirts. She hooked her arm with Rogan's and started to lead him away. "Chelsea never was one for parties. Always had her nose in a book. She was never interested in the feminine things, you know, needlework, poetry, gowns, and balls. I told her . . ."

Chelsea remained at the door, watching as they disappeared into the parlor, her stomach sick, realizing that her worst nightmare was once again coming true.

Chelsea watched her mother over the rim of her wine goblet. No one would ever suspect the woman's treachery, her artful cunning, her effortless portrayal of concern. She played the role of the doting mother well, avoiding the subject of Chelsea's hasty leave-taking from Scotland, seeming content to be with her daughter now.

But Chelsea knew the better of it. She could see it in the stern glint in her eyes and the downward tilt of her rouged mouth appeared as she conversed with her daughter when no one else was watching, as if warning her to keep her tongue at bay.

Chelsea wanted her gone. She wanted her to take her twenty trunks and leave, returning to Scotland to live out her life, as Gregor's lover, if she so desired. She didn't care where. She didn't care if she ever saw her again. She just wanted her far, far away from Rogan.

Annora laughed at something Rogan said, her light titter ringing clear across the room.

The sound turned Chelsea's stomach.

"What a witty husband you have, Chelsea."

Chelsea took a small bite of her roast pheasant. She could not taste its tender sweetness through the bitter rancor that filled her mouth. She had to think of something, some way to get Annora to leave. She lay her fork aside and reached for her wine goblet again. She swallowed, watching her mother closely. Perhaps she could bribe her into leaving, threaten to expose her affair with Gregor. She stiffened when Annora reached to Rogan and touched his hand, her laughter rioting through Chelsea's head.

"How did the two of you meet?" Annora said. She did not draw her hand away, but rather rested it on Rogan's sleeve. She peered at Chelsea from the corner of her eye as if to taunt her.

Chelsea felt the walls closing in on her. She felt as if she were going to be physically sick. Her stomach was clenching in spasms.

"Chelsea?"

The familiar sound of Rogan's voice brought Chelsea from her thoughts. It offered her comfort. She relaxed her hands which had clenched into fists.

"Is something the matter, Chelsea?"

Yes! she wanted to scream, *she bedded my betrothed and now she wants to do the same with you!*

"No. I am sorry. I am not feeling well of a sudden." She feared she would retch at any moment and rose from the table, bracing herself on the edge. "If you will please excuse me."

She did not wait for a response. She started from the room. It was happening again. Her mother was going to seduce Rogan as she had Gregor, and there was nothing Chelsea could do.

In the seclusion of her bedchamber, Chelsea leaned against the carved bedpost and stared out the window at the moon above. She closed her eyes. How could she have been so stupid, so blind to what had happened between her mother and Gregor. She thought back now, recalling the coy glances and touches, seemingly innocent, painfully real. But she could never have imagined, in her most horrible of nightmares, finding her betrothed in her mother's bed. Annora was her mother. She was supposed to love her. She was supposed to grow plump and content in years and tickle her grandchildren under the chin. Somehow Chelsea could never see Annora playing that role.

How they must have ridiculed her for her naïveté, laughing at her. And now Annora was there, in her house, doing the same with the man Chelsea loved while mocking her all the same.

A knocking at the door pulled Chelsea from her thoughts.

"Yes?"

Rogan came in then and Chelsea melted at the sight of him, so handsome, his eyes soft with concern. "Are you feeling all right?"

"Yes, I am fine. It was just a momentary pain in my stomach. It is gone now. It must have been something I ate."

He came to stand before her. "Well, it is too soon for morning illness, so it must not be that you carry my child." He pressed his hand to her forehead. "You do not feel feverish." He took her wrist. "You do still bear a pulse, so you are not dead. You must be fine, but Cook's ready to turn in her apron, worried she's poisoning you somehow."

Chelsea smiled. She stared at him and all she could see was her mother touching him. Her lips trembled and tears stung her eyes. Why? Why now? Why had her mother come now when she'd only just realized the love she felt for him?

"Chelsea, what is the matter?"

She took a deep breath to steady herself. "Nothing is wrong. I am fine."

"I will never understand why members of your sex always insist there is nothing wrong when plainly there is. You cannot hide it from me, Chelsea. I know something is troubling you. I can see it in your eyes. Tell me what is wrong."

Chelsea looked away, trying to hide the misery that consumed her. "I do not want her here."

"Who? Your mother?"

She nodded.

"Why? What has she done?"

"I . . ." She hesitated, avoiding the truth, trying to find an excuse, any excuse except what had really happened. How could she tell him the truth? If he did not believe her, she would die of the humiliation. Finally she blurted out, "I am frightened."

Rogan came to her then, covering her hands with his large ones. "What frightens you?"

"She arranged for me to marry Gregor. She wanted the match. She could give proof that I was betrothed to him long before I married you or had even met you for that matter."

Rogan smiled.

Why was he smiling when she was going to drop at any moment?

"I do not think you need to worry yourself over that."

"Why? You do not know my mother. She is sly and deceiving and will do anything to get what she wants."

And she wants you.

"It does not matter."

"Yes, it does, Rogan. You do not understand."

"It does not matter, Chelsea. None of it matters anymore."

She looked at him in frustration.

"I did not think I would need to tell you this at all, but since you are so beset over this. . . ."

"What?"

Rogan led her to the bed and motioned for her to sit beside him. He took her hand with his.

"Early this morning Fredric paid me a visit. He came to bring me the news of a law that was passed by the House of Lords. It is called Lord Hardwicke's Marriage Act."

"Hardwicke?"

"Aye. Like its creator, who is a very dear friend of our Fredric, it is a very long-winded, complicated law, with a number of different provisions. It is one of those provisions which should prove to be of significant interest to you."

Chelsea was staring at him now, waiting for him to continue.

"Among other things, it abolishes a long-used custom called a spousal."

"Spousal?"

"A promise to marry much like the one entered into between you and Gregor. Lord Hardwicke was also gracious enough to have the foresight to declare any spousal made prior to this law invalid. So your mother can shout it from the rooftops if she so pleases, Chelsea. It will do her no good. Gregor can no longer claim you. He has no more right to you than a thief would the Crown Jewels. He is absolutely powerless to take you."

Chelsea could not believe what she was hearing. "You mean I am free?"

"As be the birds that in the air fly," he said, quoting a sixteenth-century play by Heywood, "so you needn't worry about Gregor or your mother ever again."

"Oh, Rogan." Chelsea threw her arms around him and buried her face in his chest. For the moment she forgot all about her mother. Joy surged through her as the chains that bound her to Gregor and her past began to release their burdensome hold. A small sigh escaped her as she melted into Rogan's embrace. "Thank you."

Rogan tightened his hold on her, staring over her head at a fleck of dust on the floor. He frowned. That was not all of it. There had been more. There had been another provision to Lord Hardwicke's Act, a provision that had been the real reason for Fredric's visit to Rogan, a provision that Rogan kept from telling Chelsea.

With the abolition of the spousal also came the end to another long-practiced custom: the "Fleet" wedding ceremony, the one that had joined him to Chelsea. He remembered the words he'd told her when he convinced Chelsea to marry him that night. If she ever wished to leave, she would be free to go whenever she pleased.

Free as be the birds that in the air fly.

If Chelsea ever learned of the provision, she would know that she could be free from him and their marriage as well. She could dissolve their union if she so chose, go on with her life without any further fear of Gregor, and he would lose her, unless . . .

Rogan released Chelsea. "Well, now that I am quite certain you are well and all your fears have been laid to their final rest, I am afraid I must leave you, though reluctantly, for a short while."

"Leave?" Chelsea was just as reluctant to let him go. "Why, Rogan? Where are you going?"

"There are some pressing business matters I need to discuss with Fredric. I may be late in returning, so do not wait up for me. Sleep in your chambers tonight so I will not wake you when I come in. Pleasant dreams, love. I will see you in the morning."

He kissed her forehead and turned to leave, then came back and kissed her again, this time deeper, pulling her into his arms, leaving her head light and her knees weak.

Chelsea watched him go. She could never lose Rogan. And she would not lose him. Even the room seemed to chill without him there and she wrapped her arms around herself as her thoughts turned once again to her mother's displeasing presence.

Why had she suddenly come to London? Chelsea had been gone from Scotland for months, ample time to take two trips to London and back again. Had she hoped somehow to halt her daughter's wedding and force Chelsea back to marry Gregor instead?

Her mother had not seemed too displeased when she learned she had arrived too late. And how had she known where to find her? Who had told her?

Perhaps Annora had somehow learned of the attempt to restore Damson's name and return him to England. Perhaps she had come not to find her lost daughter, but to keep her husband from returning. She had to stop her, but how?

The handkerchief.

Chelsea rushed to her writing table and removed the fine white cloth from where she'd hidden it far back in a small concealed drawer. She stared at the oddly stitched flower, the elegant golden scroll, thinking back to their meeting at St. George's churchyard that day.

James had said to use it to summon him.

Only once.

She folded the crisp white linen. There had been so many places Chelsea could have gone, so many towns, so many houses. How had her mother known where to find her? Someone had warned her, someone who knew how to reach Annora, someone who could also know about the efforts being made for Damson's return. Chelsea found it amazing, and greatly suspicious, that her mother had ears even as far away as London.

She glanced to the window. The sky was dark with the dusk and overcast with thick clouds, the air heavy with the promise of rain. The leaves on the birch trees in the back garden rustled in the briskly blowing wind. Rogan had said he would be gone for hours. She had to take the chance while he was away. She grabbed her cloak and headed for the door.

"Going somewhere?"

Chelsea halted atop the stairs, her backbone stiffening at the sound of her mother's voice behind her. Inwardly she cursed her own bad fortune. The time had come for their confrontation. There was no escaping it.

She responded without turning. "Out."

She started down the steps. She hadn't taken two before Annora appeared behind her.

"And where shall I tell your husband you are when he returns to find you gone?"

This time Chelsea did not stop to reply.

"Newly married and already sneaking off to a lover, and with such a young and handsome husband. Take care, my daughter, else you might find him sneaking off in the dark of night to be with another himself."

Chelsea whirled on Annora. "And who might that be, Mother?"

Annora smiled, chilling Chelsea to her toes.

A silent moment passed as they faced each other in the solitude of the darkened stairwell.

Finally Annora spoke. "I certainly would not know."

Chelsea could not believe that this person, this calculating and vicious person, was her mother. Mothers loved their children. They nurtured and protected them. They did not rend their hearts in two. But she could not allow Annora to see the effect her words had. Before she could shed the tears burning at her eyes, Chelsea turned and descended the steps, the drawstring of her reticule clenched tightly in her hand as she headed out the door.

A quarter of an hour later, closeted inside a creaking hackney coach, Chelsea was speeding to St. George's Church. It was growing darker by the minute. The moon was up now, full and white in the night sky, peeking out only occasionally from behind the expanding clouds. She urged the driver to hurry, fearing Rogan would return and find her gone. Would he demand to know where she had been, who she had been with? She wished she'd been able to find Rogan's pistol. She needed its security with her now.

The courtyard of the small church was deserted, a small lantern flickering in the wind above the wide wooden door.

She climbed the four steps to the door and tugged at the rusted door handle, pulling it open wide. She stepped inside.

Two small candles lit the tiny antechamber at the rear of the dark and silent church. She walked in. The heels of her shoes clicked noisily along the wooden floor. She pulled her cloak closer about. Candles flickered at the end of each row of weathered pews to light her way along the narrow center aisle. She could hear the wind outside, amplified through the tiny crevices in the walls around her.

No one was about.

The building, like her knowledge of the stranger's true name, seemed empty.

James had said to leave the handkerchief at the third row. She stood there now. Each seat had its own missal, its own kneeling stool, just as the chapel in Castle Drummore. She thought back to when she had been a child, how her father would tap her sternly on the shoulder when she dozed off in the middle of a sermon, his eyes scolding as sharply as if he'd spoken aloud. How she missed him. Soon they would be together.

Chelsea heard a door close behind her. She spun about, searching. It was quiet. She could see nothing save the darkness that lay beyond the candlelight. She loosened her reticule and fished for the handkerchief inside, thinking whoever had been there had been leaving.

She heard a single footstep scrape roughly along the floor. She looked again, narrowing her eyes at the shadows. Had there not been a candle lit at the last row of pews when she had come in?

Another footstep and the shadows wavered as the candle lighting the next row blew out. A form emerged from the shadows, tall and large and frightening. She could not see its face, but its black silhouette filled her with apprehension. She squeezed her hand around her reticule, wishing it were a pistol.

"Who is there?"

Her voice sounded frightened, and rightfully so, for her heart pounded with fear. Perhaps the church was closing for the night, she tried to tell herself. She searched for the handkerchief again, wanting to leave quickly.

Another footstep. Another candle.

"Excuse me?"

No reply. Something deep inside told her to run, to get out swift as her feet could carry her, but whatever was there, that faceless, oblique shadow, stood between her and escape. She looked about and spied a small door nearly hidden at the foot of the tall pulpit. She took a step toward it.

The intruder stepped forward, extinguishing another candle at the next row of pews.

"Who is there!" she repeated, her voice echoing through the smoke-blackened rafters. She felt a moment of panic.

Chelsea took another step. At the sound of the intruder's advancing footstep, she turned and bolted toward the small pulpit door. She heard the footsteps advance behind her, nearer now, and she grasped the door handle with both hands. It would not budge. She rattled it frantically, terror rioting through her as the footsteps closed in on her. She pounded on the door with her fists.

"Someone, please help me!"

Two very muscular arms closed over her, pinning her arms to her sides and lifting her feet from the floor. A sour-smelling hand covered her mouth, stifling her screams. She could not breathe. The stale odor of whiskey and body sweat assailed her, the rough stubble of his beard scratched against her temple. He whispered to her.

"Hold, lass. Will do you no good to scream."

Gregor.

Chelsea went numb at the thought. She twisted and squirmed, kicking at him with her legs, but could not break his unrelenting hold. He lifted her higher, dropping one thick hand to the lacings of her gown.

Oh, God, no. She fought with all her strength now as he started to pull at the front of her gown. She bucked and writhed. She clawed and pulled. When the knot at the lacings would not release, Gregor forced her around to face him, taking her bodice with his meaty fingers.

"Stop your struggling, lass. 'Twill do you no good. Just lay back and take it."

With one swift yank, he rent the delicate fabric to her waist. Chelsea screamed as his hand closed over her breast, squeezing the tender flesh beneath the thin covering of her shift.

He covered her mouth with his free hand and spun her about to face him. His dark eyes glinted at her dangerously in the low candlelight.

"I tried to treat you like a lady. I tried to treat you proper. Now I'll show you how a whore should be treated."

His mouth covered hers with bruising force, his tongue thrusting deep within her mouth. She bit his tongue. He howled and grabbed her by the hair, squeezing her jaw with such force that she could not close it. She could feel the hardness of his sex swelling beneath his breeches. Thoughts of him covering her, taking her viciously on the church floor filled her with a fear so real her blood ran cold through her veins. Somehow she managed to break one arm free and struck him hard against the side of his head. He merely grunted, his eyes glinting black with rage like coals in a fire.

"I'll teach you to fight me."

Gregor brought his arm back. He cracked her soundly against the chin and Chelsea fell back like a broken doll, striking her head against the hard stone floor. She tasted blood at the corner of her mouth. The ceiling blurred above her. She tried to lift her head, but a blaring pain consumed her and she dropped back in a crumble.

She could not move. She saw Gregor rise above her and was helpless to fight him, unable to do anything but stare while he unfastened the closures of his breeches, his eyes filled with burning intent.

Chelsea could not turn her head away. She managed a low moan as he pushed his breeches down over his hips. The sight of his stiff rod jutting out from his body paralyzed her. He was massive. He would rip her in two. The muscles in his legs rippled and she felt the sour taste of bile rise in her throat as his red and engorged organ came toward her.

He was going to take her now, on the stone floor of the church, and there was nothing she could do to stop him. She commanded her limbs to move, to fight him, to somehow get away, but her body would not heed her will. Her vision obscured, she blinked against the darkness that threatened to consume her consciousness. She fixed her stare on a golden crucifix that glimmered in the candlelight above her, trying to draw strength from its sacred presence.

Please, God, help me . . .

She felt Gregor's hands pushing her skirts over her knees. She wanted to scream, but saved her strength. She took an even breath, gathering her senses and waited while he pulled her legs apart. His hands grabbed her thighs and yanked her toward him. Her bare legs scraped against the floor. She fought to remain still. She had to wait just a little longer. . . .

Gregor had pushed her skirts over her thighs now and his fingers were touching her as he lowered his body over her. Only when he was kneeling above her, his eyes burning with raging lust, his member stiff and throbbing with desire, did Chelsea finally move.

She drew every last bit of strength she had and brought her knee upward, striking Gregor directly between the legs. He howled with pain, covering his groin with his hands and doubling over in agony. She scrambled to her knees and stumbled down the aisle. She could hear his pained cries echoing through the rafters. She wrenched the church door open and ran, never looking back, running toward home and escape.

Chelsea stared at the decorative plasterwork on the ceiling above her bed. Her head pounded, her limbs screamed in protest each time she moved, as her mind played over the terror of Gregor's attack.

She still did not know how she had ever found her way back to the town house. For all she knew, she could have run through the streets the whole way. She'd lost the handkerchief, dropped it somewhere with her reticule, so her purposes for going had come to naught. She thanked the heavens that Rogan had not been there when she'd returned. Had he seen her, her lip bloodied, her gown ripped clear to her waist, he would have howled with rage and then killed her for her stupidity in going out alone and unprotected.

She'd washed every inch of her body with the pitcher of icy water left at her washstand, but no matter how hard she scrubbed, no matter the amount of soap used, she could not erase the feel of Gregor's dirty hands touching her. A purplish bruise shadowed her chin where he struck her. She hoped Rogan would not notice, for she could think of no excuse to offer for it.

A sudden rapping at her chamber door startled her from her thoughts.

"Just a moment," she called, fearing it was Rogan.

Before she could rise, the door flew open and Anne, her bedclothes disheveled, her mobcap awry, came rushing through in a flurry.

"Milady! Milady! There's two of the King's men at the door demandin' to see you!"

Chelsea blinked against the light of Anne's candle. "What time is it?"

"Past midnight! I told them you'd retired for the evening, but they said it was urgent, and if I didn't come to get you, they would wake you themselves!"

"Where is Lord Ashbourne?"

"He's not come home from Master Fredric's yet. Do you want I should send Will to fetch him?"

"No, that will not be necessary." Chelsea rose from the bed. "I will see to what they want. Show the gentlemen into the parlor and offer them some refreshment. I will be down directly."

Anne muttered something about them not being gentlemen at all bothering ladies at such an ungodly hour, and left, her mobcap now hanging over one ear.

As Chelsea opened the doors to her armoire she spotted the dress she had worn to the church lying in a heap on the floor. She looked away. She would make certain Anne burned it. She never wanted to see it again. She slipped on a clean gown of peach- and white-striped muslin, fastening it quickly at the front, and left her chambers. Annora stood atop the stairs. She did not say a word. She followed Chelsea as she proceeded down to meet her guests.

"Gentlemen . . ."

The men rose to their feet. They were dressed in uniforms that looked much the worse for wear, their coats faded, the breeches thin in the knees. One man, the taller of the two, with straight dark hair and eyes the color of wheat, stepped forward. His skin was craggy from the pox. He set his wineglass aside, sloshing some wine on the burled mahogany side table.

"Are you the Countess of Ashbourne?"

Chelsea stopped but did not sit down. "Yes, I am."

Annora came forward then. "What business do you have to disturb two ladies in the middle of the night?"

"Mother, I am certain this is not a social call, is it, gentlemen?"

The tall man nodded. "Lady Ashbourne, have you knowledge of a man named Gregor Moultrie?"

Chelsea grew wary at the mention of Gregor's name. "We are acquainted. . . ."

"And have you seen Mr. Moultrie of late?"

An ominous chill came over her, but she pushed it away. They could not possibly know of Gregor's attack. "Yes, I have. . . ."

"When did you last see him?"

"Perhaps I could ask the purpose of this inquiry or at least your name and what business you have that necessitates questioning me at this hour?"

The man removed his hat, lowering his eyes. "My apologies, ma'am. I should have introduced myself. I am John Ames, and this"—he motioned toward his companion—"is Horace Burke. We are constables for His Majesty, King George the Second. Something has occurred, a crime has been committed, and we are simply trying to establish Mr. Moultrie's whereabouts earlier this evening."

"But why are you questioning me?"

Mr. Burke broke in then. "You were, uh, familiar with Mr. Moultrie, were you not?"

"It is no secret here in London that Mr. Moultrie and I were at one time betrothed, but I am married to Lord Ashbourne now. I no longer have any association with Mr. Moultrie."

"But you did see him earlier this evening?"

"I did see him, but only in passing."

John Ames nodded again. "Where did you see him last?"

Now Chelsea did take a seat. She did not like where his questions were leading. "I saw him at St. George's Church."

The two men looked at each other. Ames turned to Chelsea. "Would you be willing to accompany us to St. George's?"

Annora stepped forward. "At this hour? Absolutely not!"

"May I ask why, Mr. Ames?" Chelsea broke in.

"They have found a body at the churchyard. It is believed to be this Moultrie fellow. We cannot be certain until we have him identified by someone who knew him."

Chelsea was taken by surprise. Gregor? Dead? Surely they must be mistaken. She had just seen him, plainly alive. It must be someone else.

She turned to her maid, who lingered in the doorway. "Anne, please fetch my cloak and summon Krune to accompany me with these gentlemen to St. George's." She returned her attention to Ames. "When I saw Mr. Moultrie earlier, he was very much alive and well. I am certain the person you have found is not he, but I am willing to come with you to verify it."

"Your cloak, milady."

Anne held the black velvet cape out to her, but Ames intercepted it. "Allow me."

Chelsea turned for him to place the garment over her shoulders. She heard him emit a pained oath.

"Damn! Something just pricked my hand." Turning toward the lining of the cloak, he searched through the folds of fabric.

"Here, let me." Chelsea stopped when Ames reached into the pocket at the inside lining.

He removed a long pointed dagger from inside, its blade stained with what appeared to be dried blood. Before Chelsea could utter a word, he handed the dagger to Burke and grasped Chelsea roughly by the upper arm.

"Lady Ashbourne, I arrest you in the name of King George the Second for the murder of Gregor Moultrie."

Chapter 15

Chelsea sagged against the stone wall, afraid to move, unable to see anything but the blackness that overwhelmed the tiny chamber. Her hands were chained to an iron ring in the wall, the shackles that bound her wrists chafing her skin raw. The air was rank with the smell of decay. In the distance she heard the anguished moan of another prisoner. She closed her eyes.

Newgate Prison. Its formidable stone walls were covered with thick ivy and topped by rusted pikes that looked like sharpened teeth. As a girl, she had heard the tales of those who entered, never to be seen again, swallowed by the villainous black mouth that served as the entrance gate. Never had she beheld its frightening form.

They had taken her with only the gown she wore, and she shivered now from the damp cold. They'd shoved her into the back of a wagon as she futilely proclaimed her innocence, her mother screaming like a banshee behind them. Ames and Burke had laughed at her cries, pushing Annora to the ground when she tried to impede their leaving, then prodding Chelsea up into the crude wagon with their booted feet. They'd chained her like an animal, leaving her to crouch in the filthy straw that covered the wagon's bottom, telling her if she treated them to a little "rompin' " they might give her a nice clean cell.

Chelsea refused their offer, and for it, they dragged her through the dank halls of the prison, her knees scraping on the rough stone floor as she tried in vain to kick her way free. They locked her in this tiny chamber and she pounded on the door, crying out helplessly as their footsteps retreated down the long corridor.

And then she was alone.

The dark had never frightened her as a child, but unable to see where she was and what might be scurrying at her feet, she now trembled in terror. She started to rock slowly forward and back, longing for Rogan's arms around her.

Stabbed through the heart, they'd said, found lying on the stone floor of St. George's Church only moments after she'd left him. A newspaper page bearing the announcement of her marriage to Rogan had been stuffed in his pocket, her name circled, as if declaring her his killer. Her reticule was lying beside him in a pool of his blood.

No matter how Gregor had hurt her, no matter what had occurred between them, she could never have killed him. Chelsea tried to pull the folds of her gown closer about her trembling legs. It was a mistake. It had to be a mistake. Gregor could not be dead. Still, she had seen the dagger they'd found in her cloak, the bloodstained blade glinting dully in the light. How had it gotten into her pocket? Who had put it there?

She had never been taken to identify the body they'd found at St. George's, but after finding the dagger in her cloak, she did not doubt it was Gregor.

She leaned her head back against the rough wall and closed her eyes, trying to fight back the lump of fear that rose in her throat. The stench of the prison was so strong, so utterly offensive, it nearly overcame her. It burned in her lungs, stinging her eyes to tears. She did not know how much time had passed since they'd brought her to the cell. Her head felt heavy and her eyes threatened to close as exhaustion crept up to take her, but the fear of what could be lying beside her made her struggle to stay awake.

Surely Rogan had returned to the town house by now. Was he trying to gain her release at that moment? What would he think when he learned that his wife had been arrested for the murder of her former betrothed? Would he denounce her before society and leave her to rot in this filth-ridden cell?

Chelsea pictured her mother, innocently informing him of her unexplained departure to the church alone earlier that evening. Would Annora offer to take her daughter's place?

She shook her head against the thought, knowing she must surely be going daft in the solitude of the cell. If there was just one thing of which she was certain, she knew Rogan's honor to be without question. He would stand up for her. He would know she had not killed Gregor. She was innocent. Innocent people could not be hanged.

But then, her father had been innocent and he would have hung if not for his escape.

Matters did not look favorable for her. She had only her word as evidence of her innocence. And it would be her word against the presence of a dead man and the evidence of the dagger that had killed him in her pocket.

"Get up, girl!"

A booted foot prodded at her side, jarring Chelsea from sleep. She looked up at the face peering down at her in the lamplight.

A large man, his double chin sporting two days' stubble and the dribble of tobacco spittle, loomed above her. He had small piggish eyes and a spot of drool forming at his lips.

It came back to her then, her arrest and the cell. "On yer feet, missy. I'm here to release ye. Ye'r free to leave."

Chelsea tried to scramble away from him, but the chains at her wrists jerked her back.

"I'm not goin' to bite ye." He chuckled. "Lessn' ye wants me to. Though from the looks of ye, ye'd need a good scrubbin' first."

Chelsea glanced down at herself. Her gown was sullied and reeked of the prison, of mildew and rot and stench. Her fingernails were broken from when she had been dragged down the hall. She itched to wipe the dirt from her face but was afraid to touch it with her grimy hands. She could only imagine what the rest of her looked like.

"Afeared I don' have a bath for ye, lady." He reached out to take her arm and she pulled it away.

"I'm not goin' to hurt ye. I'm just goin' to take you out of 'ere. Not many get to leave Newgate long enough to tell about it."

He reached forward and grabbed her shackled hands. It would be foolish to try to run, for besides being chained to the wall, she was half the size of her jailer and she knew not where to run.

"I'll unlock yer shackles at the gate," he said, and led her down the gruesome corridor toward a huge door at its end.

"What time is it?" she asked, noticing the torches that lined the walls around her.

"Aye, the torches," he said. "It's eight o'clock in the morn. The torches burn all day and all night. Not much light reaches inside Newgate."

Suddenly Chelsea realized fully what was meant by the saying *black as Newgate's knocker,* for 'twas true, no light could pervade the dark walls of the prison. When they reached the end of the hall, the guard knocked twice on the heavy wooden door, calling. A key grated in the rusted lock and the door creaked open, revealing yet another long corridor beyond. They walked through an open courtyard and two more corridors much like the first before stopping at what Chelsea remembered as the entrance gate from the previous night. Had she one hundred years left in her life, it would be impossible to forget.

Huge torches burned along the moss-stained walls that rose at least thirty feet, the pikes that lined its top rusted from the river's mist. The guard took her hands and unlocked the shackles. She rubbed the skin at her wrists as he signaled for another guard in the watchtower to open the huge gates. The portcullis raised before them.

When Chelsea saw the street beyond and the people and carriages going past, she wanted to run, but held herself back as the guard led her through.

"Chelsea, oh, thank God you are all right."

Emma was suddenly at her side, embracing her tightly.

Chelsea began to sob.

Fredric was there as well. "Let her breathe, my dear. Surely she could use it after being in such a place all night."

"Why have they let me go, Fredric? Have they found who really killed Gregor?"

He lowered his eyes and he looked to Emma nervously. "Not exactly."

"What do you mean not exactly?" She glanced around, suddenly missing Rogan. "Where is Rogan? Has he not been told of my arrest? Did he not come?"

Emma suddenly burst into tears. "Oh, Chelsea . . ."

"What? What has happened? Why is Rogan not here? Has something happened to him as well?"

"Rogan is not here because . . ." Emma hesitated, her voice cracking. She pointed toward the prison. "He is in there. Oh, Chelsea, Rogan confessed to Gregor's murder early this morning."

Rogan confessed to Gregor's murder.

Chelsea stared out the window as heavy droplets of rain pelted the coach, splattering in muddy puddles along the cobbled streets and trickling down the mist-frosted pane like tears down the cheek of a crying maiden. Despite the cloak Emma brought for her and the warming brick Fredric thoughtfully placed at her feet, Chelsea felt cold, her teeth chattering from a chill settled deep within her, an inner chill that could not be warmed.

She closed her eyes. How she wished it were all a bad dream. How she wished it would all go away.

"Why would Rogan confess to a crime he did not commit?" she said aloud, more to herself than to anyone else.

Neither Fredric nor Emma offered her a response.

She could not bear the thought of Rogan locked away in the horrible prison. It was suicide, his confessing. He had signed his own death warrant, they would need no proof to sentence him to die, and all of London would turn out to see the hanging of a nobleman.

She could not allow it to happen. There had to be something, some way of proving his innocence while sustaining her own as well. But how, when the evidence weighed so heavily against them?

The coach came to a halt before the Doraunt town house. Chelsea rose as the coachman opened the door to allow her out.

"Chelsea," Emma said, taking her hand, "are you certain you would not like me to stay with you?"

"You go on home. I will be fine. I've things to do, and if I sit and worry over it all, I will not be doing Rogan a bit of good." Squeezing Emma's hand, she turned toward Fredric. "Will they allow Rogan any visitors?"

"For a price, they will allow just about anything, sometimes even escape, excepting in this case. With nobility comes notoriety, I'm afraid."

Chelsea thanked him and stepped from the carriage. She gazed at the town house before her. She stared up its full three stories, the red brick now dark with the rain. She stopped at Rogan's chamber window. How strange it would be to be in that house without him there.

She thought back to the first time she had climbed the three small steps leading to the front door she now faced. How frightened she had been, running from Gregor with nowhere to hide and no one to turn to. Except Rogan. He had always been there for her. And now she had brought him to Newgate.

If only she had not run down that alleyway that day. If only Rogan had not stepped forward to defend her. Perhaps she should never have left Drummore, perhaps she should have forgotten what she had seen in her mother's bedchamber that night. Damn her for her jealous curiosity! She should have stayed in her bedchamber that night instead of following Gregor down that corridor, but then she would now be his wife, her mother still his lover.

She swallowed back the sour taste in her mouth. Nay, she did not regret her decision to leave Drummore, for with it she had found Rogan and the love for him that filled her to her very soul. He had saved her, without knowing who she was, and now she owed him the same in return.

She closed the door behind her and removed her rain-dampened cloak. She heard the sound of someone clearing their throat rather loudly, as if trying to gain someone's attention. Chelsea turned and was not at all surprised to find her mother waiting for her at the foot of the stairs.

Her dark eyes stared daggers at Chelsea, her lips pursed into a sour frown. She was garbed to go out, her woolen aubergine-colored cloak draped softly over her shoulders. She tugged on one black kidskin glove.

"Hello, Mother, going somewhere?"

Her trunks were at the entryway, stacked and waiting to be loaded into a departing coach. Odd, Chelsea thought as her gaze flitted over them with little interest, she had not noticed them upon entering.

She did not care. She would be glad to see her go.

Chelsea handed her cloak to Moller, who took it to the back of the house to dry in front of the kitchen fire. A confrontation was brewing, and in no mood to exchange retorts with her mother, Chelsea smoothed a hand over her skirts and moved up the stairs.

Before she could pass, Annora snaked out a hand, grabbing Chelsea by the upper arm.

"I will not allow that man to die for a crime he did not commit."

Chelsea looked to where she held her, then directly to her mother's eyes. "How good for us both since I will not allow Rogan to die either. It is very kind of you to be so beset, Mother, but there is no need for you to concern yourself so. Rogan is my husband, not yours."

"I do not know what you did to conceal the truth that it was you who killed Gregor. Probably opened your legs for every guard in Newgate to gain your release."

"I am my mother's daughter in that respect."

Annora drew back and cracked her palm against Chelsea's cheek. The blow caught Chelsea off guard, and she fell back. She grabbed the banister to brace herself and straightened stiffly, refusing to show any reaction other than the inflamed imprint of her mother's hand that rose to her cheek. She fixed Annora an icy stare, as if looking straight through to the wall behind her.

"It is so good you are leaving. You have saved me the trouble of ordering you out."

"You will regret your words, daughter. You have your father's sharp tongue." She turned to leave. "He gave you everything you wanted, indulged your littlest whim, but he is gone now and I am not so easily influenced. I know it was you who killed Gregor and I will see that you pay for your crimes, that you are made to repent what you have done, if I have to punish you myself."

"Did you ever think for one moment that I might be innocent? Your own flesh and blood?"

"What?"

"I am your daughter. How could you treat me as if I were some beggar child on the street?"

Annora's face twisted in disgust. "Do you know when I learned I was expecting you, I tried to kill you, even as you flourished in my womb? I threw myself down the stairs, hoping you wouldn't live, but you did. I prayed I would miscarry, but damned your stubbornness, you stayed. You came into the world against my wishes and when you did, you were the very image of your father. Everything about you was him. Even after he was finally gone, you were there, his living image."

Chelsea fought the pain those words brought to her heart. "How you must have hated me." As Annora turned to leave, Chelsea remained, watching as her mother turned and left in a flurry of purple wool. Chelsea stood there long after the trunks were removed, long after the coach had pulled away with the sharp crack of the coachman's whip.

Chelsea raised her hand and pounded on the heavy door. When the small side door at the entrance to Newgate swung open, it revealed the same guard who had released her that morning, his chin still stained with tobacco, his body still reeking of stale whiskey.

"Forget som'thin', lady?" His breath reeked of another foul, unidentified odor, causing Chelsea to draw back.

"Yes," she said, forcing him back as she stepped through the doorway, "I did forget something. My husband."

The guard chuckled. "Oh, so that nobleman everyone's makin' a to-do over is yer husband? Mighty lucky man,

I'd say, seeing you now after takin' yer bath."

Chelsea did not respond, just regarded him as if his opinion mattered nothing to her.

When he did not get a rise out of her, the guard pointed down the hallway. "Well, he be in the condemned cell there and ain't allowed no visitors."

Chelsea sighed impatiently and thrust her gloved hand from behind the folds of her cloak. The guard smiled in greediness at the shiny coins she held and Chelsea would have sworn she saw him lick his lips before he snatched them from her grasp.

"Mayhaps fer a minute ye can see him. But only a minute."

He turned down the corridor. Assuming he expected her to follow, Chelsea complied. She wanted to run to the door to assure herself that Rogan was all right, but slowed her stride to keep pace with the jailer's lumbering gait. They seemed to be going to the very bowels of the prison. Finally they stopped outside the heavy iron door. The smell of the prison was stronger here and Chelsea wrinkled her nose in distaste as the guard searched for the proper key. He fumbled with the long chain and her nerves stretched tighter and tighter until she felt certain they would snap.

"Ah! 'Ere she is!" The guard turned the key in the lock and pushed the door inward. It screeched on its rusted hinges, reverberating through the long prison halls. The guard motioned for her to enter.

As she stepped through, a strong odor of mildew assailed her, causing her to draw back a moment. She covered her nose with her gloved hand and proceeded forward, swallowing back her distaste.

She squinted, unable to see beyond the doorway inside.

"Where is he? I cannot see him."

"Lightin's extra."

Chelsea took another coin from her pocket and the guard furnished a small lantern with a half-burned candle inside. She nearly expected him to request another coin to light it, but he struck a flint without comment and handed her the dully glowing lamp. She turned from him then, searching the shadows, and gasped aloud as her gaze fell on Rogan's form slumped in the corner.

He was alone in the large room, chained to an iron ring that protruded from the moss-covered wall. Water dripped slowly from above in a pool beside him. His coat and shoes were gone, leaving him with only his breeches and shirt that had been rent at the sleeve, giving Chelsea the impression that the other items had been taken against his wishes.

He groaned then and turned his head toward the light. A large bluish bruise colored one eye. A splotch of blood had dried at the corner of his mouth, and the chains that bound him rattled as he attempted to shield his eyes.

"Chelsea . . ." he managed, his voice a rasping choke.

Setting the lantern upon the floor, Chelsea knelt beside him, touching his forehead lightly. He was shivering from the cold, his teeth chattering uncontrollably. She pushed back his hair to reveal an angry-looking gash on his temple.

"Oh, Rogan," she said again, examining his bruises tenderly with her fingers, "can you hear me?"

"Hmmm."

Furious, Chelsea turned on the guard.

"It is freezing in here and he has not been given a blanket to keep warm. Where has his clothing been taken?"

The guard smiled, his piggish eyes near vanishing beneath the bulging folds of his face. "Most the prisoners in 'ere don' take kindly to no nobleman comin' in wearin' nice clothes. They gets real envious of them fine silk britches and velvety coats."

"Why has he been beaten?"

He chuckled. "Sometimes, like in 'is case, the others have t' do a bit o' convincin' for 'im to share 'is togs."

Chelsea had to clutch her hand into a tight fist at her side to keep herself from slapping his face. "Why has he not been put in a decent cell?"

The guard's grin went wide, and Chelsea instantly caught his meaning.

"How much?"

He stroked his chin. "Fer 'alf a crown, I can put 'im in the Master Felons side with the others. He may not get a bed. I think they be all taken. And he'd have to pay extra fer coals fer a fire."

"Is there nothing better?"

"Well, there's the Press Yard and Castle."

He searched her face for some sign of interest.

"Which is?"

"He'll 'ave his own room and bed, and a pot to pi—uh, a chamber pot. For more he might even get a window. He'll 'ave to buy 'is own flint and coal, but he'll 'ave a hearth all to hisself."

Chelsea regarded him with skepticism. "And how much would this cost?"

The guard rubbed his grizzled jaw. "Being as how ye've been so nice and all, I could let 'im in for, say, seventy pounds, but it'll cost two crowns a week t' keep 'im there."

Chelsea emptied the contents of her reticule into her hand, mentally tallying their worth. "Fifty pounds to get him there and a crown a week to keep him. Take whatever is left for flints and coals. I will have all his food delivered and fresh clothing and linens brought daily, or is that not agreeable to you, Mister . . . ?"

"Gibbs," he said, removing his crooked hat. He bowed his head. "Elias Gibbs, at yer service, Your Ladyship." He pocketed the coin and scratched his balding head. "Crown a week it is. Jes' ask fer Elias Gibbs at the gate."

Chelsea returned to Rogan, who still lay slumped on the floor. Her heart twisted at the sight of his battered face. She did not want to leave him. She wanted to take him into her arms and soothe his pain, attend to his injuries, but she had to set her other plans into motion first, and time was quickly running out. Fredric had told her without a trial it would be only a matter of days before they scheduled an execution. She pushed that thought back. There would be no execution.

"See that he is moved immediately, and please have the chains removed from his hands and feet. It is obvious in his condition that he cannot escape. I will return later this afternoon to be assured that my coin has gotten what it has paid for, Mr. Gibbs."

When Chelsea returned to the town house, she instructed Moller to send for Fredric and set Cook to preparing a basket of food for Rogan. With Anne packing a valise and the other housemaids gathering clean linens, Chelsea set out for Rogan's study to see if she could find ample coin to keep him in the cell until they could gain his release.

She refused to believe he would hang. Innocent people did not hang. Somehow, someway, they would find who had truly committed the murder and Rogan would be freed. He had to be freed, so she could touch him and hold him and tell him just how very much she loved him.

Chelsea hesitated at the study door when she found Beecher rifling through Rogan's desk drawers. He did not see her, so frantic was he in his search as he slammed the desk drawer shut.

"Damn it!" He began pulling books from the shelf behind him, thumbing quickly through the pages.

"Is there something I can help you find?"

He froze and looked at her much like a thief caught holding a bag of gold. Chelsea suddenly remembered they were alone, and if he wished, he could easily harm her. She backed away.

"Oh, I did not know you had returned." Beecher stumbled over his words. "Lady Ashbourne." He crossed the room to her, taking her hand. "Or may I just call you Chelsea, since we are cousins now?"

The tone of his voice had changed markedly from when he had been cursing moments before. Chelsea pulled her hand away, wishing she could wipe off the touch of him. She glanced toward the desk where he had been searching so desperately and started toward it, curious to see what was so important to him and wanting to put as much distance between them as she could.

"I was just . . ." Beecher followed, passing her before she could reach the desk. Papers were hanging from the drawers and Rogan's account book lay open on top, conspicuously out of its usual place on the adjacent bookshelf. He shoved the papers back inside the drawers. "I was trying to find something that would help prove Rogan did not kill that bast—" He glanced at Chelsea. "Excuse me. I did not mean to offend you. I had forgotten he was your betrothed."

"No offense taken. Any feelings I might have had for Gregor vanished when I married Rogan." She moved to the other side of Rogan's chair. "You were saying?"

"Oh, yes, well, I was looking for something that might prove Rogan's innocence."

His tale interested her, and Chelsea wondered just how far he would take it. "Such as?"

"A—a theater stub, perhaps. I had seen him the night of the murder at Garrick's Theatre with Lady Lampley." As he realized what he'd said his eyes grew wide and he turned quickly toward the door. "Or perhaps I was wrong. I must have been mistaken. I was mistaken. I'm certain now it was someone else."

He started for the door. "And, well, I did not find anything anyway. Sorry to have disturbed you. I can see that you wish to be alone. I shall leave you to your peace. Good-day."

Chelsea remained at the desk as he grasped his cloak from Moller, who had suddenly appeared at the door. She smiled to herself. She had not been as alone as she'd thought.

"Thank you, Moller."

"Of course, sir."

"I meant to ask you," Beecher went on, "did they ever find the hackney driver who took you to the church that night? Perhaps he could tell them . . ."

Chelsea did not hear him. Her mind had wandered back to Beecher's earlier statement. Theater? With Lady Lampley? Rogan had told her he would be at Fredric's that night discussing some business. She thought back. It had been well after midnight when the constable's men had arrived. Midnight was a bit late for business, but not too late for the theater.

"Chelsea?"

She looked up. "Huh? Oh, no, they could not find him."

The look that crossed Beecher's face was one of relief. "Well, I've taken enough of your time for one day, so I will be off. My best to Rogan."

Chelsea did not bother to see him out, but turned back to the desk.

Theater? Diana?

"Chelsea, my dear," Fredric said, suddenly crossing the threshold, "you sent for me?"

"Oh, Fredric, I did not know you had arrived."

Fredric. He would tell her where Rogan had been that night.

"Before I begin with my reasons for asking you here, can you please tell me something?"

"Certainly."

"Did Rogan come to your house the night Gregor was killed?"

Fredric reflected for a moment, his eyes rising heavenward. "Let me think . . . yes, yes, I believe he did. We went over the quarterly statement for the shipyards."

Relief washed over Chelsea in a tidal wave. Beecher had been mistaken.

"Came and left about half past nine," Fredric went on. "Said something about having to keep another appointment."

Chelsea stiffened. As quickly as her hopes had soared a moment earlier, they dropped to the very pit of her stomach. Another appointment. With Diana. She cringed as if she had been struck.

"Is something wrong, Chelsea?"

"No, nothing," she lied, "I was just trying to remember where he had been that night." She raised her chin. "Now, the reason I called you here. I have been to Newgate and have exhausted all of the household funds to rent Rogan a decent cell. In order to keep him there, it will cost more than I have access to."

Fredric smiled, setting his arm reassuringly around her shoulders. "Well, you are Lady Ashbourne now, wife of one of the wealthiest, if not the most notorious earl, in London. A short sojourn to Rogan's bank should remedy your shortage of funds. Would you like me to accompany you, my dear?"

Chapter 16

When Chelsea stepped from the hackney coach in front of Newgate three hours later, her face was drawn, her eyes blank, unable to believe what had become of her life in so short a space of time.

After Fredric had helped her secure enough coin to keep Rogan in his cell for at least a week, Chelsea had returned to the town house to collect his clothing and the basket of food. If only she had not gone back into the study, if only she could have forgotten Beecher's words. But the thought of Rogan meeting with Diana nagged at her and she returned to Rogan's study to search for the supposed ticket stub.

Instead she had opened the lid to her own Pandora's box.

She did not know why when she saw the rolled and bound parchment stowed far back in the bottom drawer, she had taken it. It was not a ticket stub. It was not what she had been looking for, but something drew her to it, some invisible hand gripping her and leading her to its secret hiding place.

It had taken her only a few moments to realize its intention. It was Townsend's will, written only weeks before his death. She'd almost returned it to its place to continue her search through the desk, if not for the three small words that had caught her attention.

Certificate of marriage.

It was then that she learned of the condition forcing Rogan to marry. It was then she realized why Rogan disliked Beecher so much. It was then she realized the true purpose behind Rogan making her his wife.

The words had stunned her at first, causing her to drop back into the chair and take several deep breaths. Their union had never been because of any feelings Rogan had for her. It had not been because he had wanted to help her escape from Gregor. Rogan had married her only to keep his inheritance out of the hands of his cousin. Her situation had simply, and conveniently, provided him the opportunity.

Still, she could not fault him. Her reasons for wedding him had been less than respectable. The only difference between them was that hers were recognized and accepted. He had never told her about his father's will. He had never told her he wanted to marry her so he could keep his inheritance. Still, her inner voice cautioned, he had taken the blame for a crime he hadn't committed.

She was silent as Gibbs lead her through the prison to Rogan's cell. The chamber was small, not what one would call clean, though it was far better than the one he'd occupied earlier, and at least it was Rogan's to have alone. A fire burned in the equally small stone hearth, a damp breeze blowing in from the tiny window high above their heads. Rogan sat on the narrow straw pallet that was to serve as his bed.

Chelsea waited while Gibbs, after giving her a leer, left without comment. She then turned to the basket she had laid on the table and started removing its contents.

"Cook packed you enough food for three days, but I will have a fresh basket brought to you on the morrow."

She avoided looking at him and began arranging the dishes on the small, rough-hewn table. In the corner of the cell, Rogan wondered at her sudden change of mood, from gentle and caring about his wounds only two hours earlier, to skittish and detached.

"Chelsea, is everything all right?"

She ignored his question, but the nervous tremor in her voice did not pass unnoticed. "Anne packed you some clean clothing and a flagon of water with a bowl and cloth with which to clean yourself. If you like, I will see if I can purchase water daily from the guard, although it would most probably not be very clean."

"Chelsea?"

"And here are some clean linens."

Rogan reached out and took her hand. Chelsea stopped unpacking the basket. She stood still for several moments, then turned to face him. Her lower lip trembled.

Rogan knew her well enough to know that if he were to ask what was troubling her, she would deny being troubled, so he decided to try a different course. "Will you help me clean my wounds?"

He saw uncertainty in her dark eyes and wondered at it, but kept the thought to himself. Chelsea nodded and returned to the table. She emptied a bit of the water from the flagon she'd brought into a bowl. She sat beside him then, placing the bowl between them on the straw mattress. As she dipped the cloth into the water, she would not look at him. She raised her hand to his forehead. He was staring at her and he knew she was aware of it.

Chelsea gently cleaned the dried blood from his temple, noting that the gash there was not so deep as she had at first suspected. In fact, it was more a scrape. The corner of his mouth was split, but had stopped bleeding. As she rubbed his lower lip with the cloth, she found herself remembering the way his kisses felt, the taste of him. Her hand stopped moving. So entranced was she by her thoughts, she did not notice when he leaned toward her to kiss her. She closed her eyes as he touched his lips to hers.

Her heart was beating strongly. She felt him deepen the kiss. Her resolve melted when his hand cupped her breast, while his lips branded a mark of fire on her mouth. With his other hand, he held the back of her head and she grasped the folds of his shirt, holding, clutching to him. How she wished it would never end. How she wished she could forget what she had found. How she wished the will had never existed. The will . . .

Chelsea turned her head so that her cheek was against his mouth.

"Please, Rogan . . ."

It took every bit of strength she had to pull away from him. She stared down at her hands folded in her lap, at a loss for words to explain her actions. She thought to everything he had given her, and had given up himself to marry her. He did not deserve her disdain. He deserved his freedom.

"Why do you pull away from me, Chelsea?"

She would not tell him about finding the will. "I have been thinking, Rogan . . ." She paused. "I owe you a great deal for saving me from Gregor and marrying me to keep him at bay." Her stomach twisted at her next words. "And I have thought about it a great deal." She raised her eyes to him. "I have decided that once Fredric and I find a way to gain your release, I will leave London so that you may go back to the life you had before I came."

She stared at him, searching for something—sorrow, mayhaps an indication of love—in his eyes. They remained blank.

Rogan did not speak for several minutes, and when he did, his face tensed visibly. "Is it that you believe I murdered Gregor?"

"No, I know you did not." She did not want to tell him why she knew he was innocent, that she knew he had been with Diana that night and could not have been the murderer. "When I saw Gregor at St. George's that night . . ."

"What?"

Chelsea did not speak. Rogan's eyes turned a darker shade of gray, the color of the sky just before the raging storm.

"You saw Gregor at St. George's that night?"

"Yes."

"You were out at night alone? Why did you go to meet him?"

She could not tell him she had gone to summon the stranger, James. He did not even know of his existence.

"Why, Chelsea?"

His voice was rising now. Chelsea could not think of a response. She knew Rogan was forming one of his own.

"Chelsea, answer me! Why were you with him?"

She jumped up, spilling the bowl of water on the mattress and across Rogan's legs. "I cannot tell you."

"You cannot tell me. I confessed to a murder I did not commit to save your life and now you tell me you met the man you were accused of killing that night, at the place he was killed, but you cannot tell me why?" He rose. "I want an explanation, Chelsea. Now."

Chelsea backed away. "Why? It matters naught. I do not want to involve you further. I have already involved you far too much. Fredric and I will find a way to free you. Let us just forget this ever happened. I will leave and you may go on with your life. I am sorry for the trouble I have brought on you. I never meant to hurt you."

Rogan was beside her in two long strides. He took her by the shoulders and shook her. "Damn it, Chelsea, tell me. Why are you doing this? I will not let you leave until you answer me."

Her head was spinning. Her insides twisting. She suddenly shrieked, "He was my mother's lover!"

Rogan released her as if she'd stung him. At the expression that came over his face, Chelsea silenced, raising her hand to her mouth in instant regret of her words.

"That is why you left him?"

She nodded, tears brimming at her eyes.

Rogan came and took her in his arms. "If he were still alive, I would kill him." He stroked a hand over her head. "I never would have thought it, Chelsea. I can only imagine the pain you must have gone through. I am so sorry."

Chelsea squeezed her eyes shut. She wanted to believe him. "I know about your father, Rogan."

"What of my father?" He pulled her back to look in her eyes. "What of my father, Chelsea?"

"I know why you married me, Rogan. I know all about the will. I know you only married me because you had to take a wife before your father died or you would lose your inheritance. But it is all right. We each served a purpose for the other, Rogan, nothing more. I do not know why I would expect more. I had hoped that perhaps . . ." She hesitated, refusing to admit her love for him, afraid to see the absence of returned love in his eyes. "Now that your father is gone and you have what is rightfully yours, you may go back to your life, to your friends and your mistr—" She paused. "I will leave. I will remain your wife. You will still be married, and thus no one can ever contest the provisions of your father's will."

A pain fierce and raw surged through Rogan with each word she uttered. Damn his father's will! Why had he not burned it to perdition long ago? Did she not realize he could have dissolved their marriage had he wanted? No, she would not, for he had not told her that part of Hardwicke's Law, afraid she would leave him. And he could not tell her now. It would sever the only tie he had left to her. He would not allow that, could never allow her to leave.

Gibbs, summoned by the racket, suddenly opened the door. "What's going on in here?"

Chelsea wriggled free of Rogan's grasp. She grabbed her cloak. "Nothing, Mr. Gibbs. I was just leaving."

"No, Chelsea!"

"I am sorry, Rogan. As soon as this is over and you are released, you will be free to pursue your own interests. You can go back to what you had before and forget you ever met me."

And I will strive to do the same, though knowing I will never succeed.

Her heart was twisting and tears ran down her eyes in long rivulets. "You offered me my freedom once. You said I would be free to go if I chose to. I want my freedom, Rogan. Please give it to me now."

She turned to leave.

"No!"

Chelsea rushed through the door.

"Chelsea!"

Rogan started after her, but Gibbs stepped in his way, blocking him from leaving. "Now, where might you be goin', Mister?" He shoved Rogan back. "Back in yer hole where ye belong." He slammed the door behind him.

No! Rogan pounded at the door with his fists. He grabbed at the door handle, pulling it, yanking it while he yelled Chelsea's name over and over. He could still see the pain shining in her dark eyes at his inability to deny what she had read in that will. Perhaps what she believed—that he had married her only to secure his inheritance—perhaps even he had thought it true in the beginning. But now he knew there had always been something, some invisible tie that pulled him to her.

From the moment she had first come crashing into his life, he had been possessed by this unknown force. It had led him to taking her into his home that day and led him to making her his wife. Each time he saw Chelsea, the force grew stronger, taking him more and more under its power. Each time he kissed her, touched her, held her, loved her, it tightened its unrelenting hold on him. He had tried to deny its existence at first. He had thought it lust, figured after he'd bedded with her, it would fade as it had so many times before, with so many women before.

But it had not faded. It had only grown stronger, and more real, until he'd become intoxicated with her as if she were some sort of drug. His addiction to her was stronger than any opium, her hold on him more powerful than gin. Her dark haunting eyes, that rich ebony hair, her skin that felt smoother than a rose petal. He wanted Chelsea, needed her, and his addiction would only grow stronger each day.

Aye, he had tried to deny it at first, telling himself this feeling did not exist, even as it possessed him with its blinding force. But the moment when she had stood before him, accusing him with the words of Townsend's will and then leaving him there powerless to go after her, he knew the force existed, knew it more than he had ever known anything.

It would never leave him, this all-consuming feeling—and for the first time in his life, Rogan knew love.

"Beecher Prestwood has arrived, sir."

Fredric looked up from the stack of papers that blanketed his desktop. He nodded to his footman, an aging man named Josiah who had a limp from the gout. Josiah moved to retrieve his expected guest.

He had come quickly, Fredric thought as he removed his spectacles, rubbing the bridge of his nose. He was so tired. He felt ready to drop, so exhausted from hours of examining books of law that his vision was blurred. Volumes and volumes he had pored over, scanning each page, trying to find something, some small word in the law that would help them somehow. He had to build a defense for Rogan, one to keep him from being hanged, but it was proving quite difficult since Rogan had pleaded guilty to the charges. Fredric's only hope was that his hunch would be proven correct by the visitor now coming to see him.

Fredric rose as Beecher entered the room, watching him carefully. He had dressed very quickly, judging from the sloppy knot at his cravat and the mussed bag wig he wore. Fredric smiled. Perhaps his hunch was right after all.

He motioned for Beecher to take a seat at the chair before his desk. "Thank you for responding so quickly to my request," he said, trying to mask the distaste in his voice.

"Your note seemed urgent. Has something more developed in Rogan's case?"

How concerned he seemed about his cousin's welfare. How false his concern truly was.

Fredric took his time in responding. "Actually I have summoned you here for two reasons. First, as you know, Rogan is still incarcerated at Newgate—as we know, for a crime he did not commit." He rose then, and crossed the room to the sideboard. He poured himself a glass of sherry, then held the bottle out to Beecher. "Care for a glass?"

Beecher nodded. He was watching Fredric with interest now, obviously intrigued as to why he had been summoned, perhaps beginning to worry just a little bit, too.

Fredric took a sip from his glass, allowing the sweet liquid to soothe his weary head. He handed the other glass to Beecher. "Tell me, Beecher, did you see Rogan the night of the murder?"

"Yes," Beecher said, taking a deep swallow that left a few drops at the corner of his mouth. He set the glass on the mahogany side table beside him. "Yes, I did see him. He was at Garrick's with Diana Malcolm, and from the looks of it, they seemed to be engaged in a rather intimate conversation. You know, I had always suspected them of being lovers. I mean, it's no secret her aging husband can't satisfy her, but I thought that their liaison would have ended after Rogan married Chelsea."

When Fredric did not respond to this, he added, "Obviously it didn't."

Fredric began drumming his fingers on his glass, staring at Beecher in silence, using his lawyer's tactics to unsettle his witness.

His ploy succeeded. Beecher began to fidget, glancing at his time piece and nervously taking two more sips of sherry before Fredric spoke again.

"At what time was this that you saw Rogan with Lady Lampley?"

"That would have been around ten, just after the second act, but I already told the authorities all this."

Fredric nodded. "Just humor me. I am trying to retrace Rogan's steps that night in order to build a better defense."

Beecher looked taken aback. "Build a defense? But I thought Rogan had already confessed to the crime. Has he changed his plea?"

Fredric did not confirm or deny. "Did you speak with Rogan at all that night?"

"No. He was too far away. As I said, the second act had just finished and it was too crowded for me to reach him."

"What play was it?"

"Huh?"

"What was the name of the play?"

Beecher loosened his collar. "Why do you ask?"

"No reason, just curious as to what Mr. Garrick is putting on these days."

Beecher swallowed nervously. "I do not recall. I had gone to meet someone and . . ."

Or follow someone, Fredric thought, taking his seat again. He propped his glass of sherry before him on the desk.

"And where did you go from Garrick's?"

"I stopped at the Fleece for a tankard and played a few hands of whist, then I went home for the night, around eleven."

Fredric leaned forward, his sparrow's eyes watching Beecher closely, missing nothing. "Did you stop anywhere else that night?"

"No."

"With whom did you play whist at the Fleece?"

Beecher's voice rose defensively. "I do not recall. Why am I suddenly the one on trial here?"

Fredric settled back into his soft leather chair. "No one is on trial, Beecher. I am simply confused on a few small points. You see, Rogan's valet, Moller, stated that you came by the town house at approximately a quarter hour after eleven. I am confused as to how you could have done this if you had gone home for the evening."

Beecher stared at Fredric a moment. Fredric could see the damp sheen of perspiration begin to bead at his brow in the candlelight. Beecher twisted his cravat with trembling fingers.

"Is it warm in here to you?" Fredric stood and moved toward the window. He pushed it open a few inches to allow the cold night air inside. He turned back to Beecher.

He repeated the question. "Were you at the Doraunt town house that night?"

Beecher assumed a look of cognition. "Oh, yes, now I remember. I did stop there on my way from the Fleece to see if Rogan had returned. I wanted to extend my sympathies over his father's death."

Fredric smiled, nodding his head slowly. "Ah, yes, Townsend." He opened his desk drawer and removed a bound roll. "I was going through some of Rogan's things and I found a most interesting document. . . ."

Beecher glanced nervously to the door. Fredric made as if reading the document. He did not offer it to Beecher. There was nothing written on the parchment. The original was where it belonged, in Rogan's desk drawer. If not for Chelsea finding it and questioning him about it earlier that day, he would have never come to the conclusions that he had, conclusions that would save Rogan's life.

"Did you know that Townsend had attached a codicil to his will before he died?"

"No . . ."

"Yes, he did, and it states, in effect, that should Rogan not have married by the time of Townsend's death, all his monies, excluding Ashbourne, of course, since it is passed along by primogeniture, but everything else would have reverted to"—he looked up—" . . . you."

Beecher actually looked startled. For a moment, Fredric began to doubt his hunch. "I had no idea. . . ."

As an actor, he was accomplished. Fredric went on. "You would think that if Rogan were to hang, this would leave you as the inheritor . . ."

Beecher's eyes lit in the candlelight.

" . . . unless, of course, the child Chelsea carries is a son."

Now Beecher's surprise was genuine.

"Chelsea is with child?"

Again Fredric did not confirm or deny. It was a lie. He knew it was a lie, but he had to instill the right amount of doubt in Beecher's mind. "Funny how this little document can affect so many people's lives."

Realization began to dawn on Beecher at Fredric's carefully placed words. "Well, as I already told you, I had no idea about the will."

"Oh, I think you did have an idea about it."

"What?"

"I think you had an idea about a lot of other things that have occurred of late as well. Tell me, Prestwood, how did Gregor know that Rogan and Chelsea were at Lampley that night he brought the authorities in to take her? And how did you know that Chelsea had gone out the night of Gregor's unfortunate murder? No one, with the exception of myself and Chelsea, knew that."

Beecher flew from his chair. "I do not have to listen to this! I've done nothing." He started for the door.

"It is locked, Beecher."

Despite the warning, Beecher tried the handle then pounded his fist upon the door when it refused to open.

He leaned his head against the door. His voice was muffled against the solid wood. "You cannot prove anything."

Fredric stood from the desk. "Do not be so certain. We have found a church boy who will swear that he saw you stick that knife into Gregor's chest at St. George's that night. We have Moller, who places you at the town house the same night, giving you the opportunity to put that knife in Chelsea's cloak. You say you stopped there to see Rogan on your way from the Fleece, but the town house is in the other direction from there to your flat, and—"

"You cannot prove anything," Beecher snarled, turning from the door to face him. "You have nothing."

"And," Fredric went on, dealing his final blow, "we have Gwyneth."

Beecher fell mute, staring at him in disbelief.

Behind his back, Fredric gripped his pistol, uncertain of how Beecher would react, prepared should he react unreasonably.

"Ah, yes, Gwyneth. Do you know she has agreed to testify in a court of law that you confided all your plans in her, every little detail down to how you contrived to name Chelsea as the murderer, knowing Rogan would never allow her to hang? Also, that if he didn't confess to save her life, you threatened to kill Rogan so you could inherit the family fortune?"

"That bitch! I never told her about any of that!"

Fredric smiled, sensing victory. "She has also signed a written statement attesting to all of this, which, as we speak, is in the hands of the authorities." He saw the darkness of defeat begin to shadow Beecher's eyes. Now to play his trump.

"Which brings me to the second reason I asked you here this evening." He paused to move back behind his desk. "In exchange for your confession, I will personally see that you do not hang."

Beecher's hands were trembling now. "How?"

"Your sentence would be transportation to the Colonies. You would live out your life in servitude to another, but you would be alive. I understand Virginia is a most beautiful place to live. Mild winters, summers not too unbearable.

The Indian threat seems to have died down considerably as well. Keep in mind as you make your decision that if you do not agree to a full confession, you will be tried, and you may be certain, Beecher, you will hang. I will be one of the thousands there to watch you dance at the end of the noose at your execution."

Fredric paused to give Beecher a moment to consider his offer. He already knew what he would decide. Beecher was a coward and could never face the thought of public execution by the hangman's noose.

"What do I have to do?" Beecher said, his voice submissively low.

Fredric withdrew a parchment from inside his desk drawer. "I have drawn up a confession for you to sign, outlining everything we have discussed here. And so there will be no question . . ." He rang a small silver bell on the wall above his head. The door swung open to reveal four of the King's soldiers waiting in the entryway. "These fine gentlemen will bear witness that you were not in any way coerced or forced into signing this confession. After you sign, you will be remanded to their custody, where you will then be taken to Newgate and held in a cell to await your transportation to the Colonies."

Beecher stared at the soldiers, his Adam's apple bobbing nervously as he tried to swallow back his rampant fear. He looked at Fredric, eyeing the confession with interest. "Where do I sign?"

Fredric motioned toward the bottom of the document, providing a quill.

Beecher's hand quivered as he scribbled his name across the bottom of the page. He did not read the confession, just stared at it a moment as if he couldn't believe what he had done. He closed his eyes and returned the quill to Fredric.

Fredric stood, taking the signed confession. Relief fell over him like a warm cloak. "You have done the right thing, Beecher. I wish you well."

Beecher did not speak. Fredric doubted he could had he tried, so choked was he by his defeat. He stood then, his tricorne clutched in his hand, and turned. The soldiers came to meet him before he reached the door.

Beecher just stared at Fredric while they chained his hands and feet. He did not look away even as they led him to the door.

When they were gone Fredric returned to his study and fell into his chair, placing his pistol in the drawer, relieved he'd not had to use it. He leaned his head upon his hands and closed his eyes.

A soft knock on the door pulled him from his recollections. He looked up and smiled, a warmth spreading through him, as Emma, her belly swelling with his child, came slowly into the room.

"Did it go as you expected?" she asked as if fearing his response.

Fredric nodded. "Aye. Your cousin is now in the hands of the authorities, where he belongs, and will soon be on his way to a life of servitude in the Colonies."

"I am sorry he is my relation. How could he have done such a thing to his own family?"

"Greed sometimes makes men blind."

Emma came up behind Fredric's chair and placed her hands on his shoulders. "So Rogan will be freed?"

"Yes, most probably before dawn."

Emma moved across the room to the hearth. She stared

pensively at the wavering fire. "Has Chelsea been told?"

Fredric rose to join her. He set his arm about her shoulders and pulled her gently against his side. "No. I thought it best not to tell her until we were certain Beecher would confess. I will go to her in the morning."

Emma nodded. "I just hope it is not too late, Fredric. Rogan does love her, I know it, and she loves him as well."

"Aye, but Chelsea does not know he loves her. She believes Rogan only married her to keep his inheritance. If only I'd known he had not told Chelsea the truth about Hardwicke's Law, if only I hadn't opened my mouth."

The look on Chelsea's face earlier that night came to him as clearly as if she were standing before him.

Emma reached up to touch his cheek. "Fredric, you had no way of knowing."

"Yes, but I only confirmed that which she already believed. She truly believes he did not tell her about the law because he does not love her. Without that, there is nothing holding Chelsea to him, nothing except the feelings neither has acknowledged for the other. I do not know if even that will be enough to overcome all the adversity."

"It must be, Fredric. Chelsea brings out something in Rogan I've never seen before. He cannot lose her now. Not after all they have gone through together. They must look beyond what brought them together and hold on to what they now have. Love is too precious a thing to discard so easily."

"It is not for us to say, my love. It is for Rogan and Chelsea to decide. We can only hope they will realize what they have together."

Emma rested her head against Fredric's chest, wishing

there were something she could do, something more she could say to convince Chelsea of her brother's love. She watched as the last flame in the hearth flickered out. She hugged her arms around herself and shivered against the sudden chill.

Chapter 17

Dawn was streaking over the rooftops, its muted pink rays breaking through the fog that shrouded Grosvenor, when Chelsea finally rose from the settee in the parlor before the wall of windows that faced the square. She moved slowly. She was mentally and physically exhausted. Her eyes were red-rimmed and swollen from crying, at knowing there was no hope, no possibility of Rogan ever returning the love she had for him.

She started slowly up the stairs to her chambers knowing what she had to do. She would collect her things, and she would leave this house. The thought made her tremble, but staying, knowing she was not truly Rogan's wife any longer, was an impossibility. Every room, every thing reminded her of him. She simply could not take the pain of knowing he would never love her.

When she reached her chamber, the sun was still hidden behind the trees. Chelsea lit a small candle on her dressing table, her hand quivering as she touched the lighted spill to the wick. She turned to the armoire. She realized now it was over between them, though she was not even certain it had ever started. The only thing of any certainty in her life was that if she stayed any longer, the pain of loving him would surely choke her.

She began to retrieve her gowns, tossing them on the bench beside her in a pile of silks and satins. She took her valise from where it had been pushed far, far back in the armoire, nearly hidden behind her shoes.

She had to leave. It was his lying she could not accept. For as surely as he had not spoken the entirety of Lord Hardwicke's Law, he had lied about the validity of their marriage. He knew it no longer existed; he knew they were no longer wed.

She tried to think of why he would not have told her that their marriage was a fallacy, but the only thought that came to mind was that she had accomplished her purpose, he had gotten his fortune, and their marriage was no longer of any importance to him.

Tears began to trickle down her cheeks anew and Chelsea swallowed back the sob that rose in her throat, steeling herself and her heart against him. Why did she have to love him? Why had she allowed him to enter her heart?

Without even pausing to fold her gowns, she began to stuff them into her valise, and with each one, the tears fell more heavily, her sobs growing louder until, when she could not fit another dress into the bag, the tears were flowing down her cheeks in a rush.

She took the rest of her belongings, her ribands and hairbrushes. As she searched the bottom of the armoire, she spotted a single shoe lying there. She picked it up and closed her eyes against the anguish the sight of the slipper brought to her. He had never returned her other shoe. She stood there staring at the one remaining, her arms falling weakly to her sides.

"Looking for this?"

Chelsea spun about, her breath catching in her throat. Rogan sat on her bed, his feet crossed before him. In his hand dangled the other shoe, her shoe, the shoe he'd refused to return so long ago.

"You?" she whispered, blinking back her tears to assure herself he was not an apparition. She clutched the side of the armoire to keep herself from falling. It could not be. He was a ghost before her and she was surely losing her mind.

"I am afraid I cannot return this to you," he said. "I told you once I was keeping it to assure you would not run off again."

Rogan rose from the bed. Chelsea dropped the valise at her feet and rushed across the room into his arms. She buried her face in his chest, unable to believe he was standing there, in her room, somehow gloriously released from Newgate. He felt so warm, so alive, and she just wanted to breathe in the scent of him, feel his warmth around her. . . .

And then she was pushing at him, striking her fists against his chest, and shoving him away.

"What the hell . . . ?"

"Let me go!" she choked. She backed away. "I am leaving, Rogan. I only came here to retrieve my things and then I will be gone from your life. You can live as you please. I care not."

"Why?"

"Why? I should be the one asking that of you. Why, Rogan? Why didn't you tell me about the provision of Hardwicke's Law that invalidated our marriage?"

Rogan released her abruptly, taken aback. His silence confirmed her worst fears.

"You knew our marriage wasn't really a marriage anymore, but you chose not to tell me. Why, Rogan?"

Rogan moved toward her. "Chelsea . . ."

She backed away. "Why did you continue to live as my husband, knowing what you did?"

Rogan took her by the shoulders. "I did not tell you about that part of Hardwicke's Law because I did not *choose* to dissolve our marriage. Yes, Chelsea, I knew of the provision, and I hated knowing it. I would have done anything to have changed that, had I been able. I continued to live as your husband because I was your husband and I still am. I did not want our marriage ended. I meant to keep that part of the law from you only until I could marry you legally and finally.

"There is another provision of the law, Chelsea, a provision that requires parental consent for anyone wishing to marry under the age of one and twenty."

"But I will not turn one and twenty for five more months. Did you mean to keep it from me that long?"

"No. Just until I could gain consent from your parent."

Chelsea shook her head. "My mother would never consent to our marriage."

"No, but your father already has."

Chelsea fell dumbstruck. "My father? But he is . . ."

"He *was* in exile for crimes against the Crown, crimes which he never committed. Tomorrow a royal edict will be read exonerating your father of all charges."

Chelsea could not believe what she was hearing. "And he will come home?"

"He already has. He has been staying at Ashbourne since the night of Gregor's murder. I took him there myself."

"But Beecher told me you were with Diana that night."

"Aye, but only because she was working with us to secure your father's freedom. She convinced her husband that Damson was innocent, and along with Fredric, they were able to urge the King into releasing him from exile. That is why Beecher saw us together that night."

Chelsea was smiling now, tears running down her face, tears of joy and happiness. "And Fredric knew this?"

"Yes, he has been instrumental in gaining your father's release, he and many others. They have been secretly trying for years. When I told him your name, your true surname after our wedding, he told me of a league of others who were working to return your father to England. They were able to sail him to England and bring him in disguise to London. No one would think to look for him at Ashbourne, so we have kept him there until we could gain his release."

"Then you know of James."

Rogan looked confused. "No. I have not met any James. Who is he?"

Chelsea shook her head. "I do not know. He contacted me and told me that he was working to gain my father's release. He told me he was watching out for me. He was why I went to St. George's that night when Gregor attacked me. I was trying to warn him of my mother's arrival in London. If only I had known that you were one of the others helping to bring my father back . . ."

"I could not tell you because I did not want to raise

your hopes in case we were unsuccessful. Once he was settled and proclaimed innocent, I had planned to tell you everything and wed you properly—with the blessing of your father." Rogan took her hands. "Why do you think I confessed to killing Gregor? Why do you think I did not tell you about the rest of Hardwicke's Law? I love you, Chelsea. And I never want to lose you."

Chelsea looked up at him and ran her hand lightly against the side of his face. How she had waited to hear those words from him. "Oh, Rogan, I love you. I wanted to tell you, but I was afraid, so afraid you did not feel the same."

He gathered her into his arms. "Now, let me show you just how much I feel the same."

Chelsea nodded, her lips trembling with emotion as Rogan very slowly placed his hands on her shoulders and pulled her back just a few inches from him. Placing his hands gently on either side of her face, he brushed his thumb over her cheek to wipe away her tears.

She did not speak, still dazed by his admission. Nothing mattered any longer, nothing except the love they had for each other.

Rogan made love to her as the sun's light poured in through her chamber window, bathing them with its golden warmth. He watched as her passion gave way to climactic release, her eyes filled with the wonder, mystery, and pleasure of it, as wave upon wave of sensation swept over her, rocking her to her core. He loved this woman, as sure as he loved the life she brought to him. He wanted to spend the rest of his life with her, loving her, protecting her.

A surge of emotion, so all-consuming it made him shudder, filled him at the thought of Chelsea bearing his child.

He wondered if she could carry it at that moment, a tiny being created solely from their love.

Chelsea felt as if she had never truly lived before. He was everything to her: life, and laughter, and complete happiness. Nothing mattered more. She would never again consider leaving his side; how could she when she would surely perish without him? There would be no more lies, no more betrayals, only love and trust between them. If ever she had a purpose in life, it was Rogan's happiness, and she would spend the rest of her days showing him just how very much she loved him.

Rogan's eyes snapped open at the sound of the pistol cocking. The carved steel barrel staring down at him glinted silver-blue in the midday light. Beyond it, Beecher smiled, pushing the gunpoint against Rogan's temple.

"Sorry to have disturbed your sleep, cousin. I grew weary of waiting for you to awake."

Rogan stared at him. He did not respond. The pistol, he realized, was his grandfather's dragoon piece, the piece his father left to him. He wondered where Beecher had found the pistol. He wondered if the tiny switch beneath the hammer was in place. He shifted slightly, keeping his arm around Chelsea's shoulders to shield her. Her soft hair draped across his chest. He knew he could not do anything at that moment. He would have to wait, wait until he was certain the switch was in place, until he was not in such a vulnerable position.

He felt Chelsea stir beside him. "Rogan, what is it?"

Her voice sounded sleepy. He tightened his arm around her. "Keep still, Chelsea. We have a visitor."

Chelsea opened her eyes, blinking against the sunlight.

She gasped when she saw Beecher standing over Rogan with the gun.

"Good morning, dear cousin-in-law. How very lovely you look in the morning, fresh from a romp with my cousin."

Chelsea slowly pulled the coverlet to her chin.

Beecher chuckled. "Seems whenever I find the two of you, it is in the most inconvenient of positions." His smile faded. "Get up."

Rogan did not move.

Beecher prodded his arm with the gun. "I said get up!"

When Rogan still did not move, Beecher reached for the counterpane to pull it back. Rogan shoved him off. "Don't be a fool, Beecher."

"No, don't you be a fool, cousin," Beecher said, lowering the pistol to Rogan's chest. "I am the one holding the pistol. And I will be the one to kill you and then you will never know what I did to your wife. And the plans I have for her . . . Now get out of the bed," he said. "Both of you."

"I will get up," Rogan muttered, "but you will allow Chelsea to remain in bed while I dress. When I am finished, you will then turn your back to her while she does the same." He did not ask, but rather expected Beecher to comply.

"Whatever for? We are all family now. Why don't you share a little with your cousin. You cannot have everything and Chelsea won't mind, I'm sure."

Rogan did not rise to his comments. "You will do it."

Frowning that he did not get the expected reaction from Rogan, Beecher backed away from the bed. Still holding the gun at Rogan's forehead, he cast a quick glance at

Chelsea. "If you even try to run, you may mark my words, I will kill him."

Chelsea returned a stiff nod and remained sitting, the coverlet clutched to her chin as Rogan flipped back the counterpane and rose from the bed. He did not hurry. He moved slowly, unconcerned with his nakedness, and retrieved his breeches from the floor. Chelsea looked around, trying to find something, anything to use as a weapon. With the exception of her hairbrush, which she doubted would do anything more than anger Beecher more, there was nothing. She looked to Rogan. He was watching her as he donned his shirt and boots. He said nothing, but somehow his eyes reassured her. He was planning something. He turned toward his cousin.

Beecher glared at Chelsea. "Now you."

He turned to the side, the gun still pointed dangerously at Rogan's chest, and Chelsea rushed from the bed. She slid her chemise over her head and reached for her gown, then paused, remembering the hooks that lined its back. She would not be able to fasten them herself.

"What is taking you so long?" Beecher barked at her over his shoulder.

"I have to find another gown. This one fastens up the back."

Beecher chuckled. "Would you like some assistance?"

Chelsea did not think to respond. Her heart was racing so quickly that she hurried across the room and grabbed one of the gowns lying beside her valise. She stepped into it.

"That is long enough," Beecher said, turning just as she fastened the last button at its front.

Chelsea fled to Rogan's side.

"No, no, dear cousin-in-law. That will not do. I want

you over here with me. You and I have not had time to become better acquainted with one another."

Chelsea did not move.

"Now!"

She looked to Rogan. He nodded silently. She stepped forward.

Beecher grabbed her by the arm. "Now, cousin, you move on ahead of us. We are going to your study. Remember, if you make one false move, I'll put this shot in her lovely little head."

Rogan knew he could not take the chance that the switch was in place; he wouldn't gamble with Chelsea's life. He would have to wait.

The three of them walked down the corridor slowly. There was no sound coming from the bottom of the stairs, the house conspicuously absent of servants. Even Moller who seemed always afoot was nowhere to be seen.

As they started into Rogan's study a knock suddenly sounded on the front door.

"Get over there," Beecher said to Rogan, pointing toward the wall adjacent to the door. "One move and she dies."

He shoved Chelsea forward. She stumbled on the thick carpet and he grasped her by the arm, twisting it painfully behind her back.

Beecher's breath crawled over her when he whispered in her ear. "Now, you are going to answer that door as if it were any other day. Tell whoever is there that no one is home. Tell them that Lord and Lady Ashbourne are out of the country. Just get them to leave. One trick, one false word and your husband dies."

The knock sounded again, more insistent this time.

Chelsea's heart pounded.

Beecher lifted her arm higher, sending a jolt of sharp pain through her. She gasped. He pushed her toward the door.

Chelsea reached for the door handle, her entire body shaking. The door handle rattled in her hand. She tensed her hand to still its trembling and pulled the door open. Beecher blocked it with the toe of his boot, allowing it to open just enough for her to look through a tiny crack.

Chelsea bit her lip, her chin trembling at the sight of her father standing on the other side. She nearly cried out and ran into his arms.

Her father looked older, his hair peppered, his eyes crinkled at the corners. His face was bronzed from the sun. In his hand he held a bunch of flowers. For her. He smiled at her and it was as if he had never been gone. Her heart surged at the sight of him.

"Hello—" her father started to say.

"Yes," she cut in sharply, "what can I do for you?"

Her father looked confused. "I was looking for Lord and Lady Ashbourne."

Beecher tightened his grip on her arm, squeezing it fiercely.

She tensed against the pain. "Lord and Lady Ashbourne are not in this morning."

Her father's brow drew downward. "I believe they were expecting me."

"As I said, Lord and Lady Ashbourne are out. You will have to call another time. Good-day." She stepped back just as Beecher kicked the door shut with his foot. The door handle rattled noisily.

"Very good, cousin-in-law." Beecher pulled her against him, his hand running caressingly down her side. "I knew you could do it. Perhaps when this is over, you and I can have a little sport together. If you're good, I might even keep you."

Chelsea shrank away from his touch.

Beecher pulled her back, glaring at Rogan. "To your study, cousin, and remember, my gun is still pointed at her head. It would be a pity to stain your fine carpeting with her brains."

Once inside Rogan's study, Beecher released Chelsea and propelled her against the desk. She broke her fall by grasping its edge.

"Well, cousin, it seems your little scheme did not work. Life in the Colonies did not suit me at all. I had to kill two guards in order to escape. Did you truly believe you could get rid of me so easily?"

"Scheme?" Chelsea said. "What does he mean, Rogan?"

Rogan came to stand beside her. "Chelsea, meet Gregor's murderer."

Her mouth fell open. "You?"

Beecher smiled, seemingly proud of his new distinction. "Yes, me. I killed that idiot knowing my honorable cousin would never allow you, the wife he barely knew, to hang for the crime. Then I planted the dagger in your cloak pocket. And it would have been perfect had that fool Fredric not figured everything out."

"Fredric?"

"Yes," Rogan broke in, "Fredric became suspicious when he overheard Beecher talking to you about Gregor's murder. Beecher knew you had gone to the church that night, which only Fredric, you, and I knew of, and the guilty party, of course. He did some searching and found a church boy who had been roused by your screams, who told him it had been a man that killed Gregor, a man very much fitting Beecher's description."

"And if it hadn't been for that bitch, Gwyneth, betraying me," Beecher snarled, "you would be hanging at Tyburn right about now."

"She didn't."

Beecher stared at Rogan, his eyes widening with rage.

"She never said a word," Rogan went on, provoking him even more. "She stood by you till the end. Fredric only lied to get you to confess."

Beecher's face turned red. His hand was shaking when he lowered the pistol to Rogan's chest. "Shut up, cousin, or I will have to kill you now."

Rogan stared at him. "Go ahead, but it might prove difficult. That gun hasn't worked in nearly a century."

Beecher's eyes grew wide and he looked at the gun. He pointed it at Rogan again. "Do you think me fool enough to fall for your lies twice? I loaded it myself. Used quite a lot of shot so that I would not have to load it a second time."

He pulled the trigger. It clicked, but did nothing more.

With a growl, he swiped his hand across a vase on the edge of the desk. The flowers it held flew through the air, the vase crashing to the floor, breaking into a million pieces. He bellowed out loud and threw the pistol across the floor, springing on Rogan like a panther. The two went down, crashing against the furniture, locked in combat.

Chelsea bolted across the room and grabbed the gun. She found the tiny switch beneath the trigger Rogan had showed her and hit it. She raised it in two hands and turned. Rogan and Beecher had separated, circling. In his hand, Beecher held a long-bladed knife. He raised it on Rogan.

"No, Beecher!"

He looked to where she stood holding the gun.

"Drop the knife or I'll shoot."

Beecher laughed. "With a broken gun?"

She cocked the hammer. "Don't make me shoot you."

Beecher lunged at Rogan. Chelsea closed her eyes and pulled the trigger, falling back when the gun discharged. She heard a scream and realized it was her own. Across the room, Beecher crumbled to the floor.

"Chelsea . . ."

Rogan raced across the room and took the gun from her trembling hands, dropping it and pulling her into his arms.

"Shh, it is all right . . ."

She closed her eyes, holding on to him, breathing in his scent. He was alive. Her body began to tremble at the thought of Beecher killing him, at how close she'd come to losing him again.

She heard a noise behind them and whirled around, thinking Beecher had somehow escaped her shot.

Her father and the stranger—James—stood waiting in the doorway.

Epilogue

Chelsea stood at the back of the church at St. George's, hidden from view behind closed double doors and flanked on each side by footmen dressed in silver and royal blue livery. Her gown, the palest ice-blue watered silk which Madame Dussault had gone to Paris to find, shimmered in the brilliant sunlight streaming through the windows above as she smoothed a gloved hand down over her stomach to calm its nervous flutter. Madame, standing behind like the omnipresent mother hen, clucked about her, reminding her to stand straight and still. She pushed an errant cork-screw curl behind Chelsea's ear and bent once again to arrange Chelsea's long, lace-trimmed train behind her all at one time.

Chelsea stole a glance at her father standing at the door. His back was to her, one arm leaning against the door jamb as he stared out to the street. He'd given up trying to stand anywhere near her, for every time he'd come within two yards of the pristine hem of her skirts, Madame shooed him away as if he were an overzealous suitor. He'd finally called Madame a "bothersome beldam" and retreated to the far side of the tiny chamber.

It had been nearly two months since he had come back to her, two months since he'd been freed from exile and proclaimed innocent by the King, and still she could not believe it true. The ten years they'd lost could never be regained. Only knowing she would have the rest of her life with him helped to ease the regrets of the past.

He turned to her then as if realizing the direction of her thoughts.

"What is it, *dautie*? This is your wedding day. You should be happier than you've ever been. Why do you look so grim?"

"I am happy, Papa. I love Rogan. I was just thinking of all the time you and I have lost, all the events in my life you missed. Do you remember how frightened I was to dive in the tarn? Every summer you would take me there and show me how to dive from that tall rock. Every summer I refused, claiming a sea creature would eat me. Do you know I finally did dive in when I was ten? When I surfaced again, without the sea creature, I even looked for you on that mossy knoll you'd sit on. You weren't there and I had no one to tell. I knew if I told Mother she would fall into an apoplectic fit at the thought of her daughter diving naked into the tarn. You've missed nearly half my life."

He squeezed her hand gently. "I know, Chelsea, I regret it, too. Unfortunately your mother cared more about her own wishes than of the happiness of her daughter. I used to try to picture you each year on your birthday, what you'd look like, how much you had grown. I always knew you would be beautiful."

"You were nearly hanged, Papa. She had you sent away, ruined your name, and if not for Uncle Leland and Fredric and the others arranging to bring you back, I most probably never would have seen you again."

Damson nodded. "All because I opposed the match she'd made for you with Gregor Moultrie. I can only thank the heavens you left Scotland before that marriage could be made. Although, in truth, it never would have been. You did not know it, but your great-uncle Leland was there, ready to stop the wedding at all costs. I am only sorry you had to learn the truth about your mother yourself."

"I try not to think about it, but I'm not sorry it happened. It brought me to Rogan and I cannot truthfully imagine living without him. I just wish Uncle Leland would have included me in bringing you back instead of disguising himself as a stranger and leaving me to wonder if I'd ever see you again."

"He wanted to, truly, Chelsea, but he could not tell you for fear of exposing their plans. These people, your great-uncle Leland, Fredric, and countless others, they risked their lives to help me. And if it hadn't been for Rogan convincing Lady Lampley to persuade her husband to speak with the King, I might never have been able to return. They did not want to put you in any more danger than you were already in with Gregor and then your mother so near."

"I am just so happy you are back."

Damson reached down and hugged her tightly to him, much to Madame's utter chagrin.

Inside the church, a baby began to cry and Chelsea was not at all surprised to see Emma sneak through the doors moments later. She smiled.

"You look so very lovely. I cannot wait till we become sisters-in-law again."

Her infant son let out a wail then, as if to remind her of his presence. She glanced down at him, her eyes lit with motherly affection. "Yes, I know Master Christopher Townsend Fredric Ellingsford. You shall have your breakfast directly."

She handed him over to the wet nurse who waited.

Chelsea's insides fluttered at the sight of Emma with her child. She had not yet told Rogan the secret she held—the child she carried. Their child. She would wait until they were alone that night, lying in each other's arms, husband and wife again, as before. She would tell him she carried his son, for she felt certain it would be a boy, and it would be the last secret she would ever keep from him.

Damson took her hand and placed it at the crook of his arm. "Are you ready?"

Chelsea nodded.

As she walked up the aisle on her father's arm, even the sour look she received from Gwyneth could not dampen her spirits this day. Chelsea merely smiled. Gwyneth was herself a new bride, her marriage hastily arranged by her father to a close friend and colleague, a man of two and fifty years, the aging Earl of Stoddard.

And then she saw Rogan, looking so very handsome in his suit of navy trimmed with silver braid. His eyes never left hers for a moment. The love she saw there filled her with a feeling of complete happiness, and she knew she'd never forget this moment for the rest of her life. Nothing could ruin this day.

"Stop!"

Chelsea froze at the cry that suddenly brought chaos to the peaceful ceremony.

"Stop this at once!"

All heads turned. The crowd stared. Chelsea's breath stuck in her throat at the sight of her mother charging up the aisle toward them, her hair flying out behind her, her eyes wild and bright.

"I demand that this wedding be stopped immediately. This marriage will not be performed." She pointed a finger at Chelsea. "I am her mother. She is not yet one and twenty and I do not give my consent to the marriage!"

Chelsea did not know what to do, what to say.

"Aye, you may not give your consent, but, as her father, I do."

Annora spun about. Her face dropped as if she'd seen a phantom. She had never noticed Damson standing there.

"Hello, *wife*."

"Wh-what are you doing here?" Annora turned to the assemblage. "Someone! Arrest this man! He is a traitor!"

No one moved or uttered a sound.

Annora's voice took on the pitch of desperation. "What is wrong with you? He is a criminal! Seize him before he escapes again!"

"No, Annora. You are the criminal and you have gone too far."

Two soldiers came up from behind and took Annora by the arms.

"What? No, not me. It is him. Let me go, I tell you!

You are arresting the wrong person. He is the traitor, not me!" She turned on Damson. "You will hang for this. I will see to it."

"A moment, gentlemen." Damson stepped before his wife, his voice low. "Listen to me, you pernicious shrew. Apparently you do not read the newspapers, for if you had, you'd have seen my name has been cleared by the King. Now, as your husband, which I still have the misfortune of being, I am ordering you sent back to Drummore, where you belong and where you shall stay in solitude for the remainder of your days."

Annora spat at him. "You cannot do this. You have no right!"

Damson turned away and did not look back as the soldiers escorted Annora down the aisle and out of both his and Chelsea's lives for good.

"You may proceed," he said to the minister who was looking quite startled at the strange interruption.

The minister cleared his throat. "Doth thou, the Honorable Chelsea Estwyck, take this man, the Right Honorable Rogan Doraunt, Earl of Ashbourne, to be your lawful husband?"

When he pronounced them married and Rogan bent down to kiss her, he turned first and whispered in her ear. "I had a horse waiting outside just in case we needed one."

Chelsea laughed and tilted her head back as Rogan took her into his arms and pressed his lips to hers. She felt her heart soar to the heavens. Tears pooled in her eyes as she once again became Rogan's wife—for the second and final time.

Mail To: **True Value Home Subscription Services, Inc. P.O. Box 5235**
120 Brighton Road, Clifton, New Jersey 07015-5235

YES! I want to start previewing the very best historical romances being published today. Send me my FREE book along with the first month's selections. I understand that I may look them over FREE for 10 days. If I'm not absolutely delighted I may return them and owe nothing. Otherwise I will pay the low price of just $4.00 each: a total $16.00 (at *least* an $18.00 value) and save at least $2.00. Then each month I will receive four brand new novels to preview as soon as they are published for the same low price. I can always return a shipment and I may cancel this subscription at any time with no obligation to buy even a single book. In any event the FREE book is mine to keep regardless.

Name

Street Address — Apt. No

City — State — Zip Code

Telephone

Signature
(if under 18 parent or guardian must sign)

966-8

Terms and prices subject to change. Orders subject to acceptance by True Value Home Subscription Services, Inc.